Prisoner in the bordello

As ROSCOE FRALEY sauntered into the bordello bedroom, Lucia glared at him, making no attempt to conceal her hatred. She had been revulsed by this man from the first—and Bat Masterson had warned her that he was dangerous.

"Still lookin' for yer ma?" Roscoe leered.

"My ma is a damned murderer. She's wanted by the law. And I've got a hunch, Mister Fraley, who she is, where she is, what she is—and who her friends are." Lucia's face was flushed with anger. "Now, what is it you want? Kindly say your piece and get out!"

But Fraley wasn't ready to get out. He saw this girl as a danger, a serious threat to his plans. He was going to have to hurt her bad—that'd teach her who was boss.

"I don't reckon I'm ready to leave, just yet," Fraley growled. "I guess I'll just check out the merchandise first."

Lucia felt a tremor of fear give way to terror as Roscoe began to undress. She knew that here, even if she fought to her last breath and screamed her lungs out, no help would come. Lucia gritted her teeth and backed slowly toward the bed, saying a silent prayer as Roscoe Fraley moved menacingly toward her . . .

The
WOMEN WHO WON THE WEST
Series

TEMPEST OF TOMBSTONE

DODGE CITY DARLING

Dodge
City
Darling

Lee Davis Willoughby

A DELL/BRYANS BOOK

Published by
Dell Publishing Co., Inc.
1 Dag Hammarskjold Plaza
New York, New York 10017

Dell ® TM 681510, Dell Publishing Co., Inc.

ISBN: 0-440-01965-6

Printed in the United States of America
First printing—March 1982

Prologue

IN THE FALL of 1865, with the war ended, three Chicagoans decided to take advantage of the opportunities that the western frontier offered. They were a heavy-set, black-haired, small-eyed, broken-nosed young man named Nathan Budde; a good-looking dark-haired woman in her mid-twenties named Jenny Parker; and another woman, blondish, good-looking in a different way, and also in her mid-twenties, named Maggie Franklin.

Where they'd met, where they'd first come together and decided to join talents, was anyone's guess.

They drove a carriage southwest out of Chicago as far as Peoria, Illinois, where they set up for the winter.

They established a bordello on the outskirts of

Peoria. The man's skills were nefarious, if not downright criminal, and the women's didn't appear to be much better, although the dark-haired Jenny seemed to have a touch of class. Jenny ran the bordello while Budde and Maggie searched out a location for a saloon and gambling den.

By the time spring arrived, though, they'd all tired of Peoria, which was a far cry from the frontier, and they moved on further west.

They settled later that spring of '66 in the town of Hannibal, just across the Mississippi into Missouri. Again they established a bordello run by Jenny Parker, but this time Budde opened an adjacent saloon.

Business was good that summer of '66, very good —as it turned out, too good. The son of Hannibal's leading family was lured into the toils of Budde's saloon, and from there it was just a short step to the bordello and the tender ministrations of Jenny's young girls.

The ministrations were up to snuff but, unfortunately, violence reared its ugly head in the form of a jealous, drunken farmhand, and the boy died of gunshot wounds inflicted by that jealous suitor.

The forces of good, led by the boy's family, descended on Budde's evil establishments. Budde and his female associates were not only told to clear out, but their capital investments, the saloon and bordello, were reduced to ashes.

Budde was incensed, particularly since the boy was not the only member of that family to patronize the saloon and bordello. Both the father and the boy's uncle had been regular customers. The women counseled caution, Jenny especially, wanting only to clear out with their skins whole and while the getting out was good. But Budde wouldn't hear of it, and he drove them in their carriage out to the home of that leading family, where he planned to either extract money or get his pound of flesh.

An argument got out of hand and Budde, Maggie, and Jenny had to settle for flesh, or, more precisely, the lives of the family. Budde initiated the killing. The women may not have approved the bloody resolution, but once begun it had to be completed. Afterward they took what they could find, which amounted to a tidy sum of money and considerable jewelry.

Fortunately for Budde and his women, the bodies weren't discovered right away, by which time Budde *et al.* were halfway to Kansas City. Unfortunately for them, though, one of the bodies was still alive, if only barely, and their names and descriptions were circulated.

But by the time word had gotten to Kansas City, Budde and his women had, too, and they went to ground in that rough city for a few months, through the winter of '66–'67.

Come spring, though, they were on their way again, but this time by train, with different names, subtly different appearances, and with Jenny Parker—having cranked her class up a notch or two—as the figurehead leader of the trio. It was a role she played with surprising ease.

They reached Abilene just as Joseph McCoy was transforming his "small, dead place, consisting of about one dozen log huts" into the rowdy, rich "Queen of Cowtowns".

Again they repeated the saloon-bordello ploy, and again business was good. The Texas cowboys had their pockets full of trail wages and were ready to cram two months' worth of fun into a single night.

Budde & Company remained there for four years. Then, in '71, a Deputy U.S. Marshal showed up in Abilene, and began paying them very close attention. Their names were different, but they could change their appearances just so much.

The handwriting was on the wall, in more ways than one.

Foremost, of course, was the fact that their blood-thirsty past, especially that one mad night (which is not to say that that was the only time they were responsible for deaths, but never in so gratuitous and insane a fashion), seemed to be catching up to them.

Secondarily, though, was the sense that Abilene had run her course. Farmers were filling the area and had just about had enough of splenic fever, carried by ticks on the Texas cattle, infecting and killing their domestic animals. Bills were in the works to prohibit those Texas cows from certain Kansas counties, one of them being Dickinson, for which Abilene was the county seat. Furthermore, the railroad had pushed west, and there were plans to run another railroad line southwest, along the old Santa Fe trail. Other towns would soon replace Abilene as the cowtown queen.

Budde made plans quickly, and one night soon thereafter, both the saloon and the bordello burned down.

Three men died in the saloon fire, burned beyond recognition; one of them the deputy marshal. Since neither Budde nor the Franklin woman were anywhere to be found, it was assumed that two of the bodies belonged to them.

One person died in the bordello fire. From the location of the body it was thought to be that of the originally named Jenny Parker. It wasn't, but she'd not escaped scot-free. In setting the blaze, a coal oil lamp had fallen, exploded, and badly burned one side of her face. She'd barely managed to crawl to safety and go into hiding.

One further casualty of the saloon fire was a considerable amount of money. There was a shortage of banks on the frontier, many towns lacking them completely, and monies were often held for safe-keeping by town merchants, especially when the depositor was a transient. When the depositor was a cattleman who had just sold a large herd of cattle, the monies could be considerable. In the case of Nathan Budde, he could be ingratiating, and was considered competent, reliable, and trustworthy.

In the ashes of the burned saloon one of the bodies was found lying, scorched, by an open safe. All the money had been burned. There was speculation that the dead person had, while robbing the safe, somehow started the fire, and, in his greed, failed to escape. Some suggested that it had been a depositor, or more likely Budde himself, caught by the flames as he tried to save the money.

Whichever the case, several thousands of dollars were lost.

Life went on. The times may have been changing, but Abilene still had a few months left as the queen of cowtowns. The bodies were buried on Boot Hill and soon forgotten. ⇔

1

THE TRAIN TRAVELING west slowed as it approached the town. It was close upon midnight of a summer's day in 1878, and this would be the last train through on the Atchison, Topeka & Santa Fe line until morning.

The train rolled slowly past the buffalo bones piled high beside the track. Buffalo bones were used in the sugar-refining process, and also as fertilizer. There were not as many bones piled along the track as there had been in the heyday of buffalo hunting, but there were still enough to have prompted a traveler, one Jim Thompson (who at first thought them to be human bones) to refer to the town's violent reputation, and remark that people were dying faster than they could be buried.

But, just as the buffalo trade had been succeeded

by the cattle trade, the train now rolled past a number of large cattle pens, holding areas for the cattle that were trailed north from Texas.

The train slowed further and finally came to a stop beside a depot. The depot was at the eastern end of town and dead in the center of a street that was one hundred yards wide. The tracks ran along the street and out the western end of town.

To the north lay most of the town, three blocks in a row solid with varied businesses, and behind them some dozen more blocks that were primarily residential.

To the south lay a single row of buildings of businesses, broken by two street intersections.

Beyond those buildings lay the Arkansas River.

A sign on the depot read DODGE CITY.

The conductor watched as several passengers disembarked. Travel was not heavy at that time of night, and he'd recognized them all. There was one person he looked for and didn't see.

He climbed back onto the train, and, entering the first car, he spotted her, curled up in a forward seat. She was by the window, with two carpetbags taking up the rest of the seat. Her head rested in the crook formed by window and seat, cushioned by a rolled-up quilt blanket.

Her hair, blonde and wavy, was pulled back from her face and tied, not in a tight curl or knot, but in a way that made it resemble a pony's tail. A number of fine, silky strands fell playfully across her face.

Her face was slender and well-boned; she'd keep her looks a good long time. Her features were regular, her nose small, her eyebrows darker than her hair, and her mouth wide and expressive, tending toward fullness. At least, that was the way her mouth was when she was awake. At the moment it was loose and subtly responding to each intake and expulsion of breath.

She wore a deep-yellow full-length cotton dress with a delicate rust pattern. In the east, the skirt would have demanded hoops, but not west of the Mississippi. She wore a tan cape, rib-length, which was embroidered with yellow roses. Beside her, resting atop one of the bags, was a yellow slat bonnet.

None of the clothes looked new but, upon close inspection, one would notice that they were very clean.

The conductor gave them that close inspection as he leaned close. "Miss—"

The girl's eyes popped open. They were sky-blue, with coal-black irises that seemed to sparkle.

"You're here, young lady. Dodge City."

The girl blinked for a moment as she tried to remember where she was.

"Oh! Don't let the train go."

"It won't, not until I tell them to."

The girl quickly gathered her things. It didn't take long. The conductor wondered if she was carrying all her earthly possessions.

The bonnet sat crookedly on her head.

"You won't need that," said the conductor gently. "The sun's been down for hours."

She shot him a look—she knew *that*—but then she smiled.

"I can't carry it. I've run out of hands."

"I'll carry it," piped up a young man seated nearby. The conductor regarded him crossly.

"Your ticket's not for here," he reminded him coldly.

"It could be, if the lady so desired," said the eager young man.

The girl's face had closed up fast, distinctly forbidding. Hers was the kind of beauty that could go cold with quick ease.

"You just settle back, son," advised the conductor, "and dream on."

He escorted the girl down the car, and, as he helped her off the train, he asked her a question that he'd been saving.

"How old are you, young woman?"

She flashed him an indecipherable look.

"It's just that you seem awfully young, and mighty pretty, to be traveling alone in these parts."

The girl stared at him. She could see that the man did not affect the randy posture or the hot eyes she'd become accustomed to. She smiled, but she only answered, "Old enough." To forestall further inquiries, she asked, "What time is it?"

The conductor made a production of hauling the large watch from his vest. "Near upon one o'clock," he answered, making it somewhat later than it was.

"Well," said the girl, "I do thank you for waking me. I don't know what I would have done if you hadn't."

"Gotten a good night's rest, I 'spect," said the conductor drily. He'd seen the shadows beneath the girl's eyes. He'd noticed them when she had boarded.

"I must have put your train way behind schedule."

The conductor nodded solemnly, looked up and down the train, and signaled ahead. As the train began to move he hopped aboard. He stood on the stairs and watched the girl as the train pulled away.

He was near thirty, though his face looked older, and the uniform made him look positively antique. The girl had appealed to him strongly, but he was a man of great restraint, and now he cursed that restraint.

The train picked up speed as it rolled through town, heading for the black prairie beyond.

"Goodbye, li'l darlin'," he crooned, but only the wind heard him.

The girl stood by the tracks, looking around. She saw a sign proclaiming that where she stood was Front Street. Directly in front of her, close to the corner of Front and Railroad Avenue, was a large building. A sign identified it as Dodge House.

It looked grand—probably too grand for her pocketbook.

To the left of Dodge House, across an alley, was a restaurant named Delmonico's. It looked closed. Hell, it was late; it should be closed.

Darn it, Lucia, she thought, you'd better watch your tongue. Dirty words bespeak a dirty mind. She smiled and corrected herself out loud. "Goodness, it should be closed at this hour."

A person, lying by the tracks, sat up and looked at her. Then he lay back down. Lucia didn't see him.

She walked slowly west, continuing to look north at the buildings.

Mueller's Boot & Shoe Shop . . . a butcher shop . . . the Occident Saloon . . . another boot shop . . . and, on the corner of Front Street and First Avenue, the Old House Saloon.

To Lucia the saloons looked subdued; sedate. And they were. Those establishments were where Dodge City's better element went to drink and talk and play some quiet cards and shoot billiards. She heard a piano, faintly, playing something she associated with chamber music.

She could hear other music, of a more raucous variety, but she was willing to bet that it didn't come from that stretch of buildings.

She stepped back and looked further along Front Street's northern facade. By the moonlight she could barely make out the names of the establishments: Kelley's Opera House, the Alhambra Saloon, the Lone Star Saloon, and more beyond that.

Lucia looked across the tracks to the south. The music was coming from one or another of several buildings some hundred yards or so distant.

She watched as a couple of men careened out of one of those establishments. They staggered off to the side, bent down as if they were throwing up, and then careened right back inside.

She stepped off in that direction, southwesterly to be precise, taking care not to trip over the tracks.

As she drew closer she made out the name of the establishment. The Crazy Hors Saloon. The "Hors" had no "e" at the end, but it appeared to be a deliberate misspelling, as there didn't seem to be enough space between Hors and Saloon to accommodate an "e".

Clearly, that was where all the excitement was; there and in the brightly lit saloons on either side. She could make out the name of another one down the street. The Lady Gay.

She certainly couldn't lug her bags all over the town—her arms were already tiring, and so she was grateful to discover that among south Front Street's attractions was a hotel, the Great Western. She went there.

The night clerk eyed her narrowly, noting her proper but worn clothes, her well-traveled carpet bags and the rolled up quilt over her shoulder. He especially noted her good looks. His was a lonely post, and nice girls didn't trot around at night unattended.

"Kin I help you?" he asked, and Lucia found the hot eyes she'd missed in the railroad conductor.

"No," she said sharply, "I enjoy walking around town late at night carrying heavy bags."

The night clerk's face clouded. That sure was a funny thing to enjoy doing.

Lucia read his confusion and despaired. "Yes, you can help me. I'd like a room."

"Ah," said the night clerk brightly, "then you've come to the right place. I kin give you"—he studied a sheet—"number foh-teen. That's one flight up toward the rear. Got a big bed, pitcher of water, basin an' fixin's fer you-know-what, case you should need 'em."

"I'll take it. Should I pay now?"

"How long you stayin'?"

"Few days, maybe longer."

"Naw, you kin pay later. Jes' sign the register."

She did. The clerk studied her signature.

"Lucia Bone. That's a nice name." He got no reaction. "That's a funny name, too. Had a dog named Bone once. Fetch, Bone!" He cackled. "Wal hell, guess yer too tired to laugh. I'll help you fetch yer bags upstairs."

"Could I leave them here?"

"What fer?"

"I thought I'd go down the street. There appear to be some lively places there."

"You mean them *saloons*? An' *hurdy-gurdies*?"

Lucia knew that *hurdy-gurdy* was what dance halls were often called. "Yes. Do they permit ladies?"

"Ladies?!" he squawked. "Hell, I don't figger no lady'd wanta be caught dead in them." He suddenly colored. "But they do got some gals," he finished lamely.

"I see . . . would you call me a lady or a gal?"

"Gol-leee, don't rightly know. Gal, I guess—"

"What?!"

"*Lady*! Fer sure! Don't know what I was thinkin', ma'm."

Lucis eyed him harshly. "Don't call me 'ma'm'. I'm not that old. Miss Bone will do nicely."

The night clerk nodded hastily. When he got through bobbing his head he asked, "Uhhh—yer goin' down the street, is that it?"

"Yes," said Lucia sweetly, "with your permission."

The clerk swallowed. "Well then, maybe you better pay now."

Lucia smiled to herself. "Very well. Will one night do?"

The clerk bobbed his head.

"But the night's half over," she observed in a soft voice.

The clerk swallowed again. Hard. "Guess yer right. Gimme half, plus a full night's, an' that'll take you through two nights."

"Well, sir, that sounds eminently fair."

The "sir" would have been plenty, but the look and smile she gave him really finished the job. "You're sure my bags will be safe?"

The clerk was ready to die defending them.

Lucia Bone walked west along Front Street's south side. She walked easily. She'd grown up in the east, and knew how to walk and liked to walk. She also knew how to ride, and rode well. She'd been something of a tomboy at a younger age and she enjoyed physical exertion.

She swept on past the Crazy Hors Saloon. Two angular, rough-looking men were outside the saloon, but by the time they were sure they'd seen what they'd seen—a beautiful young woman—she was gone, and they were too unsteady to follow.

She paused outside the next saloon, Cattle Annie's Dance Hall, and glanced inside. She saw a long room with a long bar. There was space toward the rear for billiards and dancing. A door at the far end led, no doubt, to several rooms that were available to the dance hall girls.

Those girls, in this instance, were all dark-complected. Lucia's childhood friends had called them niggers, and the nuns at Sacred Heart school had called them, rather archly and deliberately, Neegroes. Lucia'd split the difference and called them colored.

Lucia'd heard rumors that about one out of every four or five cowboys was colored, and about the same number, if not more, were Mexican.

Of the men in long, narrow Cattle Annie's, about half were white, half colored. She didn't see anyone who looked Mexican. She walked on.

Near the southeast corner of Bridge Avenue and Front Street, she passed something called the Comique Theater. She looked in, but it was dark. Attached to it, though, and probably part of it, was the Lady Gay Dance Hall. It was right at the corner.

She looked into it. The girls were white, the men were white, the music was loud, the setting was raucous, and she walked in.

Or rather, she ventured in. Whereas her manner on the street had seemed assured, if not bold, upon entering the Lady Gay she became tentative, if not timid.

And well she might. The men were rough and rowdy for the most part. Trail-crazy cowboys blowing a month or two's wages; gamblers and confidence men bent on slickering them out of that money; roughnecks simply ready to take it; soldiers from nearby Fort Dodge, eager to have a good time, their steady income the town's steady income, one way or another; respectable businessmen who, after a sedate evening on the north side of Front Street and after their wives were safely tucked away, had crept south of the tracks for some excitement (as one Dodge City wag had commented, *"It was only a few steps from the Long Branch to*

*the Lady Gay, but every step was paved with bad
intentions"*); and then there was a generous sprin-
kling of Dodge City's minor employees and various
riff-raff. Then, above all, and seeming to tie all
these establishments together with a common
thread, were the women.

They were a prepossessing lot, those women,
bold and fierce. By and large they were not the
youngsters to be found in the west's bordellos.
They were more mature and were relatively independent entrepreneurs. They were called "soiled
doves" by those of delicate tendencies, but their
very names put the lie to the gentility that "soiled
doves" evoked. Big Emma, Squirrel Toot Alice, Big
Nose Kate, French Mary, Lillian Handie. . . .

Some chose those names to prevent their families
from finding them living lives of shame, but not
many, for they were often as crude and thick-
skinned as their customers. Big Nose Kate Elder
fought off unwanted males with a meat cleaver.
Josie Armstrong was jealous of her sister "doves"
and pulled hair and kicked shins. Frankie Bell often
drank too much and fought anyone near her, male
or female. Those women didn't care who learned of
their profession, and they chose their names to appeal to the prospective client.

Their language, too, said much about their characters. One court affidavit said, *"Annie Lewis . . .
said that . . . one Sallie Doke did use indecent
language toward one Annie Lewis in that the said
Sallie Doke called affiant a dirty-bitch, a whore and
that affiant was afflicted with the clap, all of which
was done in a loud and boisterous manner."*

They often took southern names, such as Dixie

Lee, to appeal to the cowboys, whose sentiments were often Confederate.

When business was slow in town, the girls made money by visiting nearby Fort Dodge. The Fort's commanding officer was not happy with these girls slipping into the barracks, and he issued an order that "no wagons containing prostitutes are allowed to be driven through the Fort Dodge garrison". But a lot of good that did! These women were enterprising, and possessed amazing ingenuity.

Little wonder, then, that Lucia Bone might appear cowed.

But she didn't have time to change her mind. A group of randy, disheveled, hard-drinking cowboys invited her to their table, enforcing the invitation physically. Lucia did not resist, nor flinch at the cowboys' bawdy comments, but neither did she enter fully into the spirit of the occasion. She remained relatively prim, reserved, and cautious, but she did have a gentle smile for the cowboys, who were thereupon temporarily confused. Considering their drunken condition, that was not surprising. They did realize that if they'd been sober and had encountered such a pretty young thing on the north side of Front Street, they would have made straight for a tub and the barber shop, and would have fallen all over themselves making a good impression. But here in the Lady Gay it was different. There weren't any *ladies* here, or at least there weren't supposed to be. Yet, the girl behaved like she was attending some sissified tea party, and damn, she sure was pretty; a feller couldn't risk a misstep with something that fine, or wouldn't if he wasn't drunk.

They called for drinks. "And brandy for the lady, gawdammit!"

One of the "doves," eyeing the action from afar, raised an eyebrow. The girls, while nominally independent, had working arrangements with the saloons. In exchange for use of the premises, including the rear rooms, they were expected to charm customers into buying them drinks, which "drinks" would be tea. It was a custom as old as time itself. The "dove" Aggie wondered what the bartender would send this young thing for her brandy.

The bartender, House Harry—called "House" for the four-shot, .41 caliber, two-inch-barreled Cold Cloverleaf House Pistol he always packed—wondered also.

"Whaddya think, Brooker?" he asked the man who sat across from him at the bar—the tall, well-dressed man who'd been asking all the questions thus far.

"I'd say she wasn't playing the game," said Paul Brooke. "Not the same one everyone else is playing, at any rate. I'd send her some brandy. She might object to tea, and those punchers might make trouble."

"Let 'em," said Harry, patting his side significantly. But he sent brandy.

Lucia Bone tasted it and made a face. She'd expected, or hoped for, tea. She'd always used brandy as a code, and so had others. She shot Harry a look, which he misinterpreted.

"Hell," he grumbled, "what's she complaining about? That's the best we've got."

Paul Brooker had read the look differently, and he set about readjusting his impression of the pretty, tender young thing, who looked as out of place as a fresh rose out in the badlands.

"What's wrong, Bonesy," asked one of the cowpokes, "ain't it—"

"Miss Bone, if you please."

"Miss Bone my royal red—"

"Lucy, then."

"Thash better. Now, whaddya say we drink up, an' ah'll order more. Then, maybe, we kin all sashay out back." He grinned foolishly.

Lucia's head spun. It was happening too fast.

"Now please, let's not be too hasty. A lady needs time to think, and there are so *many* of you—" Five were at the table, but only the three with money left figured they were in the running. "Now I just got to town, just this minute really, and I. . . ." She fluttered her eyes and hands helplessly. "Tell me, how long have *you* all been in Dodge?"

They discussed it. It had been about a week.

"Have y'all been all ovuh town?" Her southern inflection sharpened subtly. After all, these were southern boys.

"Hell, we 'bout *live* heah."

"Do tell. You do mean north of the tracks, too, don't y'all?"

"Wal natcherly. They got saloons there, too. An' they got a passel of *houses*, iffen you know what I mean."

"Oh I do indeed."

Chortles and guffaws were heard all around.

"Wal, 'course, them places is a mite fancier'n this, quiet'n everythin', but yes ma'am, you better b'lieve we been to every lick-splittin' one of them."

"Well then—" she dug in her handbag, opening it

just enough to allow her hand to slip in, and drew out a sheet of paper with the likeness of a woman sketched upon it "—have any of you seen a woman who looks anything like this?"

They all passed the sheet around. All shook their heads. Of course, they'd drunk so much they could barely focus.

"But thet's just a *haid*," crowed one. "Ah never looks at *haids*. Show me her tits, or her—"

"Now you just shut your mouth," Lucia cut in. "I won't hear any talk like that." She retrieved the sheet of paper and stuffed it back in her handbag.

She looked around. Some men at a nearby table returned her look eagerly. They already had a woman with them, Fat Fran, a fairly decent looking woman of ample proportions. She just wasn't ample enough for all four of them.

Lucia's cowboy companions spotted the exchange and glares abounded.

Paul Brooker, at the bar, had also spotted the exchange, and his impression of the young blonde girl was undergoing further adjustments.

Now complicating matters was Private Burt Samuels from nearby Ford Dodge. He had taken a shine to the new arrival, as had all within reach of her charm, and he'd decided that she was much too good for the cowboys.

Samuels was not an innocent, but he did come from a large, religious family that included five sisters in its number. He'd never expected to find a girl in the Lady Gay that reminded him so much of his youngest and gentlest sister, but his eyes did not lie. Nor did his groin. Private Samuels had always nursed an incestuous passion for his little sister Poteet, a passion his father had either shared or despised, for it was his father that had driven him from their home.

Paul Brooker saw the man in faded Army blues, forage cap cocked crazily on his head, edge towards Lucia's table.

Brooker leaned over the bar and motioned to Harry for a refill.

"I've got a feeling that this girl doesn't belong here, Harry. Got an idea she's just looking for someone—she's got some drawing that she's been passing around amongst those cowpokes. I've also got an uneasy feeling that there's going to be trouble as long as she's here."

"So there's trouble—that ain't nuthin' new fer the Lady Gay," Harry said.

"I understand this place got busted up two weeks ago. You want to replace everything again? That private's heading for trouble. And that other table, with Fat Fran, they're gonna jump right in. Winner takes all, you might say."

House Harry remembered the aftermath of the last fracas. Repairing busted fixtures meant a lot of extra work.

"Deke!"

Deke, a young, gangly, pimply fellow, was staring towards Lucia's table.

"Deke! Unfasten yer eyes and git over here."

Deke shuffled over to the bar.

"Run over an' ask the Sheriff t'drop by. Tell 'im we got this young flower of the plains, so t'speak, what gonna get plucked, after one hell of a fight, lessen he makes his presence known and felt. If he don't we may have to close this place an' he won't have a place to deal an' his brother'll lose money." Harry winked at Brooker. "His brother's the goddamn co-owner here."

Deke ducked out the door and ran for the Sheriff. The jail and the city offices were right out in the middle of Front Street, just south of the tracks and halfway between the Lady Gay and the Great Western; centrally located, one might say, and not very far away. But they were too far away to save Private Samuels.

Samuels had edged to Lucia's table and hovered over it. He waited for a break in the conversation.

"Perhaps the lady would care for some moments of quiet, *sober* talk." He smiled winningly and swept his forage cap off.

Lucia looked up at him kindly, but decided the army wasn't her answer.

"Whyn't you stuff it, soljer?" sneered one of her companions.

"I was speaking to the lady."

"What lady? Ain't no lady here, just us'n Bonesy, ain't that right, Bonesy—Ooops! Pardon me, *Mish* Bone," and he fell to cackling.

Samuels' lips tightened.

Lucia glanced around as if looking for help, at Fat Fran's table, at the bar, at Paul Brooker, and House Harry.

Paul Brooker felt something stir within him.

"Aw hell, soljer," said one of the punchers, whyn't you jes' move it on out. Head up t'Sara's, or Nellie's; find yuh some gals there yer own age, an' maybe they can teach you what to do with yer pecker, what it's *for* . . . like we're gonna show Bonesy here."

"You watch your language, you filthy sonuva-bitch," ordered Private Samuels.

The punchers rose, however unsteadily, as one.

Samuels didn't think he'd have too much trouble—a little boxing, some nifty footwork—but that was before some helpful gent behind him gave him a hard shove.

Samuels found himself right inside a puncher's roundhouse swing. The fist missed him but the arm wrapped around his neck and he was nose to nose with the cowpoke. The man's breath made his eyes water.

Then the punches he started taking all up and down his side and back, to say nothing of the knee searching persistently for his groin, did more than make his eyes water.

After being worked over from top to bottom for about twenty seconds, his eyes closed and he sank to the floor at Lucia Bone's feet. She drew her skirt in and looked coolly down at her would-be rescuer.

In the meantime, the cowpokes had no sooner reached for their bottle and begun to celebrate than the men from Fat Fran's table, excluding the gent that Fran had tight hold of, lowered the boom on them.

As the cowpokes had given they now received, in spades.

The new fighters, burly, grimy men who'd trailed stolen cattle in from the Indian Territory and were now looking for fun, may not have been better fighters but they weren't nearly as drunk. They began to make mincemeat of the cowpokes.

Gunplay might have made the contest more even but. . . .

Paul Brooker, seeing Lucia Bone trapped in the center of the seething maelstrom, reached automatically for his pistols. As his hands touched his hips where his guns should have been, he remembered that he'd left them back in his room at the Dodge House. Brooker was a law-abiding man, and there was a city ordinance that said: "Take 'em off when you come into town and strap 'em back on leavin'."

Many a cowpoke got a headstart and, feeling too goddamn good for words, shot up the town on his way out, but by and large the law was honored. Of course, the lawmen in Dodge had to get some credit for that.

The cowpokes, one by one, sank down to mingle with the sawdust, cockroaches and Private Samuels.

One large brawler took hold of Lucia Bone and began to lead her toward the rear. Everyone knew there were rooms back there for the gals and their clientele and a feeble cheer went up.

Lucia did not look happy about the turn events had taken. Not grievously shocked or horrified, either, but not happy.

Brooker took a step from the bar toward the pair, but Lucia glanced at him, registered his fine suit, neat appearance, and soft brown eyes, and she subtly shook her head.

Brooker thought he detected steel in her look.

"Gimme your gun, Harry."

"To hell with you, brother," said House Harry.

Brooker stepped forward anyway. He slid quickly between tables to block the burly gent and his beautiful captive.

Lucia had seen him move, noted the easy coordination of an athlete, and decided he might not be the soft, civilized pushover she had at first thought him to be.

The burly gent had his head down, and was about to walk blindly into a rising fist—for which action his two buddies trailing would certainly punish Brooker—when the air was rent by the sudden sound of gunshots.

Everyone froze. There was dead silence as plaster dust began to fall through the smoky air from three holes in the ceiling.

Heads turned toward the batwing front doors of the Lady Gay.

Two men stood just inside the doors.

One of the men, a pace or two ahead of the other, was of average height and unprepossessing appearance. A sturdy, compact man, he wore a derby hat tilted slightly on his head. His face was soft, his eyes gentle. His eyebrows were heavy and dark, his mustache full, and just as dark. He wore a vested suit, the jacket buttoned only at the top, over a clean white shirt and maroon tie, and two guns. One of the heavy, ivory-handled guns was still on his hip; the other was in his right hand, tilted up. He wore a sheriff's badge on his vest.

The other man was about the same height, but had a leaner, harder face. He had a very prominent nose and a handlebar mustache even grander than the Sheriff's. He wore a Stetson hat and, like the Sheriff, was attired in a vested suit with only the top button of the jacket buttoned, which made the jacket less constricting and provided easy access to his guns.

This second man, his guns both still holstered, peered sharply at the crowd from deep-set eyes. He, too, wore a badge, smaller than the other man's, which claimed him to be an assistant marshal.

The Sheriff's domain was all of Ford County, and the town marshal's was just Dodge, but in local matters they and their assistants worked together.

The Sheriff, having been filled in by Deke, looked for the girl. He soon found her, still in the grasp of the burly gent.

"This isn't your night, fella," he said calmly. "Let the lady go."

The burly gent and his friends were relatively new to Dodge, but they knew who they were dealing with. Many fights weren't fought in Dodge because of the reputation of these lawmen. The man released Lucia.

Paul Brooker took her gently by the shoulders and guided her toward the front. She started to resist, but, after looking up at Brooker, decided to allow herself to be so guided.

As they approached the Sheriff he took a long look at her.

"This is not the place for you, young lady."

He was quite ready to change his mind, but not just then, and Lucia decided it was not the time to argue.

"I'll escort you back to where you're staying," continued the Sheriff.

"I'm going along too," Brooker said.

The Sheriff waited for Lucia Bone to object, but when she didn't, he merely shrugged. "Suit yourself, Brooker."

"When you get off-duty, Sheriff," called House Harry, grinning with relief that no damage had been done that night, "I'll have a table ready for you."

The Sheriff noted the emphasis on "off-duty" and regarded Harry with a twinkle in his eye.

The Sheriff rarely visited south Front on official business. He was very zealous about maintaining order throughout Dodge and Ford County *except,* pointed out his detractors, in that part of Dodge south of the tracks. It was common knowledge that the Sheriff's brother, also a lawman, was part-owner of the Lady Gay, and it was assumed that some of the money made there went into the Sheriff's pocket. Very few people lost any sleep over it.

But while the Sheriff may indeed have been profiting from his benign neglect of south Front, he may also have been interested in maintaining a safety valve. When the cowboys hit town they were going to get drunk and raise hell, that was for sure. Better that it be contained in one area.

Of course, the Sheriff was not unique in his lax or selective enforcement of the law. Alcohol prohibition laws had long since been passed by the Kansas legislature, but Dodge City was one of several towns in the western part of the state that depended on the trade of heavily drinking cowboys. Thus, those statutes were widely unenforced.

"Not tonight, Harry," said the Sheriff.

"Get rid of them guns, fella!"

The assistant marshal, his eyes as keen as they appeared, had spotted a gent trying to keep his guns concealed beneath his coat. He'd reacted swiftly.

"Lemme have 'em. You can pick 'em up on your way out of town."

The guilty party seemed almost relieved to be rid of them.

"That's better," said the assistant marshal, taking possession of the guns.

He was another one of Dodge's lawmen who seemed to be working both sides of the street. Everyone knew that he could often be found in north Front's Long Branch Saloon, padding his lawman's wages by dealing cards. Or, some said, it was the other way around, that his wages were the lesser part of his income by far. Whichever, he was quite openly the profiteer, unlike the Sheriff, who maintained an atmosphere of mystery around his money-making ventures. "Let's go," said the assistant marshal. "I've got a game waiting."

"It's late," said the Sheriff.

"For Doc it's early."

The Sheriff escorted Lucia Bone out of the Lady Gay.

"I'm at the Great Western," said Lucia Bone.

The Sheriff pursed his lips but only nodded.

Lucia decided she'd better start getting on the good side of the Sheriff.

"My name is Lucia Bone," she said, smiling.

The Sheriff only nodded as he guided her along the wooden sidewalks. He didn't seem to be much of a conversationalist, but at length he looked at her and smiled.

"Solid name, that," the lawman said.

Lucia flared. If he couldn't manage a civil conversation, to hell with him.

"And who might you be, my brave rescuers, you and your friend—the only ones with guns," she said, laying the sarcasm on heavily.

Paul Brooker, following, winced, but the Sheriff said nothing. He'd let her cool down. A strange girl, this blonde filly.

"You didn't have to rescue me," Lucia went on. "I know how to take care of myself."

The Sheriff glanced sharply at the assistant marshal, then he reached quickly and snatched Lucia's pocketbook from her. Moments later he was quietly inspecting a Derringer-style Remington Over-and-Under .41. The pocketbook was a very effective hideaway.

"The laws apply to guns carried in purses, too, Miss. Being shot with this seems a heavy price to pay for accosting a . . . *woman* in the Lady Gay." He handed it back. "Leave it in your room. And don't worry, a filly as pretty as you, staying at the Great Western, you'll get a chance to use it."

The assistant marshal laughed and the Sheriff smiled but Paul Brooker thought it was crude and ungallant.

Lucia Bone replaced the gun in her pocketbook.

"I'm still waiting to know who you are," she said evenly.

"William Bartholomew Masterson at your service, miss."

Lucia blinked. Though new to the frontier, she'd heard of Bat Masterson but she hadn't known he was Dodge City's sheriff.

"How long have you been sheriff?"

"I filled in for the latter part of '77 but officially took office this year. I was under-sheriff before. Why?"

"I wanted to know, that's why. Who's your friend?"

The assistant marshal opened his mouth and Lucia thought he made a rude sound.

"Does he often make disgusting noises like that?"

"Real often. He doesn't waste words. That was his name. Earp." Masterson chuckled and his eyes gleamed. "Wyatt Berry Stapp Earp."

"I'll drop these off at the jail, Bat," Earp said, seeming to be in a hurry. He walked off.

"Wyatt comes and goes," said Bat. "He was here two years ago in '76, served as assistant marshal then, dropped by again last year and now here he is again. He just signed on."

"How come he's a marshal and you're a sheriff?"

Bat shrugged. The girl asked too damn many questions.

"He's an *assistant* marshal," Bat said.

They had arrived at the Great Western. Bat Masterson touched his ivory-handled guns where they nestled in the heavy silver-studded gunbelt, and put a finger to the brim of his rakish derby.

"G'night miss. Do sleep well."

"With Mister Remington under my pillow I surely will."

Bat walked off thinking that Miss Lucia Bone would probably give as good as she got. An unusually interesting and attractive girl. He would be sure to see her again.   ৵§

2

PAUL BROOKER STOOD ALONE with Lucia Bone. She didn't look at him but she knew he was there. She'd known he was there all the time. She was very aware of her surroundings.

Brooker's unease was a new feeling for him. He cleared his throat.

"Don't do that. I know you're there. And what's *your* name, Wild Bill Hickok?"

"Don't I wish," he said with a chuckle. "No, I'm just Paul Brooker."

"That's a relief."

"So you've heard of those two—Masterson and Earp?"

"Masterson, yes, a mention somewhere. Earp, no."

"They're both dangerous."

"Dangerous? They're lawmen, not outlaws."

"There's sometimes a fuzzy distinction," said Brooker. "For instance, I heard Earp was arrested for horse thieving back around '71. Near Fort Gibbon, in the Indian Territory. He vamoosed before it came to trial. After that I guess he decided the other side of the law was better, so here he is, a marshal."

"Assistant."

"But he still deals faro and monte up at the Long Branch. Makes good money. Takes a share of the house winnings. And if someone doesn't care for the way the game is going, bingo!, Assistant Marshal Earp appears and shows the gent out of town. It's a nice set-up."

"It's not illegal?"

"Not in Dodge."

"Hmmm." This was some town. "Well, are we going to stand around here all night or are you going to see me to my room?"

Paul Brooker bit his lip. He was trying to hang on to his illusions.

"Oh come on . . . Paul? Is that your name, Paul? Well, come on, I won't bite, and I was just trying to get someone to carry my bags upstairs. I left them at the desk."

"It would be my pleasure."

They retrieved her bags from the night clerk.

On the way up the stairs Lucia commented, "I can't get over how calm the Sheriff seemed. Doesn't anything bother him?"

"Did a few months ago, or so I hear. His brother Ed was the marshal. Got himself shot and killed.

April it was. Had a big funeral, and then they took
Ed and buried him at Fort Dodge."

"Isn't there a cemetery here?"

"Not for decent citizens. Just Boot Hill. That's
just for folks who don't live here, aren't respectable,
just passing through—like gamblers, cowboys, buffalo hunters. Die sudden." He grinned. "With their
boots on."

"I know why it's called Boot Hill, thank you,"
she said, beating him to the punch.

"But decent folks still have to be buried at the
Fort. You'd think they'd set aside some ground for
a legitimate cemetery here in Dodge."

"What for? All their old friends are over at the
Fort."

That was a slightly irreverent comment, thought
Brooker.

"Do you believe in ghosts?" he asked.

Lucia wasn't sure she believed in Brooker.

"Only when I think of dying. I'd like to be a
ghost." It had been a point of contention between
her and the sisters at Sacred Heart. "So Bat Masterson's brother was killed. I'll bet he cried and cried
and cried."

"Don't," said Brooker. "The Sheriff's a good man.
Stay on his good side."

"I would," she said, "if I could get there."

They got to her room and she unlocked the door.
"Would you get the lamp, please?"

" 'Fraid of the dark?"

"Don't be a fool," she snapped.

Brooker put the bags down and leaped into the
room. He lit the lamp and turned it up bright.
Then he went back to get the bags.

He toted them into the room.

"Well, I might as well get around to asking. What brings you out to this God-forsaken town, Miss Bone?"

"You don't think I came to work in the dance halls, Mister Brooker?" She smiled coquettishly and then laughed at his reaction. "You're quite right. God may have forsaken this town, but others haven't, or anyway *I* haven't. I intend to open a school."

Her bags hit the floor with a thud.

"Please. Don't just throw my bags around like that."

"A *school*?"

"Yes. You have heard of schools, haven't you?"

Paul Brooker was flabbergasted. The Lady Gay was a hell of a place to go to start a school. But, aside from the inappropriateness of such a springboard—"There already is a school."

"There is? In this town?"

"Certainly. People here out west are especially conscious of the need for education, maybe even more than they are back East. The school's up by First Avenue and Walnut Street. It was built in '73 soon after the town itself started. It's got this real stern-faced lady running it. Which reminds me, you don't exactly look like my idea of a schoolmarm. More like a pupil . . . or a recent graduate. How old are you?"

"That's none of your business, Mister Brooker. I'm old enough. And I've got enough learning to start a school of my own—probably a better one than that old fuddy-duddy runs."

"I didn't call her that."

"Yes you did. What's her name?"

"Walker. Mrs. Margaret Walker."

"A *married* fuddy-duddy. Well, I'm sure there's room for another school. If these Westerners want education so much they're going to need schools."

"They need wives and mothers first."

"What does that mean?"

"It means that men outnumber the women hereabouts at least four or five to one. You'll have a whole herd of suitors camping on your doorway any second now, especially when they learn you're a real proper young lady."

Lucia Bone nodded with enthusiasm.

"Is that your way of complimenting me?"

"No. I can do better than that."

"Then do it."

Brooker had no trouble spotting a tease.

"I don't believe a school's your only reason for coming here."

Lucia grew wary. She was bold but she was also careful and calculating. She was almost nineteen, and had been on her own for two or three years now. A girl couldn't manage that on blind trust.

She detected something stiff and very Victorian about Brooker. He seemed to be a man of his time who had a place for women and liked to keep them there. Or maybe he was just very uncomfortable being in her room—a lot of men were like that.

But she also sensed something good about him.

"Maybe it is," she said, "and maybe it isn't."

Brooker looked blank.

"The *school*, dummy."

"Oh. Right." She obviously wasn't captivated by him; he could tell that. Dummy wasn't what one called one's hero. But Paul Brooker was a patient man. He could wait.

"Sounds like you could tell me something about this town," she said quickly, before he could start prancing through his mating rite. She had misread him slightly. "I guess you've lived here a long time."

He smiled. "Just a month."

Her eyes widened.

"But I can tell you a lot about this town. I find out things fast."

Now Lucia found herself wondering about this handsome man with the good clothes and the knowledgeable look.

"What do you do?" she asked.

"I find out things."

"What kind of answer is that?"

"A good one."

"All right then. Tell me what you've found out about this town."

"I'll tell you that if you tell me about yourself. I don't believe you're just a schoolmarm."

Lucia's lips tightened.

"I don't have to tell you anything. I don't even have to let you stay in my room."

"That's right, you don't."

She picked up her pocketbook and reached into it. Paul Brooker correctly guessed that her hand had closed around the small, deadly Remington. He wondered if he'd seriously misjudged the girl. Apprehension made him twitch.

Lucia laughed shortly, withdrew her hand, and tossed the pocketbook on the bed.

Then she hauled her bags to the far side of the

room and began unpacking, emptying them into the room's single dresser.

She lingered over a small, brown, tightly wrapped package before thrusting it into a bottom drawer beneath some clothes. She looked around—

"Get your hands out of there!"

Brooker snatched his hand out of her pocketbook, then looked over his shoulder at her sheepishly.

"I was looking for that picture you were showing around."

Lucia's eyes crackled with blue flame.

"There's no money there!"

Brooker appeared profoundly offended.

"I don't need your money. I was after that picture, I swear, that's all."

Lucia tried to bank her anger.

"Why are you still here? Why haven't you run to tell the great Masterson that the slut wants to open a school?"

"I never called you a slut"—he was treading carefully since the girl was somewhat higher strung than he'd thought—"I never even implied as much."

"Well, it wouldn't be something I hadn't heard." Her shoulders slumped. "I wouldn't blame you."

Brooker saw she was vulnerable. And as she stood there, head bowed, blondish ringlets hanging down the side of her face, he could see an artery throbbing gently in her neck, a neck as fair and delicate as fine china.

He fell in love. He wanted her. His breath shortened.

"Damn," she said quietly but emphatically.

He looked again at that delicate neck. It was probably as tough as a bull whip. He sighed.

"Don't weaken," he said. "Not after you've come this far."

She looked up at him without raising her head, her eyes dark pools of blue and black in amber sockets. An especially fetching angle, Brooker thought.

"How would you know how far I've come?" she demanded, once more in control.

"I told you, I find out things."

"Just by looking?"

"Just by looking," he lied, "and listening, yes."

"Horsefeathers," she said, but she'd already made up her mind. She'd looked and listened to him, too.

"I'm nineteen, we'll get that out of the way first, but please don't spread it around."

"What age *are* you going to admit to publicly? You don't even look nineteen."

"I certainly do, but I'm not going to admit to anything. Ladies don't tell their age. And besides, I just look young. That's what you can tell them. Say 'she *looks* young, but . . .' and then just leave it hanging, all right?"

"If you say so."

"I do. Now, to make the long story as brief as possible, I was an orphan, left at an orphanage by my mother. Then I was adopted by these people from outside of Philadelphia, the Crowleys—"

A sudden thought had occurred to Brooker, an astounding thought.

He interrupted her. "Where was the orphanage?"

"That's not important."

"It is—"

"It's *not*. The Crowleys raised me. They thought they couldn't have children, but then they had scads of them. Started coming every year. They couldn't believe their good fortune, and had to test it, over and over and over. Damn near sent them to the poor house, all those kids. It was incredible . . . and very annoying, since naturally, I was no longer the light of their lives, and less so every year.

"But they did well by me. Probably felt guilty. Sent me to good schools; church schools with all those fierce damn nuns, and those *Jesuits*. 'Bout drove me crazy, but got me a good education.

"Then, about three years ago, surrounded by all those *kids*, I decided I wanted a mother of my own."

"I'm surprised you want to be a teacher," Brooker interrupted again. "With all those kids I'm surprised you even like them."

"Well, to tell the truth I'm not that crazy about kids."

"Then why—?"

"Because it's a good profession for a lady, and I can do it." She glared at Brooker. "What the hell else is there for a woman?"

"Not much when you talk like that," Brooker said.

"Oh come on, get down off your high horse . . . you down now? All right. So, I wanted to find my mother. The Crowleys couldn't have helped more. I guess they wanted to be rid of me. They told me where I'd been adopted and gave me a letter. I went there and I was lucky. The woman that had handled me, or my case I guess, was still there.

And she was still young. Of course, it had only been twelve or thirteen years. She described my mother to me."

"She remembered her?"

"Yes. Why shouldn't she?"

Brooker had any number of reasons, but he kept them to himself.

"Now, what came in especially handy was my drawing ability. I can draw anything. I probably should be an artist. In fact, when I start my school, it's going to be my specialty. It'll be an art school, too."

"Just what Dodge City needs," muttered Brooker.

"What's that?"

"I said, I thought those orphanages weren't supposed to tell a person who their real parents are."

"They aren't. That's why I was lucky. I found someone who didn't agree with the rules."

"And she gave you your mother's name?"

"Yes. She's changed it by now so that's no help. But like I said, I can draw, and I did a portrait from her description. I did several, actually. I'd do one, and Belle—that's the woman at the orphanage—she'd look at it and squint and make a face and I'd do another." It must have been fun the way she enjoyed telling the story.

"That's what you were showing around?"

"Yes."

"Could I see it? Maybe I'll recognize her."

Brooker's hand was actually shaking as he extended it to take the portrait.

But as he studied it his face slowly lost its eager tenseness; sort of fell apart. "Damn," he muttered.

"What's wrong?"

He regarded her sadly. "I thought it might be someone else. It was just a wild guess."

"You're saying you haven't seen her around town."

He blinked at her. No, he didn't mean that at all. He looked at the portrait again.

"Actually, there is something vaguely familiar about this face . . . would she be blonde, like you?"

"Yes. Have you seen her?"

He shook his head. "There's *something* . . ."

But he couldn't put his finger on it.

"She looks *exactly* like this?"

"That's what Belle remembered."

"But this woman looks old, or not as young as she must have been."

Lucia shrugged. "Maybe Belle tried to make her look older. Or I did."

"Maybe. What makes you think she's here?"

"Well, she doesn't *have* to be, of course . . . but I've been tracking her west—her and her man—"

"You have? Like a detective?"

"Sure. That's not so hard."

Brooker bit his tongue.

"At least I think I've been tracking her. She kept her name for a while, but I may have made a mistake right at the start and gotten onto the wrong person. She may not have gone anywhere near Chicago, but I've been tracking *someone*."

Amazing, thought Brooker. He also wondered how she could sound so certain, and keep on going, when she knew she could be entirely wrong.

"I tracked them as far as Abilene, anyway. Then the trail kind of petered out."

"So did Abilene, several years ago."

"The problem is, the ones I've been following, they're not such nice people. There was some bad trouble in Missouri—"

"What kind of trouble?"

"Never mind. If I catch up to them I don't want them running off to hide. But it was bad."

"Murder?"

"You're supposed to be good at finding things out; find it out for yourself. I think it almost caught up to them in Abilene; scared them out. They were supposed to have died in some fires— all three of them."

"Maybe they did."

"All three? In two different fires in two different places? They may not have been nice but they weren't dumb. No, they ran for it, and covered their tracks real good."

Brooker began to suspect that Lucia Bone had a flair for fantasy—detective fantasy.

"Tell me, Miss Bone, how is it *you've* been able to track these criminals and the law hasn't?"

"I don't know. Maybe no one cares as much as I do. They're the *only* ones I've been trying to catch."

Single-minded concentration of effort? Possible.

"So there I was in Abilene trying to figure out where they might have run to."

"Denver?"

"Maybe. It's big, but it's also kind of civilized. I looked for a place where the law might not look too close at a person's past."

Brooker nodded.

"Dodge City."

"And what you told me about that Earp fellow rustling cattle less than ten years ago—"

"Alleged."

"—that encourages me a lot."

Brooker shook his head.

"I don't know, Miss Bone. You make it sound almost convincing. But I'm a professional at this game, and it sounds just like a wild goose chase. You don't really have any concrete evidence that she's *anywhere* out here, or even that she's still alive. You yourself said that you could have made a mistake right at the start."

"I did say that, didn't I?"

"Yes. Isn't it true?"

"It was until a week ago."

Brooker had guessed Lucia had a flair for detective fantasy. If so, could a taste for melodramatic effect be far behind?

"I'd written that woman, Belle, at the orphanage. She'd implied that she'd sometimes heard from my mother. I asked her if she'd heard any more."

"She'd heard from your mother?"

"Yes. Apparently my mother was curious as to what had become of me. That's probably why Belle remembered the case so well.

"Anyway, she had gotten some letters from my mother, some that came before I started looking and that she hadn't told me about, and some that had come more recently.

"Now, Belle said that my mother didn't want me looking for her, *but,* since I'd stuck with it that long, and since I'd made it all the way to Abilene—" Lucia took a deep breath "—she figured it was all right to tell me that one of those older letters had come from Abilene."

Lucia was almost jumping up and down.

"And that meant that I hadn't made a mistake, that I was right on her trail, and since that letter wasn't the last one she'd got, *that* meant that she *hadn't* died in any fire. . . .

"And she's here in Dodge City, I'm sure she is. She's gotta be."

"Hm, you may be right," Brooker said. "Not that she's gotta be here, but you may be right. And it's funny, you and me, we're more alike than you'd guess."

"How so?" demanded Lucia dubiously.

"I've been tracking a woman, too. Or the Agency has. I haven't really tracked anyone. But the Agency's been scouring the country, moving from east to west, looking for this woman. They sent me down here. I'm not sure why. I don't know what all the other investigations turned up, but the Agency must think she's somewhere west. Of course, one difference is that I'm looking for a woman and her daughter—her supposed daughter —but actually we're in the same line of work, you and me."

"You're a real honest-to-God detective?"

"Yep."

"You're too good-looking."

Brooker, both pleased and self-conscious, tried to laugh it off.

"But I'm not too good a detective, according to my co-workers."

"I don't believe that."

"I don't either, not completely."

"What's a *supposed* daughter?"

"I'll tell you. I'll tell you all about it."

"Don't." Lucia was suddenly weary, possibly

made so by Brooker's exuberance. "I'm awfully tired." She eyed the bed on which he sat.

"Well?"

"No, you're going to have to leave, Mister Brooker."

"Call me Paul, please."

She shook her head. "For now it'll be Mister Brooker." She suddenly smiled. "Paul." She took hold of his arm and pulled him from the bed. "Oh, I know, if anyone saw you coming in here my goose is cooked anyway, but I do have to ask you to leave."

"Don't you want to hear about my detecting?"

"No, of course not, you said you weren't any good."

"*I* didn't say that," he protested. "Then I'll tell you all about Dodge. I agreed to."

"No, Paul. Tomorrow. I'm tired now."

That was funny. Paul Brooker didn't feel tired at all. But he did look very forlorn as he edged towards the door.

"Oh Paul, don't look like that. I'll see you tomorrow morning and we'll go around Dodge restoring my reputation, all right?"

He nodded and left, and she closed the door.

She leaned against the door, listening to Brooker's steps recede down the hall.

Then she turned the lamp down low, turned down the bed and began to undress.

A window was open into blackness. She didn't give it a second thought, especially since it would be impossible to sleep in there with the window closed. Summer nights on the Plains were often chilly, but not that night.

She unlaced her high-heeled, calf-high boots and removed them.

Then her dress fell, which left her wearing just a pleated petticoat. She carefully hung her dress up on a wall hook. It wasn't her best, but she had only two.

As she'd reached for the wall hook her breasts had risen some, but not much. They were already high and tight. Not incredibly large, by any means, but firm.

She noted their minimal adjustment as she stretched, and she hoped they would stay that way. She wasn't planning on any children, or not for a long while—despite what Paul Brooker had said about the need for wives and mothers and kids and all that rot. She'd seen what an unending succession of suckling babes had done to her foster mother's breasts. Great sacks they'd become, rivaling any decent cow's udder. And the large, bumpy, knobby nipples. . . .

Lucia supposed hers would get like that in time, but not if she could help it. If it was up to her, they'd stay tulip-fresh and smooth and perfect, just the way they were.

A sound came from the blackness beyond the window, startling her.

She turned toward the window, and the sounds got a little louder, more guttural. Sounded like someone was having trouble breathing.

She went to the window and boldly looked out, her breasts hanging just as boldly as she bent.

Nothing but blackness . . . but as her eyes grew accustomed to the night . . .

She turned from the window, went to the bed,

took the Remington from her bag, went back to the window, and waited until her eyes got used to the dark again and she could make out the same suspicious shadow. Then she raised the Remington and shot.

"Jesus Jumping Christ!" came a howl.

Bedlam broke out just south of the hotel. It sounded like a pack of hunting dogs hot on a scent.

Goodness gracious, thought Lucia, satisfied nonetheless. She turned out the lamp, finished undressing, reloaded her pistol, and put it under her pillow as she climbed into bed.

She lay back and stared at the ceiling, deciding that Paul Brooker was not the type of man to shout "Jesus Jumping Christ" when fired upon. At least she hoped he wasn't.

By the time the nightclerk stole cautiously down the hall, knocking quietly on doors and whispering hoarsely, "Anything wrong in there?" Lucia was sound asleep.

3

"A SCHOOL?" queried Bat Masterson. "From the way you describe her it sounds like another romantic notion. People are inclined to think schoolteaching's fun—fun and easy."

The sound of a gunshot came from the direction of the Great Western.

"And she's wrong about that being the only thing a woman can do."

"She's a girl, Sheriff," said Brooker as the dogs started howling, "not a woman."

"Mmm. More girl than I'd thought. You know, Kelley's going to have to find some way to keep those hounds quiet."

"I told her there already was a school."

"I'll bet that didn't faze her, did it? You know, if she was teaching school I might be tempted to go back myself," Bat said. "I remember I had a teacher once who had a real loose shirt and everytime she bent over . . ." Bat smiled at the memory. "But if your Miss Bone hasn't got her head in the clouds, if she really wants to teach, there's some talk of building a new school up on top of Boot Hill."

"Goodness." A chilling prospect if Brooker had ever heard one.

"Goodness?" Bat laughed. "I'm not Miss Bone, Brooker. You can curse if you want. Hell, spit on the floor if you want. But don't worry, they'd dig up the old bones first and move 'em, naturally."

"Naturally, goddammit, and who's worrying?"

"They'll find themselves another Boot Hill, on a less valuable piece of land. You may not have noticed, but Boot Hill's got kind of a nice view. I'm not sure my brother wouldn't have enjoyed it there."

"Seems she's looking for her mother."

Masterson stared at Brooker.

"*Who's* looking for whose mother?" Lucia had slipped Bat's mind.

They regarded each other silently for a while. Brooker wasn't sure he wanted to go into it just then.

Finally Bat broke the silence.

"Oh hell, it's late. Let's get some sleep."

"Before I retire, I'd like to know where those shots came from," Brooker said.

"Sounded like the Great Western."

Brooker looked at him expectantly, if not anxiously.

"Aw, come on," Bat said. "If I investigated every shot I heard I'd run myself ragged."

"But still, Lucia . . ."

Just then one of Bat's deputies entered. He'd heard the tail end of the conversation.

"That was just some gal firing her gun out a window of the hotel." He smirked. "Damn near hit me."

"There, Brooker, you see?" exclaimed Bat. "We keep a close eye on this town."

Dodge House was a two-story, wood-frame building with a peaked roof. It was perhaps thirty feet wide and about one hundred feet deep. Right next to it, easterly and apparently attached, was another structure of similar dimensions but it had a square false front. A second-floor balcony, overlooking Front Street and common to both, linked the two structures. A sign just beneath the balcony railing of the left building said "Dodge House". A similarly placed sign on the right corner building said "Billiard Hall".

The wooden porch of Dodge House was nearly four feet above ground level, gained by steps to the front and side.

The Billiard Hall's porch, on the other hand, was only about two feet high.

Between both porches and the street was a foot-high, wooden sidewalk. And a hitching rail.

One might not have guessed that the two buildings were of common parentage, but they were, and as similar and dissimilar as two brothers might be.

Paul Brooker rolled from his bed in Dodge House at around ten o'clock. He poured water into a basin and attended to his toilet, washing his hands and face in cold water, rubbing his teeth with a wet cloth, painfully shaving with that same cold water and a straight razor, and combing his hair. He dabbed at his body with the cloth and sprinkled toilet water over certain areas.

He then took the basin and set it down beside the bed. He threw back the sheet and blanket and conducted a detailed and thorough examination. Unless he was mistaken, he'd had a couple of bedbugs for company during the night. He remembered hearing how veteran buffalo hunters and mountain men dealt with bedbugs when their blankets got too infested. They'd find a lively anthill, and pile the blankets and robes atop it. The ants would take care of the bedbugs. But then, wondered Brooker, how did they get rid of the ants?

Gotcha, you bugger!

But he had to settle for just the one. He drowned it in the basin.

Then he stepped to his window and emptied the basin out.

Next, Paul strapped on his gunbelt, heavy with a pair of Scoffs—Smith & Wesson's .45 caliber pistols, Schofield models. They were a trifle unwieldy with their six and a-half inch barrels, but they were accurate. Paul Brooker stood in the middle of his room and practiced his draw for about a half-hour.

It was eleven o'clock before Paul Brooker made his appearance on Front Street. He stepped down off the porch and headed for the Great Western Hotel.

That took him by the railroad depot, where he

stopped to send a wire to his home office. It told of no luck in his investigations thus far. It also requested a full backgrounding on the investigation thus far. Brooker felt a little silly not knowing much about the background of his quarry.

He left the depot thinking that maybe one of the other operatives would get lucky, and he'd get pulled back to Denver.

That worried him. He might be able to talk Lucia Bone into going to Denver with him, but he didn't hold out much hope. Lucia Bone seemed determined in her own quest, and Paul Brooker also knew that although he was a solid, stable, and even a good-looking gent, he was not a terribly exciting one. Too serious, too sober, too careful. If he could only do something wild, but safe.

Damn. Why were the best looking women always looking for excitement, to say nothing of looking for a lost mother.

He listened at Lucia Bone's door, heard nothing, and then knocked sharply for a minute or so before concluding that she was not there, or was sleeping the sleep of the dead. Or, considering the previous night's gunshots, was indeed dead.

"That gal went out 'bout an hour ago," said the elderly desk clerk, a neatly-dressed, pleasant change from the night clerk.

"She say where she was going?"

"Nope. Heard her mumble something about those dogs making a racket."

Brooker left the Great Western and cut around back to the home, and kennels, of Mayor James H. "Dog" Kelley.

Kelley had a two-room frame structure. The back room was occupied that summer by two women, Dora Hand, an actress, and Fannie Garretson, a singer, who used the theatrical name Fannie Keenan. Kelley lived in the front room.

Outside the Kelley manse lived a pack of thoroughbred greyhounds, the town's best hunting dogs. A number of the dogs had once belonged to Lieutenant Colonel George A. Custer.

Kelley also had a bear, Paddy-the-bear, but he kept her chained up in back of his saloon on the north side of Front, where she was slipped whiskey by pranksters and teased unmercifully. She came to love the whiskey but hate the pranksters, and made every effort to hide when she saw them coming. One night she broke her chain and hid in the Dodge House, causing considerable excitement.

Paul Brooker found Lucia Bone visiting with the greyhounds.

"Hello, Mister Brooker," she greeted him brightly. "What would you think of me as a singer? Or an actress?"

Evidently she'd met Fannie and Dora. She wants to do and be too many things, thought Brooker grumpily.

"Can you sing?" he asked.

"In a choir."

"I can sing in a choir. How about acting?"

"I'm acting all the time." She smiled. "Fannie and Dora were most encouraging."

Brooker didn't doubt it. There was a shortage of women everywhere out there, and singers and actresses were in particular demand. He'd seen men of taste and refinement throw money at girls that couldn't act worth a damn and sang worse.

"Better stick to school teaching," he advised.

"Mister Brooker!"

"All right, it's something to think about . . . and you'd better keep your hand clear of those dogs. They may not have been fed."

"Well, they surely look thin enough, but they don't look mean."

"Those are hunting dogs. Greyhounds."

"These?"

"Yes. There's a story about the time back in '72 when Kelley took them out to hunt after a big snowstorm. The storm had caught and killed more than a hundred buffalo-hunters. A bad storm. The town was snowed in and they needed food. Of course, Kelley wasn't mayor then."

"The Mayor owns these? And the women?"

"Don't know about the women . . . but anyway, Kelley and his dogs got plenty of food, all right—antelope—but there was one dog that just wouldn't stop hunting. He'd run and kill and run and kill until he couldn't run any more. Kelley finally found him twenty miles up the Arkansas, collapsed beside his last kill."

Lucia Bone thought about it.

"That's an awful story."

Startled, Brooker protested.

"*I* didn't kill all those antelope."

In his heart he was disappointed by Lucia's show of squeamishness. How did she think steaks got on her plate?

"Do they still hunt with them?"

"Sometimes."

"What about you; do you hunt?"

Of course he did, but why get her upset?

"The only things I hunt are steaks and missing women. Have you had breakfast?"

"Nope. Been down here since I got up. These dogs were making a lot of noise last night. I had to see what they were."

They walked back towards Front Street. Lucia told Paul about shooting at some low-life night-crawler.

Paul refrained from telling her that the "night-crawler" had probably been one of Bat Masterson's assistants.

They had a steak breakfast at Hubbard's Restaurant.

"Well," said Brooker over coffee, "I promised to tell you about Dodge City, and I will."

Lucia, inspecting the well-appointed restaurant like a prospective buyer, looked at him without encouragement.

"Will this take long?"

"I'll make it brief," he said unhappily. "I guess you can say Dodge City is what it is because of Indians, buffalo and fever."

"It's not starting like something brief."

"Ahem. First came Fort Dodge. That was built as a base of operations and supply for soldiers fighting Indians. Then came the buffalo-hunters. Most of the buffalo-hunting in the midwest and southwest was centered around here, near the Arkansas. Of course, up until about '70, there was quite a lot of buffalo-hunting, but then they discovered a way to tan buffalo hides to make them into usable leather. The hides used to be spongy, but in '70 a dealer sent some hides to tanners in Germany and that's where they worked out the process. And that's when the killing really started in earnest."

Lucia made a face and Brooker remembered her attitude towards hunting.

"In any case, there was a lot of soldiering around Fort Dodge, and a lot of buffalo hunting, and it was pretty active. There was already talk of starting a town, but it was just talk. Then came '72, and one day Colonel Dodge, who'd assumed command at the Fort that Spring—"

"It's named after him?"

"No. Probably after General Dodge. Grenville Dodge. But anyway, this Colonel Dodge was outraged to find officers and enlisted men drunk on duty. He ordered an end to the sale of alcoholic beverages to enlisted men.

"Naturally, the enlisted men had to drink somewhere. Both Colonel Dodge and Wright, the post sutler, could see that. While they were still thinking about it, a man called Hoover arrived with a wagonload of whiskey. He kept on driving west about five miles, to where the military reservation ended, put up a tent, laid a board between two posts of sod, and opened himself a saloon. And Wright and the rest weren't far behind.

"Then, on top of that, the railroad was coming. The company building the railroad had a contract to build one as long as they reached the Colorado-Kansas border by March third, '73. If they didn't, they'd lose their land grant rights. So the railroad was laying tracks like crazy.

"Naturally, with the railroad coming, buildings started sprouting up like crazy, too. Most of these buildings on Front Street went up that first year. The railroad got here—and tore right through, needless to say—and Dodge City was born. The buffalo trade was booming, and Dodge was rich. And, incidentally, they tried to name the town Buffalo City, but Kansas already had a town named Buffalo so they had to settle for Dodge."

Brooker sipped his coffee. He observed that Lucia was not hanging on to his every word. He tried to think of something that might interest her.

"Two of the workers that showed up that first year, '72, were Ed and Bat Masterson. Bat was nineteen."

"Practically founding fathers," Lucia said sarcastically. "So all right, we've had the Indian part, and the buffalo. What about this fever?"

"Oh. You want the works, huh?" he said, and before she could stop him, he resumed.

"With the buffalo being killed off, Dodge might have died, but cattle started showing up just in time to replace them. They were Texas longhorns. They're from North Africa, actually. Moorish cows. Skinny, tough beasts; run forever and trail where there isn't any water for fifty, maybe even seventy miles.

"At first the Texas cattle, for which there wasn't a real big market, were trailed east to Missouri. To Sedalia, to be exact, along the Sedalia or Shawnee Trail. But that wasn't much of a market, and Missouri people didn't want the herds crossing their land. Pretty soon, though, the railroad pushed west into Kansas, and it made better sense to trail the cows north to a railhead. A halfbreed Cherokee scout named Jesse Chisholm blazed a trail they could follow to Abilene. And the cattle started to arrive.

"The problem was, the Texas cattle brought the Spanish fever, or Texas fever, or splenic fever—it was all the same. It was actually carried by ticks that lived on the cattle. It didn't seem to bother the longhorns, but any animal they came in contact with usually caught it, and died. That was one of the reasons Missouri didn't want the cattle. And the Kansas farmers didn't like it any better.

"But Abilene was all right for a while. There weren't *that* many farmers there yet, and the Texas ranchers agreed to pay for any Kansas animals that died from fever. That arrangement was good for about five years. After five years, though, there were just too damn many farmers, and Abilene residents were tired of all the hell-raising and shooting, and that finished Abilene.

"For a while, Ellsworth and Hays City, further west along the Kansas Pacific railroad, they were cattle centers, but then the Atchison, Topeka and Sante Fe started laying tracks down out of Topeka, southwest, and that changed things.

"Newton was on that line, and it was a cattle center, and then a trunk line was run south of Newton along the Chisholm trail, to Wichita and Caldwell, and they were shipping points for a while.

"Then a new trail north out of Texas was discovered, the Western Trail, or Dodge City Trail as it's now called, and Dodge became the most convenient shipping point. And that's how the cattle got here just as the buffalo were fading away."

"There aren't any farmers around here, are there?"

"Not many; not yet. But there will be, and lots of them. This will be good farm land. I figure three, four more years, and that'll end Dodge City as a cowtown."

"And it'll be just a farmtown, like any other farmtown." Like the one she grew up in several miles outside Philadelphia, Lucia thought. Dull.

"Guess so."

"Great future," Lucia commented.

"Could be worse. You get these mining boom-towns. Once the mine's played out there's no reason for a town. And it gets abandoned. Here, at least, there'll always be a Dodge City."

"But a lot different."

"Sure, but look," he said, smiling warmly, "if you're looking for a big, exciting city, what about Denver?"

Lucia wondered what had inspired that suggestion. "Where do you come from, Mister Brooker? Denver?"

"Shucks," he said, "you guessed."

She flashed him a smile, then got up. "Let's look this town over, Mister Brooker."

They came out of Hubbard's near the western end of Front Street and began to walk east along Front Street's northern side, arm-in-arm. "Looks more proper, Mister Brooker, me being a lady."

Behind them, beyond Hubbard's at the corner of Front and Third Avenue, was the Last Stand. Ahead of them, at the near corner of Front and Bridge Avenue, was McCarty's drugstore. "One of the originals," said Brooker as they passed.

Across the avenue, on the far corner, was Wright, Beverly & Company. "Wright was the post sutler I mentioned."

Gee, thought Lucia, who could remember that? What did he think she was?

After Wright's, in quick order, came the Alamo Saloon, the Long Branch Saloon (Earp's hangout), Hoover's Liquors & Saloon, Zimmerman's Hardware, Drummond's Tea Shoppe, the Lone Star Saloon, the Alhambra Saloon, Mayor Kelley's Opera House & Saloon and First Avenue.

Then, strutting right along, on the far corner of First and Front they found the Old House Saloon, the Dodge City Boot Shop, the Occident Saloon, a butcher shop, Shulz' harness shop, Mueller's Boot & Shoe Shop, Delmonico's Restaurant, the Dodge House, the Billiard Hall and Railroad Avenue.

"I've got a room upstairs."

"Over the Billiard Hall?"

"No, the Dodge House. Fanciest hotel in town. I've got a real nice room—"

She started dragging him on.

"—complete with bedbugs."

"Why Mister Brooker, what an awful thing to say."

"Man can't sleep alone," explained Brooker.

Lucia Bone smiled down at the ground.

They turned the corner and walked north. There was no longer a sidewalk.

"That," said Brooker, pointing, "is the Dodge House privy."

"Mister *Brooker!*"

They passed Chestnut Street and Walnut Street.

Near Spruce Street he pointed out a building and told her it was the Courthouse.

They turned west on Spruce, and back at First Avenue Brooker showed her the Union Church.

Then they turned back down south on First. On the next corner, First and Walnut, the school house was situated.

"It's not very impressive," Lucia remarked.

Brooker agreed. "But they're planning a new one —or *you're* planning a new one."

Lucia just nodded, and Brooker wondered just how dedicated she was to the task of education.

They proceeded on south to Chestnut Street, turned west, and walked on to Bridge Avenue. At the corner of Bridge and Chestnut was the Ford County *Globe*. And on the next block was the Dodge City *Times*.

"The *Times'* editor, Nicholas Blaine, is kind of a puritan, and the *Times* is conservative. But the *Globe* thinks Dodge City is fun."

They passed a large, elegant house.

"Who owns that?" asked Lucia, but Brooker didn't say.

And then they were back at Third Avenue. Brooker pointed to the northwest, towards a rise. "Boot Hill."

"Which is where I'll be," groaned Lucia, "if I don't sit down soon. My feet are killing me!" ⋖§

4

THEY FOUND another restaurant, Drummond's Tea Shoppe, squeezed in between Zimmerman's and the Lone Star, where they snacked on tea, coffee, and crullers.

Lucia, sipping her weak tea, looked with envy at Brooker's steaming mug of black coffee. Being a lady had its drawbacks.

A few other ladies, respectable Dodge denizens, were also taking tea in Drummond's. They regarded Lucia Bone with extreme reserve. Any young woman as good-looking as Lucia already had a couple of strikes against her.

"Of course, Millicent," said one, "her face is much too thin to be called pretty." The speaker was a well-fed, well-dressed woman in her late thirties, the frizzy-haired wife of a merchant. She and her friends associated a thin or gaunt look with the poor, hard-working plainswomen, out in the middle of nowhere in their soddies. The refined, spare look of the well-bred easterner, the patrician look, was not often seen out here—especially not in a young woman who'd tramped into Drummond's like a farmhand and sat down like she really meant it. Those skinny easterners, besides always arriving in their own private railroad cars, always had that delicate, superior air about them.

"Do you suppose she's betrothed to that young gentleman?"

"I should hope so," said one. "I saw them arm-in-arm."

"I don't think so," said another. "Harold knows the gentleman, and if he'd been expecting a fiancée, Harold would know. And look, her dress is really quite plain. His suit is much superior."

"What is his name?"

"Brooker, I believe."

"What is his business?"

"He's a cattle-buyer," said one of the ladies with certainty, though she had not the vaguest notion.

The "cattle-buyer" Brooker was feeling most pleased. This was the way he'd like life to be, taking his ease with a woman such as Lucia Bone. A regular couple, they were. And to him, it appeared that Lucia was quite content with the set-up, too.

"Excuse me a moment, my dear," he said, and he got up and left the restaurant.

Lucia Bone, aware of the ladies' scrutiny, studied her cup of tea demurely, privately turning Brooker's "my dear" over in her mind.

Then Brooker was back, and sitting armed with

copies of the Dodge City Times and the Ford County Globe. He began to leaf through the journals.

Lucia Bone gritted her teeth.

"Listen to this," said Brooker, suddenly smiling. He then read her the following news story:

> Yesterday we witnessed an exhibition of the African national game of lap-jacket, in front of Shulz' harness shop. The game is played by two colored men, who each toe a mark and whip each other with bull-whips. In the contest yesterday, Henry Rogers, called Eph for short, contended with another darkey for the championship and fifty cents prize money. They took heavy new whips from the harness shop, and poured in the strokes pretty lively. Blood flowed and dust flew and the crowd cheered until Policeman Joe Mason came along and suspended the cheerful exercise. In Africa, where this pleasant pastime is indulged in to perfection, the contestants strip to the skin, and frequently cut each other's flesh open to the bone.

The ladies of Dodge, overhearing Brooker's recitation, blanched. And Lucia Bone wasn't any more enthusiastic.

"I wonder where I was when that was going on?" wondered Brooker. Then he resumed scanning the journals.

"Here's another one," he said. "There—"

"Mister Brooker," Lucia broke in quietly, "who are those people?"

A theatrical-looking trio, two men and a woman, had entered and taken a table, drawing the ladies' attention from Lucia.

Brooker glanced up.

"Those are a couple of actors, and one of the women who play with them. They do blackface and what they call 'Irish humor' down at the Commie-cue." The Comique was the darkened theatre Lucia had seen alongside the Lady Gay and "commie-cue" was the way its name was pronounced locally. "One of them is Eddie Foy, the other's Jim Thompson." He tried to remember which was which.

"Anyway," Brooker announced loudly, returning to his newspaper and getting Lucia's and the ladies' attention again, "there's a story here about a dance at the Dodge House. A ball or, as they call it, a social hop. They say Dodge House is quite well known for them. Chalk Beeson provides the music. Apparently the reporter they sent got drunk and filed this (quoting the Editor), 'varied description of the paraphernalia of the Lords of Creation.' Unquote."

The ladies sat forward in their chairs expectantly. Brooker read:

Mr. J.F.L. appeared in a gorgeous suit of lin-sey wolsey, cut bias on the gourd with red cotton handkerchief attachment. Mr. H. was modestly attired in a blue larubs wool under-shirt, frilled. He is a graceful dancer, but paws too much with his forelegs. His strong point is 'the schottish my dear'. Mr. J.N.—The appearance of this gentleman caused a flutter among the fair ones; as he trimmed his nails,

picked his nose and sailed majestically around
the room, the burr of admiration sounded like
the distant approach of the No. 3 freight train.

Brooker chortled and looked up.

The ladies, despite themselves, were giggling
discreetly into their handkerchiefs. Foy was staring
across the room at him, smiling broadly. But Lucia
Bone was gone.

Lucia Bone had taken advantage of Brooker's
amused preoccupation to slip from Drummond's
and return to the Great Western. There she retrieved her purse, which contained the Remington
hideaway and the sketch of her mother. She con-
templated leaving the Remington in the room, but
decided, to hell with it. If Bat Masterson wanted
to follow her around, grabbing her pocketbook and
inspecting it, let him.

She went back down and stood just inside the
front doors of the Great Western.

"Waiting for a carriage, Miss Bone?"

She shook her head at the clerk.

"Just trying to work up the courage to step out
into that hot sun," she said weakly, fluttering her
eyelids.

She was already wearing her slat-bonnet—so-
named because it could be stiffened with wood
slats—but the clerk was determined to find some
way to express sympathy for the comely young
miss.

"If only I had a parasol," he said. "That's what
a fair young lady needs out on these plains."

Lucia nodded, then looked back outside.

She spied Brooker exiting Drummond's, some hundred yards north of her. He appeared to look her way but she was confident he could not see her. She watched him walk, slowly picking up speed, east on Front until he disappeared into the Dodge House.

"Well," she cried lightly, "here goes."

It was a waste of time, though, trying to give the impression of ladylike delicacy. It might not have been a waste had she headed for the church, or the school, or any number of places where ladies were expected and welcomed. But she angled to her right and made a bee-line for the Occident Saloon.

The Occident had been built soon after the founding of Dodge by Moses Waters and James Hanrahan. At about the time Dodge became a cattleman's town, they sold it to a German immigrant named Henry Sturm.

Sturm provided good whiskies and wines, and a dignified setting in which to drink them. He imported Rhine wine from Germany, and featured Milwaukee beer and Monogram cigars. Milwaukee beer, and any beer for that matter, was a fairly recent thing in the west. Beer, being so heavy compared to what a saloon-keeper could charge for it, simply could not pay for the animal-drawn freight charges. It was only where the railroad ran, hauling kegs easily, that beer flowed in volume. And since the railroads were recent, so was beer.

But Sturm was not content with beer, whiskey, wine, and cigars. He also had a lunch counter, where he sold sausages and cheeses. And among those cheeses was Limburger, noted for its powerful and pungent odor.

The story went that a local joker went to Sturm's, ordered a beer, a sandwich, and some Limburger and, as he awaited the order, leaned back and placed his feet on the table. When the order was delivered and set down beside his feet the joker protested that the cheese must not be good because he couldn't smell it. Sturm reportedly replied, "Damn it, take your feet down and give the cheese a chance."

Lucia decided the red-faced, portly gentleman must be Sturm, and she approached him.

Sturm regarded her somewhat askance, as did the rest of the men in the Occident. That saloon might have been a "dignified setting" for them, but in the 1870s, no saloon was a proper place for a lady.

It may have been different in Germany, but Sturm knew the ways of the frontier, and thus did not welcome Lucia warmly, although she was uncommonly attractive, and Sturm was very sensitive in matters of taste, whether it concerned whiskey, wine, beer, cheese, or women.

"*Gut'tag, fraulein.* Can I give you zumzing?"

"*Guten tag,*" replied Lucia, astonishing the Alsatian.

"You *sprech Deutsche?*"

"No," said Lucia, smiling, "just enough to say hello."

"*Ach,* too bad! Zohhhh?"

Lucia took the sketched portrait from her pocketbook and showed it to Herr Strum.

"Do you recognize this woman?"

Herr Strum studied the sketch with narrowed eyes, appeared to hesitate, but then shook his head.

"*Nein.* No."

Lucia nodded. "May I show it to your clientele?"

Sturm, though not happy about it, said that she could.

"*Danke.*"

Sturm beamed, considerably happier.

Lucia showed the sketch around. The various men studied her as much as they did the sketch. But they did give the portrait some attention and, aside from a few more hesitations, all claimed ignorance.

Lucia thanked them all and left the saloon. And there were several audible sighs of relief. Not one of the men present wanted to believe that the tender young thing was one of *those* women.

Lucia went methodically from one establishment to the next, totally oblivious to its nature or whether or not she was welcome. But others were not so oblivious, and as she progressed along Front Street, an increasing number of women began to go further and further out of their way to avoid her, as if she was slowly developing a tangible and repellent aura.

That avoidance she did notice, but she kept on going.

Finally, at the corner of Front and Third Avenue, she stood before the Last Stand Saloon. It seemed to her that she and Brooker had somehow managed to miss it on their exhausting tour. She entered.

It was much like the rest; long and narrow with a bar towards the front, billiard and gaming tables

. towards the rear, and a two-storied bank of rooms beyond that, the upper rooms gained by a staircase and balcony.

There were a few men scattered among the front tables; one man at the bar, a couple of gamblers practicing cards on each other in the rear, and one man desultorily shooting billiards.

There was no one behind the bar. It was so slow, being the middle of the afternoon, that the bar-tender had probably gone to the back to check stock for that evening.

A man emerged from a rear door and glanced towards the front, toward Lucia. He approached her.

He was a heavy-set but flat-bellied man, a bit above medium height. Thinning black hair was combed forward over a wide brow. Wide-set but small eyes were set right up on the plane of his face; he'd look pop-eyed if they weren't so small. It was a pasty face, but a hard face. And the many-times-broken nose showed, with its threads of purple and scarlet, a history of drink.

He wore a brilliantly clean white shirt, heavily starched; an expensive vest with a gold watch fob that swooped from one vest pocket to the other; and a perfectly creased pair of pin-striped trousers. He was either a compulsive dresser, or was getting an early start on the evening.

His thin black mustache seemed to suddenly take wing as he smiled.

"Can I be of service, young lady?"

The effort at politeness was there—or the words were—but the voice didn't take to it. The grating

quality of it suggested that she'd better have some
service for him to perform, if she knew what was
good for her. The voice had power, and Lucia felt
it, like the caress of a bull whip.

"You are . . . ?"

The bird on the man's upper lip flapped a few
times.

"Roscoe Fraley. I am the owner of this and the
Crazy Horse and Cattle Annie's Dance Hall and
the Drover's Rest."

Lucia frowned prettily. "Drover's Rest? I'm staying at the Great Western, and I know the Dodge
House, but—"

"Up Walnut and Bridge," snapped Fraley. "Bigger'n either one of them, bigger'n better."

"What about Nellie's?" called a voice.

Fraley's eyes half-closed. "Shut up, Jim," he
said, his eyes never leaving Lucia.

Lucia sensed her clothes being peeled away.

"You need a place to stay?" demanded Fraley,
and the invitation was so blatant it was close to in-
sulting.

This was a force Lucia hadn't encountered thus
far. Even at the Long Branch, when a man had
made a rude remark, Wyatt Earp had looked up
from his card game and said simply, "Enough!" and
that had been the end of it. Earp himself had
studied the sketch and passed it on, but not without
a look of sympathy for the girl.

But no such sympathy or understanding faced
her here. She felt like turning and leaving, but she
also sensed something she couldn't identify.

"No, I'm not looking for a place to stay, or for

work"—anticipating the predictable—"I'm looking for a person. A woman. I wonder if you might look at a portrait of her?"

Fraley licked his lips. "Lemme see."

Lucia handed him the sketch.

He eyed it for a long time, glanced at Lucia, then back at the sketch.

The same door at the back that Fraley had emerged from now opened again, and a woman appeared. At that distance Lucia could only see that her dress was flashy and clung tightly to a full and strong body; that her light hair was done up in a swirl atop her head and, as she drew closer, that she seemed to be in her thirties.

"Nope," said Fraley, handing the portrait back.

"Can I show it around?"

Fraley's eyes swept slowly over the place. "Hell," he declared loudly, "if I ain't seen her then none of these dumbheads have either." No one appeared to take offense. "But go ahead, show it."

Sure enough, none had seen her. And none wasted more than a second's glance coming to that conclusion.

"Show it to Maggie," said Fraley, indicating the woman. His eyes, growing smaller and harder, almost vanished.

Maggie studied the sketch, her lips tightening.

Fraley watched her, and a cold smile grew.

"Where are you from, Maggie?" Lucia asked.

Maggie's look was unfriendly. "What's it to you?"

Lucia shrugged, having no good answer.

"Chicago," muttered Maggie, looking back down at the sketch.

"You were never east of there?"

"Never!"

Lucia was taken aback at the force of the reply. Maggie returned the sketch brusquely.

"You've never heard the name Jenny Bone?"

"Jenny?" the woman repeated slowly, her eyes hardening.

Lucia felt a rush of something. Knowledge? Or was it fear? She wanted to push this woman, press for a truth she felt was there, but she held back.

"Never," said Maggie. "I've never known a Jenny. Never!"

"Hey," Fraley broke in, "what the hell's going on here?"

Lucia Bone turned quickly. "Nothing, Mister Fraley. Thank you for your help." And she almost ran from the saloon.

Fraley looked after her thoughtfully, then went behind the bar. He took up a rag and began to mop the bar.

"Should I get Whitey?" asked Maggie from down the bar.

"Naw, let 'im work back there. I kin do this."

He steadily mopped until he got down to where Maggie sat at the bar.

"It's goddamn spooky," growled Fraley in a low voice. "That sketch looked kinda like you."

"I think she saw that, too."

"An' you don't know her, never seen her?"

"Never," said Maggie. "Think the Pinkertons might be using women?"

"Naw, don't be stupid. An' who said anything about the Pinkertons? The Pinkertons got enough to do tryin' t'catch Jesse 'n Frank James."

"Yes, you're right, Ross, it was stupid. But when

she said *Jenny,* after showing me the picture, it gimme a chill, Ross, I'll tell you."

"Yeah, yeah, yeah," droned Fraley. He was thinking. "Now wait a minute. Maybe you ain't so stupid, Mag. That might be a nice move, usin' a girl. It may not be the Pinkertons, but who said th' Pinkertons were the only detectives around?"

Paul Brooker spent the early part of the afternoon in his room at the Dodge House, cleaning his guns and composing a long report to his Denver home office, a follow-up to the telegram he'd sent.

Just twenty-four hours earlier he'd been thinking. A few more days in Dodge and then, if no leads had turned up, back to Denver, or on to somewhere else they told him to go. East to Wichita perhaps, or south into Texas, splenic fever country.

But that had been before Lucia Bone had shown up. Now he struggled to give the impression, on paper, of having come up with a solid lead, without actually saying as much. He hated having to fool the home office, but he couldn't leave, not yet.

He stared at the paper, envying the ease with which, he imagined, those journalists churned out their scintillating columns.

Maybe it'd be easier if he got drunk like that reporter at the Dodge House dance.

Brooker crumbled sheet after sheet, until he'd achieved that perfect ambiguous balance between honest confusion ("I can't really make head or tail of it but I think I may have stumbled upon something") and outright falsehoods.

He didn't feel that badly, though, about the finished product. His report gave them about as much detailed information as their orders had given him. He'd received a description of a woman, and that was it; no history, no nothing. He wondered if the Pinkertons were as inefficient as his own outfit. They probably were; it probably accounted for their inability to catch the James brothers.

He sealed and addressed the envelope, tidied himself and then brought it down the street to McCarty's Drugstore, which served as the local post office, and mailed it.

That done, he spent a moment wondering what in the world had become of Lucia, and then he headed back down the street for the Occident. He'd developed a habit of snacking on cheese and wurst in the afternoon. Combine that with good Milwaukee beer. . . .

Brooker suspected that he might have added a few pounds during his stay in Dodge. But he didn't worry. He'd work it off, sooner or later. He was normally an active man and the weight never stayed on.

He was finishing off his stein of beer when he overheard talk of Lucia and her sketched portrait.   ◄§

5

PAUL BROOKER poked his head into Roscoe Fraley's Last Stand.

Whitey had come out front to tend his bar. Maggie was checking the till. Fraley was staring out a front window. He might have been checking on the Crazy Hors or Cattle Annie's, but his distant look suggested preoccupation of a different order.

"Roscoe."

Fraley's head snapped his way, eyes hot. But then they cooled. "Oh, it's you, Brooker."

Paul was passingly annoyed. He didn't think he was *that* inconsequential. True, he wasn't supposed to stand out in a crowd, not that much, but still . . . "Yes," he said evenly, "Brooker."

"Well, what can I do for you, my good man?" Fraley seemed to have a talent for false *bonhomie*.

Brooker had already noted that Lucia was nowhere to be seen. "Was there a young lady in here, showing a picture around?"

Fraley and Maggie exchanged quick looks. "Yes," said Fraley.

Brooker nodded. "I don't reckon she struck a mother lode here, then," he said, admiring his own choice of words.

"How come?"

"'Cause she'd be whooping and jumping all over."

"How come?" repeated Fraley. He'd repeat it ten times over if that was called for.

There was no reason why Brooker should have to explain, but Fraley was the kind of man that put pressure on himself just looking in the mirror.

"Because she's looking for her mother."

"Eh?" Surprise was written on Fraley's face. Also, since she obviously wasn't a Pinkerton or anyone else, sudden relief.

"She's an orphan. Decided to go looking for her mother. Tracked her as far as Abilene, solid, but now she's kind of fishing."

The mention of Abilene put Fraley right back on his guard. "Is that so?"

"But then," Brooker sailed on airily, "if she does find her it might be even worse."

"How come?"

"Apparently, in tracking down her mother she found out that she and her friends had done something pretty damn bad."

"Oh yeah?" Fraley turned away and looked out the window again.

"Back east somewhere."

"Done what?" Fraley asked.

"Don't know, exactly. Something along the line of murder, I suppose. Don't expect her mother will greet her with open arms"—he grinned suddenly—"'specially since she's supposed to be dead in Abilene."

Brooker decided that Fraley didn't have much of a sense of humor.

"Well, I'll be off. Probably see you at one of your places tonight." Brooker breezed out of the saloon.

Fraley moved slowly but threateningly over to where Maggie was fumbling with the cash and coins.

"Maggie," he growled, "are you sure you ain't got some kid you ain't told me about?"

"Honest, Ross," whispered Maggie, "I don't, I swear. I'd know about something like that, wouldn't I?"

Fraley eyed her closely. Anyone that could say what she just said with a straight face had to be watched closely.

He finally exploded, "Then what the hell?!" and brought his fist down hard on the bar.

Maggie didn't even blink an eye. "Ross," she said dreamily, "that girl did kind of look like me, didn't she?"

Fraley stared at her. "What girl?"

"The one that was in here," she crooned, "looking for her mama."

Fraley's face congested. "It was the woman in the *picture* you looked like, goddammit, not that young blonde thing!"

He was going to have to do something about

Maggie. He looked around to see if Hattie was there yet.

A half-hour later, Paul Brooker watched a train pull in. Eight people disembarked, including a rangy pair that were lugging saddles and sporting a couple of days' growth. They had the look of cowpokes, except that their guns were hung too low. And there was a feral look in their eyes that was different. Hardcases.

The two men glanced south, but gave their serious study to Front Street's north side. They shifted their saddles to their left hands and began to step slowly in the general direction of the Occident and the rest of the saloons.

The main tracks were on the south side of the depot, and some siding tracks on the north side. The two hardcases had barely stepped over the siding tracks, still moving slowly, right hands brushing their gun butts, when a familiar figure stepped from the shadow of Mueller's Boot & Shoe Shop and moved to intercept them.

Bat Masterson was nattily dressed as usual, his derby canted rakishly, also as usual. His coat, buttoned at the top button, was swept back to expose a brace of Colts Peacemakers with the five and three-quarter inch barrel and the cutaway trigger guards. These were the guns that Bat used when he was contemplating serious speed. His expression was mild, if not benign.

Brooker saw one of Bat's assistants off to the side, keeping pace with him, but trying not to be noticed.

Brooker glanced at the nearby Long Branch. It

was damn near as far from Bat as was Brooker. Earp stood in the doorway, a cardhand held in one hand down by his side, a Peacemaker with the eight-inch barrel in the other hand, also down by his side. If Earp was annoyed at having his game interrupted he didn't show it.

Bat sort of met the pair, some one hundred and fifty yards from where Brooker stood. All three adjusted their directions until they were moving parallel to the saloons and various business establishments, Bat keeping between the two hardcases and their apparent objective.

They may have exchanged words, but Brooker couldn't hear anything and there were no big gestures.

They drew closer to Brooker, and to well within Earp's range. Brooker would have liked to see Masterson work without the back-up, but watching Earp shoot was almost as much of a pleasure.

But, in the event of gunplay, a man had to look close to see anything. Once the first shots were fired, the black powder raised so much smoke it was hard to see anything. Of course, if you were in the fight yourself, and trying to hit something, it was damn near impossible. You ended up shooting at where you last saw your opponent, or where you thought he might be.

The two gents, hardcases though they might have been, may have spotted Earp and decided that they weren't *that* hard. Or maybe it was Masterson's cobra-look. Those steady, genial, slightly hooded eyes tended to unhinge a fella. In any case, the two men slowly angled back over the siding tracks, and then definitely turned and headed in the direction of Cattle Annie's and the Crazy Hors.

Brooker found that he'd been holding his breath. But he always held his breath in a fight, for a while, anyway. He felt his palms and they were dry as sand. He glanced at the Long Branch but Earp was gone. He headed for Masterson.

The Sheriff had regained the shady sidewalk in front of the Alhambra when Brooker got to him.

"What was that about, Sheriff?"

"What was what about?"

"The fight you almost had."

"Fight? You didn't hear any shooting, did you?" He smiled. "All in a day's work. The railroad wired ahead they were on their way. I had to tell them that I'd admire it if they stayed south of the tracks, where they belong." He stroked his mustache. "Also had to inform them of the ordinance regarding guns. It's funny how surprised folks are when they get to Dodge, loaded for bear, and find they have to take their guns off."

"You didn't make them take theirs off."

"No call to shame them, to look for trouble. They've got the word. If I see 'em again, wearing them . . ."

"You haven't seen Lucia Bone, have you?"

"That little gal from last night? The schoolteacher?" He laughed. "No, I haven't. Why? You lost her?"

"Sort of, and she'd been making the rounds."

Batt's eyebrows elevated.

Brooker told Bat that Lucia was searching for her mother, and how she'd pestered everyone along Front Street with her sketch.

"So that's it. They were still jabbering about her in the Old House."

"I heard about her in the Occident. Funny how everyone feels like helping that poor orphan."

"I wonder how much sympathy she'd get if she were ugly," said Bat, and they both had a laugh.

"She made the rounds, huh," mused Bat. "Wonder if she showed it to Fraley."

"She did. Why?"

Bat stroked his mustache. "There're some folks she'd best steer clear of. Fraley's got more irons in the fire'n you could count, and he's got the morals of a polecat and is about as ruthless as they come. He wants to run this town." Bat's expression said clearly what he thought of that.

"Not much chance of that happening, is there?"

Bat shrugged. "Not while I'm Sheriff. But I'm elected. I'm only here until I'm voted out or killed, whichever comes first. Voted out, I hope. But hell, when I ran for office there were two others running, George Hinkle and Larry Deger, and I only beat out Larry by three votes. Not what you'd call an overwhelming victory.

"Roscoe Fraley, he owns a couple of saloons, a dance hall, and the Drover's Rest, and though it's not obvious I figure he's got a big say in the workings of Nellie Pope's."

"Nellie Pope's?"

"You haven't been there? One of our fancier bordellos. Clean girls, most of them kids, but nice kids—considering—and the right kind of clientele."

Brooker wondered what he meant.

"Proper gentlemen what sneak by there late at night. I wouldn't be surprised if Nellie gets on their good side, so to speak, and then influences them to look kindly upon Roscoe Fraley."

"What does Fraley get out of that?"

"Nothing yet, but you see, there are two groups in town, those that want a quiet, God-fearing community, and those that want the town kept wide-open. The second group's called the Dodge City Gang, and so far, they've had their way. They backed me, and they're one of the reasons I don't mess around south of the tracks too much.

"Now, you might expect Fraley to be part of the Dodge City Gang, but he's not. He doesn't like them, and when you come right down to it, nobody likes him, either. But he's got power, he owns things. And I figure he's just waiting for the right time to make his move; get religion and join the upright folk, at the same time calling in the markers Nellie Pope's gathered for him."

"Blackmail."

"Yep. He'd end up Mayor in no time at all."

"Sounds like a sure thing," said Brooker.

"Not if I kill him first," said Bat pleasantly.

"You don't like him, personally?"

"Nope. I dislike him personally, professionally, every way there is. And he dislikes me just as much." Bat made it sound fair. "He'll try to get me. I think he's tried already. I'm pretty sure he got my brother, Ed; that he arranged it. Those two hardcases that just arrived, they were looking for Roscoe.

"But look, Brooker, just keep your Miss Bone away from him. He'll use her if he can, and if he's already seen her, I'd wager he's figuring out the ways and means right now."

"I'm afraid she's not *my* Miss Bone," said Brooker. "She's not anyone's. She's a very independent young lady. I'm not sure I know what to make of her."

"Been around, huh?"

"What do you mean, been around?"

"Which reminds me—"

"What do you *mean,* sir?!"

"Oh hell, Brooker, I don't need *you* on my back. I didn't mean anything. I was just reminded of a gal. . . ." He broke off as he saw a new expression come over Brooker's face. "Now what?"

"I was just thinking of that sketch. There was a woman at Fraley's. She didn't look that unlike the sketch."

"You're sure?"

"I'm a trained observer," said Brooker a trifle pompously.

"All right, all right." Bat fell silent for a while. "Just all the more reason to keep an eye on that Bone gal."

Brooker nodded and responded absently, "Will do, will do." He nodded awhile longer, then suddenly said, "Ah, by-the-by, Sheriff, do you happen to know of a decent dentist?"

"Well, there are a few." And he gave Brooker their names. "But, since you're staying at the Dodge House, one of your neighbors there might help." Brooker wasn't sure there wasn't a mischievous gleam in the Sheriff's eye. "That the *Times* you've got there?"

Brooker handed it over and Bat Masterson opened it to a classified advertisement. "Read that, Brooker."

* * *

J.H. Holliday, Dentist, very respectfully offers his professional services to the citizens of Dodge City and surrounding country during the summer. Office at room twenty-four, Dodge House. Where satisfaction is not given, money will be refunded.

"Is that *Doc* Holliday? He's a dentist?"

"Sure is. Comes from Georgia and practiced around there until his T.B. sent him west looking for a dry climate."

"But he's a gambler, and a drunk practically."

"True, he is now. But he's still got his tools, keeps his hand in sometimes." Bat grinned. "There's a story about him working on Clay Allison—"

Brooker knew the great gunfighter only by reputation.

"Seems Doc pulled the wrong tooth, so Allison made Doc get in the chair and knocked out one of Doc's teeth."

"Ah-ha," said Brooker. "What were those other names you mentioned?"

Bat repeated them. "By the way, Brooker, I was wondering—and I better ask you now while you can still talk—what is your Miss Bone doing for money?"

"She's not *my* Miss Bone, and I don't know what she's doing for money. I saw her hide a package in one of her drawers. I imagine that's her stake. Don't know how much it amounts to, though."

Bat nodded.

"You know, Sheriff, what this town needs is a bank."

"What for? We get a bank and the next thing you know Jesse and Frank'd be riding into town to make a withdrawal. I'd just as soon wait until they were out of the way."

"Where do you keep your money?"

"We've got a safe in the jail."

"Ah, well then, how about holding some money for me?"

Bat laughed. "Try Zimmerman," he said, "or Wright's. The merchants do all the banking around here."

Brooker thought he might. He said good-night and headed back to the Dodge House.

Lucia Bone watched Brooker enter the Dodge House. She wasn't avoiding him because she disliked him. It was simply that she had things to do, and Brooker was time-consuming. If it were up to him they'd still be sitting in Drummond's.

She'd returned to the Great Western to wash her face and hands—Dodge was dusty—brush her clothes off, and renew her scent. The small bottle was labeled "Prairie Blossom." She'd yet to cross a prairie that smelled like it did, but that was the prairie's loss.

Now, satisfied that Brooker was out of the way for a while, she headed north. She had a lot more canvassing to do.

She kept that up for two more days. She'd meet Brooker in the morning for breakfast, and join him again in the evening for dinner and entertainment, either the quiet music and performances north of the tracks, or Eddie Foy's bawdy show at the Comique, or the brand new can-can show at the

Varieties Dance Hall. But in between those times she lost him; left him grabbing at thin air as she continued her search. She retired to her hotel early, sorely frustrating Brooker, and leaving him to imagine awful things (which generally involved late visitors to her room), she had to have *some* source of income. Jealousy made his frustration worse.

In the end, though, Lucia came up as empty as did Brooker. She managed to meet most of the town's middle class, and the wealthier residents' hired help, and all were sympathetic, but none could help her. All she was left with was the resemblance to her sketch of the woman in the Last Stand.

But that was something, definitely something. The woman Maggie looked as tough as Lucia's mental image of her mother. Her mother had dumped her in an orphanage and walked off. This Fraley woman looked like she could dump an entire family into an orphanage, or worse, without batting an eye.

Lucia had no illusions about her mother. She didn't expect much, but she was determined to see just how little there was to the woman. It would remove a great weight from Lucia's shoulders. ✺

6

Lucia Bone awoke with a feeling of light-headed unreality. The previous evening she'd witnessed a scene that had brought home to her the often fleeting and witless quality of life—and death—in Dodge City. It was also a stimulating quality, she had to admit, that had left her sleepless for a while, but in the morning it was the spooky unreality that remained.

She and Paul Brooker had dropped by the Comique to catch Eddie Foy's show. The show's level of humor was crude (Foy, working with a female performer: "Belle, you are my dearest duck." Belle: "Foy, you are trying to stuff me") but fun. In the audience that night, however, was a man that Foy, for some reason, happened not to like. Ben Thompson was a renowned gunslinger, and reportedly a cold-blooded killer. Foy, foolishly, never bothered to conceal the fact that he did not like Thompson. He was a performer and a ready wit and was confident he could talk his way out of anything. And he probably thought that Thompson, like everyone else, was unarmed.

In any event, that previous night Thompson came into the Comique and sat down facing Foy. Thompson produced a gun from somewhere and pointed it at Foy's head. "Move your head. I aim to shoot that light." He meant a light right behind Foy's head.

Eddie did not move, though he was courting death, since Thompson was known to be a man of his word. Instead he stared intently into the eyes of the man he detested, Ben Thompson.

Thompson hesitated.

Then Bat Masterson was there leading Thompson outside.

Foy went to his dressing room.

Afterward, Foy spoke to a gathering that included Brooker and Lucia.

"I found my hands shaking so that I couldn't put on my make-up."

"Why do you suppose Thompson didn't shoot?"

Foy stared at the questioner, as if he wasn't about to wonder why, but just count his blessings. But then Foy's irrepressible sense of humor got the best of him.

"A man accustomed to killing tigers would feel himself belittled if he were asked to go on a squirrel hunt."

Still later, Lucia Bone asked Brooker why Bat Masterson had been able to lead such a bad man as Thompson away so easily.

"With the real gunfighters," said Brooker, "like Allison and Thompson, there seems to be some kind of gentleman's agreement, which is probably why Thompson still had his guns—they're expected to behave themselves in a town run by one of their own."

"One of their own—Bat?"

"And his brother. And Wyatt. And Doc. Besides which, Bat and his friends are good. Even someone like Thompson might bite off more than he can chew."

"That Foy's pretty spunky."

"He has to be with the things he says about Dodge. Last week a few of the boys decided to see what he was made of.

"Late one night he was grabbed as he left the theatre. They put a rope around his neck and were about to string him up from a telegraph pole. They asked if he had any last words.

"He said he had plenty of words, but they'd best be spoken at a nearby bar where he would buy a round of drinks. After that he was accepted."

"Then he is brave."

"He didn't have much choice. When he gets a chance to think about it . . .

"There's this pass through the hills, in Colorado, that the railroads have been squabbling over. One day Dodge City got a bunch together to go out and fight for the Santa Fe against an army raised by the Denver and Rio Grande Railroad. Bat Masterson asked Foy to join. Eddie said he didn't know one end of a pistol from the other. Bat said that it didn't matter, that he'd give him a sawed-off shotgun that even an actor could fire. But Eddie still managed to beg off."

"So he's not a hero," said Lucia, defensively. "Not everyone's a hero."

"Matter of fact, Lucia, damn few are heroes. Damn few."

Lucia thought about that shortage of heroes as she lay there in bed. Paul Brooker certainly wasn't a hero. He was too intelligent, too cautious, too cagey.

But did that mean only stupid men could be heroes? She didn't like thinking about that and she threw back the covers and got out of bed.

A half hour later she was wearing a split dress and striding west along the south side of Front toward Ham Bell's livery.

Hamilton B. Bell, a native of Maryland, had arrived in Dodge in 1874. His first Elephant Livery Stable, the present one, was modest in size (he was later to build the largest livery in Kansas) but he more than made up for any lack of space with trustworthiness and a largeness of spirit. Freighters knew that they could leave their wagons and animals at Ham Bell's and they'd be safe. And cowboys knew that if they didn't have money for a hotel room, Ham would let them sleep in his hayloft; during the height of the cattle season as many as fifty cowboys could be found sleeping off their drunken stupors in his hayloft.

Bell had one other noteworthy characteristic. He was a maniac on the subject of good health and

temperance, and while he was not among those demanding enforcement of the State's prohibition
laws, he did seize every opportunity to hand out
free dippersful of buttermilk. Buttermilk Bell. "It's
one hell of a lot healthier than whiskey."

Lucia Bone was feeling pangs of hunger as she
walked into Bell's livery. Ham himself approached
her. He noted her split dress, not a common sight
those days.

"Good morning, miss. Where did you get that riding outfit?"

"Made it," said Lucia shortly. She enjoyed riding
astride, and was tired of hearing comments on the
proper way for ladies to ride horseback. You
couldn't do a damn thing riding sidesaddle on a
horse.

But, she'd heard, even so prestigious a person as
Libbie Custer had had to ride sidesaddle when
others were around. It was only when she was off
riding alone, or with George or members of the
Custer family, that she could ride astride and show
what a damn good horsewoman she was.

"Wal," said Ham, smiling genially, "makes sense
to me. But don't tell the ladies I said so."

"Don't worry, I won't. But they haven't been going out of their way to talk to me anyway, so . . ."

"Independent, are you? Oh, now wait a minute,
you're not one of them gals from the dance hall,
are you?"

"No."

"Didn't think so. They're still sleepin'." He
winked broadly. "You from Nellie's?"

"No. What's Nellie's?"

"Less you know the better. What are you?"

"School-teacher."

"That so? Guess you're out of luck, lessen you're still here next year. You had breakfast?"

"No."

"Care for some buttermilk?"

Lucia frowned, trying not to salivate. "I don't think I've ever had any." Actually, she was very fond of it.

"You haven't? Well, you are in for a treat." A few moments later, he said, "Here."

She sipped tentatively, looked indecisive, and sipped some more, eventually sipping the dipper dry. "That's not bad," she pronounced a trifle uncertainly.

Bell sensed a convert. "Hell. Have some more."

When Lucia finally rode out of the livery she was practically sloshing in the saddle.

She rode over to Bridge Avenue, turned south, and quickly found out why it was called Bridge Avenue. It ran directly into a bridge over the Arkansas. A toll bridge.

The bridge had been built by the Dodge City Bridge Company and opened in 1874. It was just another way to separate the Texas cattlemen from their money, since it was the only way across the river for both the cowboys and the cattle. But there was no discrimination; everyone had to pay.

Lucia hadn't brought any money with her. Ham Bell had offered credit, but— "Oh goodness gracious, now I'll have to ride all the way back into town to get some money."

"Hell, you ain't left town yet, miss."

"Oh, it's just so much trouble."

"Wal, mebbe I'll let yuh by this time."

Lucia smiled warmly at the man. "Will you let me by when I come back, too?"

"Shucks, cain't leave yuh sittin' out onna prairie fer the resta yer life."

"Oh, you're so sweet. What's your name, in case you're not here when I return?"

"I'll be here. Been here since '74. But the name's Riney. John T. Riney."

"Golly. Been here all this time. It must be interesting, watching everyone come and go."

"Interesting? Stampedes are interesting, *too* interesting, but that's about it."

"You don't like your job?"

"Job's a job. You get used to it."

"Oh."

"Tell you what. Come time fer you to die and go to heaven, you jes' keep yer eye peeled fer ol' John T. I'll likely be right there at them Pearly Gates, collectin' tolls."

Lucia grinned. "How much do you think the toll will be? What'll it cost to get in?"

Riney tried to think of an appropriate cost. "A good life, miss, that's all, just a good life, and I'll tell you, there're damn few in Dodge that've got the fare."

Lucia rode on. John T. Riney was probably right, she thought, but she also had to admit that she might not have the fare, either.

Lucia rode for about as long as the buttermilk sustained her. She rode hard, and it felt good as it worked out a lot of the kinks. Tension had been building in her the past few days, subtly and unsuspected, and had been slowly tying her up in knots. But the jolting exercise untied them. Toward midday, since the prairie landscape wasn't all that exciting, she did not regret the reawakened hunger pangs that drove her back to Dodge.

She scarcely paused as Riney waved her on over the bridge.

She returned the horse and promised a protesting Ham Bell that she'd get him his money that afternoon, then returned to the Great Western with a good deal more spring in her step than when she'd left.

One of Bat's assistants lounged by the front door, but said nothing as she entered, only nodded, eyed her slyly, and clearly recalled her breasts hanging out the window that recent night.

The clerk gave her a worried look but she was feeling too good to wonder about it.

She bounced up to the second floor, but hesitated as she neared her room. The door was open.

Bat Masterson stood inside the room.

The room would have been a shambles had it not been so bare to start with. As it was, just the area around the dresser was a mess. All its drawers had been removed and emptied on the floor.

Lucia gasped and went to her knees, pawing through the clothes and random belongings.

She looked up at Masterson, her face drained.

"I understand there was a packet tucked away in a drawer," he said. "I poked through, and didn't find any packet."

"How did you—"

"Brooker saw you putting it away. He thought it was probably money." Masterson realized he was casting suspicion directly on Paul Brooker, but facts were facts, deal the cards and play 'em as they lay. Besides, Brooker was a big boy; he could take care of himself.

"Brooker?"

"Wasn't him that did this. A couple of fellers, which the clerk doesn't seem able to describe very clearly, came upstairs and shot the door down." He glanced toward the door which, being wide open, Lucia had failed to examine upon entering. The area around the lock had been destroyed by slugs. "Don't understand that. Could have put their shoulders to it just as easy."

Lucia's lips were colorless.

"Emptied the bureau. Didn't touch your pocketbook. That little gun I told you not to carry, it's still there."

"They knew just where to look," said Lucia bitterly.

Masterson, looking around coolly, said, "That's no trick. There's nowhere else to hide anything." He pursed his lips. "Or they'd been here before."

That didn't deserve a reply, decided Lucia, surprised that the Sheriff would even say such a thing.

"The clerk heard them," Masterson went on, "but he'd just about died and wasn't about to come up here. He did manage to send someone to get me. Gunshots, you understand, aren't that unusual hereabouts.

"About then these undescribable gents came pounding back down the stairs, and likely advised the clerk to keep his mouth shut; but maybe you know them, miss. Maybe you can help me."

Lucia frowned in puzzlement, yet was reminded of Masterson's earlier comment.

"Apparently, when they left, they said to tell you that the night wasn't worth what they'd paid, not nearly, that you'd cheated them and they were only taking back what was rightly theirs."

Lucia now understood the cool appraisal she'd been getting from Bat Masterson, the expressionless voice with which he'd noted the facts.

"On my way over here, one of those slimy gents that hangs around Cattle Annie's, he shouted, 'Looks like one of them soiled doves got cleaned up; cleaned up and cleaned out,' his very words. Have you got any comment?"

What could Lucia say? What good would it do? Masterson's mind was made up.

"I was with Paul Brooker last night."

"Oh? All night?"

"No. Of course not." Although spending a friendly night with a man like Brooker wasn't the same as selling it, it would make her a bad woman, of course; "soiled" as hell in the eyes of the upstanding, but not in the same class as the professionals; the whores. Paul, she was sure, would back it up— and probably insist on making an "honest" woman of her, one way or the other—but Lucia was angry. "No, goddammit. I don't sell it and I don't give it away for free."

An admirably virtuous statement, thought Bat, if clothed in pretty ornery language. He chewed on his lip.

"I don't suppose you believe me," said Lucia bitterly.

"Wouldn't help if I did or didn't. Won't get you

your money back. I imagine those fellers are long
gone by now, in the next county, easy."

"And this is what you call *law* in Dodge City?"

"No one got killed," observed Bat, "and a robbery
like this, it's not much worse than what happens
every night in the hurdy-gurdys. In cases like this
where things aren't so clear cut—"

"What you're saying is that you don't believe me."

"Well—" Bat pushed his derby to the side and
scratched his head "—what puzzles me is why they
would yell a thing like that if it wasn't true. And
how they knew you had money."

"Everybody knew that who wanted to know. I
don't live on air."

"Reckon you're right about that."

"But you're just putting me in a class with all
those whores."

"Not quite," but not for any reason that reflected
well on Lucia. Bat respected virtue and its cham-
pions, and could apply the double-standard as fast
as the next man—it was the way he had been
raised—but he wasn't stupid, and while he knew
that damn few whores had hearts of gold, they
often had other redeeming qualities. Loyalty, in-
dustriousness, enterprise, sometimes looks, a desire
to please a man; but most importantly an openness,
a lack of deception. A kind of honesty.

He thought about Big Nose Katie Elder, with
her meat cleaver. She was devoted to Doc Holliday,
and Doc to her, and Doc was no dummy.

The ones that bothered Bat were those that tried
to deceive themselves and everybody else.

He wasn't sure where to place Lucia in that suspect pantheon of heroines. She might be telling the truth, but instinct also told him she was no lily-white virgin. He'd known too many women in his young life to be wrong about that.

"How much was there?" he asked.

Lucia said something Bat couldn't hear.

"What was that? How much?"

"More than a thousand dollars," said Lucia in a low voice.

Bat's eyebrows raised. "Where'd you get that much?"

"I worked for it!"

Bat pursed his lips and whistled low. "A thousand dollars does seem a mite steep for one night."

Lucia's eyes were slits.

"Works both ways," Bat rambled on. "Can't imagine anyone paying a thousand dollars for a night, or for ten nights, but on the other hand, I've just got your word on the amount." He smiled genially at her.

"Sheriff Masterson," hissed Lucia, "this is my room. You get out of here or I'll take that Remington those boys so kindly left and empty it into you."

Bat shrugged and edged toward the door. "Don't know what you're planning to do," he said mildly, "without any money. I reckon you could marry any one of fifty gents, including Brooker, or open that school; you might be able to teach a few things that don't often get taught"—he knew how long it would take her to get to her gun—"or, I guess Nellie Pope could find a spot for you. Her girls are about your age, or less."

"Nellie Pope's is a . . . ?"

"Yep, fanciest in town. And Nellie herself, she's supposed to have some kind of aristocratic background, though I've got my doubts. She's tied in with Fraley, and he's bad news."

"You don't like me, do you? You like me about as much as I like you."

Bat remained expressionless. "I haven't made up my mind yet about that," he replied truthfully. "I'm inclined to respect folks that are honest, honest good or honest bad. You—"

"You've no proof I'm bad!"

"No proof, true, but none that you're good. You're not clear to me, miss. And I do know you're not exactly what you say you are." And Bat stepped out into the hall, closing the shattered door behind him.

How could he know who she was, thought Lucia, when she didn't know herself. "Well, to hell with you, Sheriff!" she shouted at the door. "And you tell that bastard Brooker that having me robbed sure ain't gonna help his case—that lousy bastard!"

Bat, as he descended to the first floor, regretted his own performance. He should have been smoother, more sympathetic; less doubting. But it had all come as a rude surprise. He'd rather liked Miss Bone, off first impression.

He glanced at the desk clerk and the man almost shriveled on the spot.

Stepping outside, he found his assistant grinning at him.

"I could hear her all the way down here."

Bat nodded.

"Damn, Bat, I shore don't see how any fellers

couldn't have been pleased by a night with that filly."

Bat's eyes narrowed. "How do you mean?"

"Wal, remember them shots the other night?"

"George, there've only been about a thousand shots this past week."

"Late? When that feller Brooker was in talkin' to you?"

Bat recalled the shots from the hotel.

"Well, that was me!"

"Shooting? Those weren't shots from a .45."

"Noooo . . . I was out in the dark while that little miss was prowlin' around her room half-nekkid. It was me she was shooting at."

Bat leveled a hard gaze at his assistant. "Don't ever do that again, George; or if you do, make sure I never hear about it."

George bit his tongue.

Bat reentered the Great Western. He would tell Lucia who the prowler had been. Bat was a fanatic about keeping things straight and above-board, out in plain sight for everyone to see.

He mounted the stairs once more, and went down the hall. He had a soft, springy walk; the walk of a well-conditioned man. Didn't make much noise.

He hesitated outside Lucia's door, knuckles raised.

From inside the room came the sound of weeping, the heavy, gut-wrenching sobs of a person suddenly hurt and vulnerable.

Bat slowly turned away and walked silently back down the hall.

* * *

"Went off smooth as silk," said the young man with the wispy beard and the close-set eyes. He handed over the money.

Fraley counted it. "Hell, I shoulda promised you a tenth 'stead of a half," he said grinning.

"Deal's a deal, Ross."

"You say what you were supposed to?"

"Hell, we made sure everybody knew."

"Anyone see yuh?"

"No one what's gonna say nuthin', an' even if they did, it's our word against hers, an' right now her word ain't worth nuthin. We saw Bat an' his man over t'the Great Western. They was laughin'."

"So," said Fraley, rubbing his hands together, "now that poor girl's gonna have to get the hell out of here, or work for a livin'." ᴈᵹ

7

THERE WEREN'T too many jobs available in Dodge City for a girl of beauty and intelligence, but limited skills.

Lucia could sew, but so could a lot of women and Dodge was overflowing with seamstresses. She was also a decent artist, but that was not a talent in very great demand thereabouts.

She briefly considered trying to work as a laundress at nearby Fort Dodge. Laundresses had been an official part of the Army since 1802. The laundress was housed, fed, given fuel, received the attention of the post surgeon, and received appropriate payment for her work, often as much as forty dollars a month for a hard worker. Since a private's pay was only thirteen dollars a month, an unmarried laundress was in great demand as the enlisted man sought to improve his own lot.

There were, however, a limited number of laundresses, a number arbitrarily set by the Army—one for every twenty men on post. And that limitation, plus the squalor in which they seemed to live, led Lucia to look elsewhere.

The obvious options of working the south side of Front Street, or being kept by a man such as Brooker, were also rejected, but not for reasons of morality. Rather, the south side saloon's rough trade did not appeal to her at all and, perhaps in reaction to her own rootlessness, she firmly believed in the legitimacy and permanence of marriage. At the same time, however, she did not feel ready to marry.

Singing and acting, while nice to think about, were fantasies. Even if Foy were to take a shine to her, she didn't think she could countenance the inane stage repartee. Besides which, a lot of those actresses weren't much better than dance hall girls.

No, the theaters, the dance halls, the saloons; she wouldn't be able to survive in those environments. She couldn't wrestle with a man, wield a meat cleaver, or drink and curse with the boys. She was tough, but not that way.

All of which considerably narrowed her options.

The house was on Chestnut Street, which was parallel to and one block north of Front Street, and between Bridge and Third Avenues. Its closest neighbor was the Dodge City *Times*. Blaine, the puritanical editor, thought it an evil gesture, plac-

ing such a house so close. But since he'd found he
could do nothing about it—his bleats before the
City Council had fallen on surprisingly deaf ears—
he ignored it, in print, at least, if not in the turgid
recesses of his own mind.

The house, two-storied, narrow, but deep with
a peaked roof, was grey with cream trim. It always
seemed either freshly painted or freshly washed.
Without the cream trim it might have seemed
somber; with it, it seemed almost elegant.

A house-wide balcony overhung the deeply re-
cessed front door and was supported by four fluted
columns that rose from a high porch. The porch
was enclosed by a low balustrade, save where six
wide steps rose from the street and gave access.

Potted vines climbed from the porch up the columns. And dense bushes flanked the stairs.

All the windows facing the street, below and
above, were thoroughly curtained. Occasionally
those curtains would part and a face would show,
but that vaguely spooky apparition never lasted
long.

The front door was rarely used during daylight
hours. The house's denizens would come and go by
a rear entrance, which opened onto Walnut Street,
the next street north. And daytime clientele, too
impatient to wait for night, would likewise use that
rear entrance.

There was an abundance of cottonwood trees at
that north end, still young and growing, that afforded some cover and discretion to those coming
and going.

There were hitching rails out back, while there

were none in front. At night, despite the rails, there
was often a hopeless tangle of horses, wagons and
rigs at the back entrance.

Deliveries were also made to the rear. Wash was
hung out to dry in the rear. And girls, in various
states of undress, often sunned themselves out back.

Thus the house was a contrast, the two ends in
apparent conflict with each other: the stately, almost ante-bellum front and the ragged, earthy rear.

It was the front facade that Lucia Bone approached, but not in ignorance. She knew what lay
behind.

Lucia was startled by her first encounter with
Nellie Pope.

Lucia's knock had been answered by a young,
slim, colored girl. The girl, named Cassie, showed
Lucia into a dim reception room. The room was
large and abundantly furnished with velvety, overstuffed sofas. There were a number of ornate, rose-
colored glass parlor lamps, but they wouldn't be
lit until later. There was a large, mirrored, hand-
carved maple liquor cabinet that must have cost a
fortune. There were Italian fruit compotes on ma-
hogany stands; the compotes would later be filled
with fruit. There were several china spitoons.

The thick maroon drapes on the windows were
velvet. The basically cream wallpaper had a taste-
ful nymph motif; slim, chaste nymphs that danced
over the walls but were unlikely to be found working at Nellie's.

Cassie left Lucia there and went to fetch the
madam, Nellie Pope. Lucia, waiting, wondered if
Cassie was one of the girls, and whether the bordello's clientele was multi-colored.

A door opened and Nellie Pope entered.

Lucia realized that Nellie had been among the ladies that had given her considerable clearance along Front Street. Not that it was easy to pick one out from so many—and Lucia had only seen her once—but Nellie Pope was unique.

There had been the obvious measures of distinction; the clothes finely tailored from expensive material, the modish bonnet, the slender but full-bosomed figure and erect carriage that bespoke good breeding. The face was mature and pretty, if not beautiful. But Nellie Pope's singular distinction lay in the fact that only two-thirds of her face was visible.

Her hair, deep brunette and thick with only the slightest wave, fell down across the left third of her face, and reached to her bosom. Both green eyes were visible, but the left one just managed to peer past the partial mask that her hair formed.

She moved slowly, gracefully, carefully. Nothing jarred that hair. Not for her were carefree tosses of the head.

"Good afternoon. I'm Nellie Pope."

Her voice was soft, with the sound of culture. No wonder the elite of Dodge City felt at home here.

"I am Lucia Bone." Her voice was unnaturally low, as if to match the other's.

Nellie Pope's mouth fell slightly ajar. Roscoe'd told her to expect a girl, but not . . . She wet her lips, and then smiled gently.

"And what can we do for you?"

"I was robbed. I have no money. I need to work."

Nellie Pope appeared to spend an inordinate

amount of time studying Lucia's obvious charms, her finely boned beauty. Nellie may have wondered if those fine bones were china, like her complexion, or delicately drawn steel. Only time would tell.

"I see. And you know what kind of—work—is performed here?"

Lucia gave her attention to the sofas, the nymphs, the heavy drapes, the thick carpeting, and smiled.

"One could hardly help but know."

"Do you mean it's gaudy? Garish?"

"Luxurious. Not a place where tea is drawn."

Nellie Pope looked disappointed. "That's too bad. I was so hoping to create an atmosphere of refinement, of genteel refinement." She smiled, amused.

There was a crash from somewhere in the house, and a brief, distant caterwauling.

"To offset, you might say, the impression given by my children. They're so . . . exuberant."

"Do you call your girls your children?"

"Yes. Do you mind?"

"To my face, yes. Otherwise. . . ."

"Is Lucia Bone your real name?"

"Yes. There's no one to care."

"How old are you, Lucia?"

Lucia thought for a moment. "Twenty."

Nellie also thought for a moment. "Oh, nonsense, you're not that old. And Lucia, in this house, age is a hindrance, not a help."

"I'm almost nineteen."

"That's better."

"Well? Do I have a job?"

"Goodness, yes. Need you ask? Don't you know how beautiful you are?"

"When do I start?"

"Tonight. I'll show you to a room. You may fix it up as you wish, as long as it's in good taste."

"Whose taste is that?"

"Mine."

"I'll go get my bags."

"What? And carry them all this way, exhausting yourself as well as announcing your new undertaking?" She smiled. "I confess it might be good advertising, but probably too good; we wouldn't be able to handle the rush. You just sit fast and I'll send someone to discreetly gather your belongings and pay off your bill, if that's necessary."

Lucia shrugged. "It is. It's the Dodge House; and send him by Ham Bell's, too. I owe Mister Bell for a horse-ride."

"I can see to that. We'll deduct it from your wages."

"What are my wages?"

"They will vary, naturally," said Nellie Pope. "There is a six dollar charge for what we call a 'quick date,' forty dollars for an entire night. Those rates are slightly higher than is customary elsewhere. We actually deserve more than that since this house is distinctly better than your normal house, and gives the client more for his money even at those higher rates. But we can't afford to price ourselves out of business, no matter how excellent our product."

Lucia thought she sounded like a Front Street merchant.

"We split the fees, you and I, down the middle. Tips you keep. We have a bar, which I will show you, and you will get a cut of the drinks you promote. There is also a buffet set-up. I buy my delicacies from Henry Sturm at the Occident. Privately. You do not, however, profit from your client's gluttony, no matter how strenuously you have performed your task—they generally eat afterward, poor dears. No, food is strictly a break-even proposition."

Lucia was busy with figures, trying to estimate a night's possible profit. The deal was as good as any she'd ever had. Not that she'd had that many.

"You pay for your room, a large room, well appointed, ten dollars a month. I also expect that you will clothe yourself fashionably. There are some dressmakers I favor. You may charge any clothes to my accounts in those places."

"I make my own," said Lucia.

"Indeed. I only hope that you are good, and that you have time."

Lucia finished her fast figuring. "The money shouldn't be bad, but a girl won't get rich here, will she?"

"Lacking lavish tips, no. You could make considerably more working the hurdy-gurdys."

"The dance halls?"

"Yes. A dollar a dance, and you set your own price for anything beyond that. I would imagine that you could make a considerable amount of money at it. Not that I'm trying to get rid of you, but I assume you've already given it some thought."

"Yes. It's too public, and too—grim."

"And not as safe. There are men here that will protect you."

Not to mention whatever she paid the law to step in and help out, if necessary.

"You mustn't expect to retire quickly upon a fortune amassed here. The best you can hope for are a number of steady, generous clients, and possibly an acceptable marriage proposal, which are not uncommon."

"That wasn't what I had in mind."

"What did you have in mind?"

"First, finding my mother. I'm an orphan."

"Aren't we all," said Nellie coolly. "But yes, that is a worthy endeavor."

"And then I want to open a school."

"I beg your pardon?"

"A school."

"Here? Don't be ridiculous!"

"But I like teaching, and I can teach, I know I can, and"—she suddenly grinned—"I guess I like being a boss. How many things are there that a woman can do, boss or no boss?"

"Not many," agreed Nellie Pope. "We can't even vote. Women can vote in Wyoming, but not here."

"Then let's change that."

"We will, Lucia, we will, but not right now. Right now I'm going to show you to your room, and then we'll see what you've got to wear." She rested her arm on Lucia's shoulders as she led her from the room.

"Lucia Bone, I think we are going to get along very nicely, very nicely indeed."

Maybe so, thought Lucia. Nellie seemed nice, and she'd seen no sign nor heard any word of that Fraley character that the Sheriff had characterized as "bad news". Maybe this would be good for a while.

And so, Lucia Bone began her new career as a *nymph du prairie*, a "soiled dove", or, just as euphemistically, one of Nellie Pope's "boarders".

And quite a career it quickly became.

Lucia, shrewdly, declined to sell herself as just a beautiful young girl, eager to please. Instead, she assumed all the reserve and hauteur of a girl's finishing school product, a perfectly mannered young lady but, once you got behind the cool exterior, sweet and gentle. If she did not seem eager to please right away, she was willing to be coaxed, cajoled and bribed into giving pleasure—and such keen and exhilarating pleasure it was.

Naturally, every man that passed through had to stare at the sketch of her mother.

In time, a few select and well-placed gentlemen came to know of her school-teaching ambitions. All —after their initial shock—expressed approval and a willingness to help her get a school started, but not in Dodge City.

"Why, I have a daughter school age," said Henry Pomeroy, the proprietor of a saddle shop. "Little Amy. I couldn't . . ."

"Let her be taught by me?" completed Lucia. She was tempted to argue, but Pomeroy's expression told her of how little use he was going to be. She could write him off as far as the school was concerned.

"It'd be a good school," she said seriously, "good for her. She'd learn her basics, but also sewing, drawing, how to conduct herself as a lady and, most importantly"—she ran her hand down to where Henry was most alert—"how to please a man."

A strangled sound emerged from Henry Pomeroy's mouth. His—his—*Amy?*

Pomeroy knew that Lucia meant well, the poor, dim creature. It was just too much to expect that one of these—girls—could understand about the finer, more ethereal things in life; could appreciate real refinement and social grace. These poor girls were so deprived—expert in physical skills, but otherwise deprived. And in order to lessen Lucia's deprivation, Pomeroy lavished a grand tip on her.

Lucia accepted it with minimal gratitude. And that, of course, drove Pomeroy into a frenzy of insecurity.

"Here, take this, this will be a down payment on next time, all right?"

Lucia nodded coolly. "I think you'd better go now. Won't your daughter be missing you? Little Amy?"

"Oh I didn't mean that, Lucia, what I said before. You mustn't always take me so seriously."

She didn't. But she took his money seriously. So, as he stood there, delaying his departure, she treated him to a reverse strip, slowly covering up those delightful privacies that he'd just shared so intimately, one by one.

A breast, so sleek and tight and perfect, slipped from sight, possibly never to be seen again.

Never? Oh God!

"That school's a wonderful idea, Lucia."

Lucia pushed him out the door.

"I can help. We must talk—"

She closed the door on him and leaned against it, smiling. She'd get her school yet. That is, if she decided she really wanted the damn thing.

Whether she really wanted one or not, as a by-product of those several confidences to the well-placed men, Lucia came to be known as "the school-marm."

It wasn't until later that she became known to the clientele in general, as "Nellie's Li'l Darlin'."

And still later, she took sole possession of the title, no person's chattel and bigger than any one establishment. Thus she came to be known, affectionately, as "the Dodge City Darling."

It was a fast transition, taking no more than a couple of weeks. Life in a boomtown was hectic, and things happened fast. So it was with her career. But so it was also with the events that transpired in connection with that new life.

It was late one night, not long after Lucia had begun working for Nellie, that Roscoe Fraley showed up at the bordello.

Nellie Pope, who had herself received and entertained Barton Clay, a member of the City Council and a representative of eastern meat-packing concerns, was at that moment in the bar, helping Clay restore his diminished strength with food and drink.

"A man like you needs extra fuel," crooned Nellie, her way of saying he was fat.

Clay ate like he was preparing himself for a visit to the slaughterhouse. All he needed, thought Nellie, were horns and a tail. He'd bring a good price.

Cassie, the colored girl, who'd turned out to be

a maid, came in and told her of Roscoe Fraley's arrival.

"Fraley frequents your establishment?" asked Clay with wonder.

"You don't see anything as good as my girls at any of his places, do you?"

"Indeed not!" snorted Clay. "But Nellie, tell me, when are you going to let me sample your newest young prize, the—"

"Hush yo' mouf, Senuhtuh Clay." Nellie knew Clay imagined himself distantly related to Henry Clay, the great southern senator and orator. "Aren't these old bones of mine good enough for you?"

Clay fluttered his hands and, his cheeks bulging with cheese, tried to reassure her. "Of course, of course."

"Now you just stay put while I find some company for Mister Fraley."

She slipped forward to the front room.

"Mister Fraley. So pleased you could find time to favor us with your presence this evening."

Fraley glared about. He didn't see anyone listening.

"If you'll follow me, Roscoe, I'll do my best to find you some company."

He followed her out of the room and up some stairs.

"Goddammit," Fraley grumbled, "it ain't like it's such a big secret, me'n you an' this place."

She didn't respond, but simply led him toward a room at the front end of the second floor. She opened the door.

"Wait in here. I'll be along as soon as I get rid of that pig Clay. That's if he ever stops eating."

"Hell, slip 'im some laudanum an' send 'im trottin'."

Her lips compressed briefly. "He'd trot right into a tree. Just stay put, I'll be along soon."

"What the hell am I gonna do?"

"You can keep your voice down for one. And look through that notebook on the stand. There are some new entries."

Fraley brightened, and Nellie left him.

She found Barton Clay right where she'd left him, wiping his mouth and burping contentedly.

She smiled at him and winked mischievously.

"Maybe you'd like to go back upstairs with me, Barton?"

Barton Clay could barely rise from his chair. "You should have your strength back now, Barton, and the night's still young."

"What do you mean, the night's still young? The night's almost over. Kathryn will be wondering just what manner of inventory I am conducting."

"Then perhaps you'd better run along, Barton." Run? That was a laugh. "Time certainly does fly when you're having fun."

Clay made some grunting sounds as he jerked himself upright.

Nellie leaned close and kissed him on the cheek. "Button yourself up before you go."

Clay reddened and fumbled with his fly all the way to the door. He was all thumbs, though, and exited the back door with his fly gaping.

"There's no one up at this hour," he shouted back to Nellie, "and who knows, I may have to pee along the way."

He disappeared into the night giggling.

Nellie glanced at Giovanni, the tough, wiry Italian bartender, and shook her head slowly. Then she went back upstairs.

Roscoe Fraley looked up from the notebook as she entered.

"This stuff you've got on George Emerson Asshole Carter, it's for real?"

Nellie nodded. "According to him he's got wives, satisfied wives he says, spread all the way across the continent. Not the sort of thing one would invent."

"Sure he ain't one of them Mormon fellers?"

"Not yet. But if he ever gets caught you might expect a quick conversion."

"You got any names an' addresses on them wives?"

"Not yet, but I've got something about our fat friend Barton Clay you'll enjoy hearing."

They discussed her latest intelligence gathering. Fraley's smile grew. He was happy. None of those bastards was any better than him.

8

WHAT'S THIS?" asked Lucia.

"I was shot there."

"And this?"

"There, too."

"How about this one?"

"Nasty ol' bull caught me there. Critter had horns 'bout twelve feet wide."

"Really?"

He laughed. Normally he would have lied himself blue in the face, like any other cowboy, but with this girl . . .

"Naw. Lots of boys will swear they're that long, or longer . . . though they usually stick to something reasonable, like nine or ten feet. But the widest spread I've ever heard of was measured at just a hair over eight feet. Most of the cows we trail north ain't got spreads more'n four feet, if that much. But cowboys do like to tell stories." He laughed again.

She smiled at him. She liked him, this young cowboy. He seemed brighter than the usual run, and didn't try any rough stuff; in fact, he was real considerate.

"And what's this funny ol' thing? Who gave that to you?"

"Hell, my mama gave me that." Lucia was touching his navel.

"Your mama's mean, too? Got horns fifteen feet wide?"

"Naw, my mama's an angel. She'd kill me if she knew where I was, though I guess by now she knows about these things."

"If she had you she does."

"You know that ain't what I mean."

"When was the last time you saw your mama?"

"Oh, 'bout a month ago."

"That recent? Don't you live on a ranch? I thought all the cowboys—"

"They do, 'ceptin' those that get signed on just for the drives. But sure, I live on the ranch."

"And your mother lives nearby?"

"No." He tried not to grin. "She lives there, too."

"They allow that?"

"Aw hell, darlin', my folks own the damn place."

"Oh." That made things a lot clearer. "Dumb me," she said and smiled.

"You couldn't know."

Lucia looked into his eyes. They were dark and had depth.

"Why'd you call me that, call me darlin'?"

" 'Cause that's what they said you were. Nellie's li'l darlin'."

Lucia liked the sound of it, but with reservations. "I don't belong to her."

"It's not important."

"I—no, you're right, it's not important." She ran her finger down his body. "You're awfully young to have all these scars, to be shot up so much."

"I'm older'n you."

That still didn't make him any less young, thought Lucia.

"What's your name?"

"About time you asked. Tom. Tom Beaumont. My father's Bayard Breckenridge Beaumont. And the spread's the 3–Bar–B." He grinned. "Lucky I don't stutter."

"What's your mother's name?"

"Beauty."

"I asked your mother's name," said Lucia, "not your horse's," but she regretted the joke as she saw Tom's face cloud.

"That *is* her name. Beauty Jo Forrest. She never liked it, but she got used to it, 'specially after she kinda grew into the name. She's real pretty."

"I'll bet she is."

"So why'd you have to joke?"

"I'm sorry, Tom."

"That's better."

"You're lucky you have a mother," she said.

Tom nodded, then smiled brightly. "Hell, she's lucky she has me."

Lucia's finger resumed its travels.

"Want to do it again? For Mom?"

Tom tried to work up some outrage, but couldn't and laughed.

"Love to, darlin'."

"Lucia."

"Lucia—love to, but it's late and I got a ride ahead of me an', well, I only paid for a quick date."

Lucia reached out to the nightstand and fingered the brass check, a metal token the client bought downstairs and gave to the girl. A single token was worth a quick date.

"So you did," Lucia said, "but like you say, it's late and I don't figure there's anyone waiting in line. . . ."

Tom Beaumont was sorely tempted.

"Come on, Thomas Beaumont."

"I don't guess I better. I—I better wait."

He wasn't committing himself. And neither was Lucia. She'd pushed him hard enough. Pushing harder would hurt. She'd pull back. Let him come to her.

He was a rancher's son, which meant there was money. He was real good looking, he was bright, and he might be a terror with his friends, a mean sonuvabitch, but with her he was sweet. He was worth cultivating. It might turn into something.

And besides all that, she liked him.

She got out of bed and threw on a silken robe. He got up more slowly and gathered his clothes. She started brushing her hair.

He dressed, waiting for her to speak. Finally, he broke the silence. "Aren't you going to say anything?"

She glanced at him, smiled, and shrugged. Then she bent over, brushing her hair over her head.

"This your room? You live here?"

The head of hanging hair bobbed in confirmation.

"Then hell, I'd better get movin' so you can go to sleep."

The brushing stopped, then started up again.

"Well, I'm dressed. . . ." He watched her brush, brush, brush. "Uhhh, you mind if I come back?"

She straightened, tossing her hair back and looked at Tom Beaumont.

"I'd like that a lot, Tom," she said softly.

Tom's hair practically stood on end as current surged through him.

"Then you count on it, darlin'—or Lucia—you count on it. And next time I'll be plannin' on a full night, you hear?"

She nodded, holding back the smile.

He opened the door, but paused in the doorway, as if having second thoughts. Lucia pushed him out the door.

"Now you get, Tom. I've gotta get my beauty rest, and so do you."

He grinned foolishly and walked on down the hall.

As he was descending the stairs, a door at the far end of the second floor opened and Roscoe Fraley emerged. Roscoe closed the door behind him and walked toward the stairs.

Tom Beaumont went on down and paused at the bottom, waiting for the man to come down after him. He wanted to see the expression on the man's face, see if he looked as happy as he himself felt.

But Fraley didn't descend after Tom. Instead his steps continued on down the hall. Tom Beaumont wondered where he was heading. Maybe there was a rear staircase. There probably was.

The door suddenly opened and Lucia Bone looked up, startled. Her first thought was that Tom Beaumont had changed his mind, but the sight of Roscoe Fraley wiped her mind clear of such warm and cozy thoughts.

"What do you want?"

Fraley stepped inside. He looked around.

"This used to be Angel's room. Stupid kid got herself in trouble, tried to get rid of a baby all by herself, messed it up, and died." He grinned at Lucia. "When she was dyin' she was callin' fer a doctor, callin' fer Holliday. Holliday's a *dentist*!" He seemed to find that very amusing.

"What do you want?" Lucia asked again.

"You still lookin' fer yer mom?"

How did he know that? wondered Lucia.

"Or was that just an excuse to look over the town real close, pick yer spot, so to speak?"

"I was robbed," said Lucia sullenly.

"Was yuh now? Ain't that a shame."

"And I'm still looking," she added quietly.

"Are yuh now? An' what're yuh gonna do if yuh find her, give'r a big ol' sloppy kiss?"

Lucia was getting angry. "If I find her," she said tightly, "I'm going to find out who she is, what she is, let her know I'm the kid she got rid of, and then I'm going to turn her in to the law."

"What?" Fraley showed alarm—or was it astonishment?

"She's a damn murderer. She's wanted by the law, her and some friends of hers."

Fraley drew shallow breaths. "That any way to treat yer own ma?"

"She's never been a ma to me." Lucia realized Fraley was pushing her to say things she didn't mean, but she couldn't help herself. And in the warm afterglow of Tom Beaumont's visit she felt safe. Invulnerable. "And I've got a hunch, Mister Fraley, who she is, what she is, where she is . . . and who her friends are."

Damn, thought Lucia, she didn't know she had that hunch until just then.

Nor, apparently, did Fraley, whose features congealed.

"Now," said Lucia, on the attack, "what do you want? Say your piece and then get out!"

"Not so fast, darlin'—"

"Don't you darlin' me." She was rapidly coming to loathe this man with his leering aggression.

"I'll call you what I damn well please," growled Fraley, and the power, the force, was back in his voice.

He'd dropped by the room as much to question the girl as anything else. But now he decided she was a danger, and he wanted to hurt her; to warn her. He grinned sadistically.

"I reckon I'll jes' check me out the merchandise."

Lucia felt the first vague tremor of fear, but she didn't fully credit his meaning until he began to take off his shirt.

"The hell you will!" she said, as much in fright as anger.

"The hell I won't."

"I'll scream."

"You go right ahead. Scream yore pretty little head off."

His confidence told Lucia that screaming wouldn't do any good. The Sheriff had said that Fraley was somehow tied up with this place.

She glanced longingly at the room's heavy oak dresser, in which her Remington was secreted. If she could only get to it . . .

"Yer a little too smart fer yer own good, darlin'," growled Fraley. "Git down an' spread 'em—I'm gonna cut you in half."

Lucia despaired. If she fought to her last breath, screamed for help where there was no help, it was more trouble than it was worth. If she even survived.

But she had one last card to play. "You're not getting nuthin' for nuthin'!"

Fraley grinned triumphantly, took a handful of brass checks from his pocket, and flung them at her.

Lucia gave up. She carefully gathered the checks.

"Leave 'em lay!"

Lucia gathered the checks and stowed them away in her dresser. She stared down at the Remington where it lay atop some underwear.

To grab the gun, throw the bastard's checks back at him—it might cause more trouble than she could handle just then.

"Turn the lamps down," she muttered, feeling more abandoned than she ever had.

The light dimmed. And she turned and let the robe fall and stood naked.

Fraley's breath grew shorter.

Lucia grit her teeth, climbed onto the bed and closed her eyes, praying that the sonuvabitch was clean.

An hour later Lucia walked down the hall. She was hurting, bleeding actually, but she was tough, and she walked steadily.

She stopped outside Nellie Pope's room and knocked on the door.

After a few moments a slurred voice came through the door.

"Yes. What is it?"

"It's me, Nellie, Lucia. If that man Fraley ever comes by my room again, I'll kill him."

Would she? She didn't know. She'd had her chance and hadn't done it.

Inside, Nellie Pope shook her head slowly but said nothing.

Lucia waited awhile, then walked away.

"I'll try to help, Lucia," said Nellie slowly, struggling with the words, "but it's not an easy life. Lucia?"

But Lucia was downstairs by then, and Nellie waited in vain for a response. She finally returned to her pipe.

Lucia went into the bar, where chairs were stacked on tables, and asked Giovanni for a drink.

He gave it to her. He noticed that she looked ten years older, and that her eyes were rimmed with red.

She squirmed, trying to find a comfortable position in which to sit. Giovanni's mouth tightened.

Two men came in, both bouncers. One was JB, a huge mulatto with soft brown eyes, and the other was Red, a short, wiry, ugly man with the gimlet eyes of a gunfighter.

Giovanni inclined his head toward Lucia as he gave them both shots of rotgut.

They didn't need the clue; they knew what went on in that house. They both downed the shots.

Finally, Red spoke.

"You say the word, Lucia, I'll kill him." He smiled coldly. "I'd have to get out of town real fast, but he'd be on his way to hell even faster."

"Sheeet, Red," growled JB, "they'd prob'ly make yuh Mayor. Ah'd vote fo' yuh."

Lucia looked at the three men. All were eyeing her with sympathy and devotion. To men like them, a beautiful and gentle whore was the ultimate.

Lucia nodded, smiling tightly to acknowledge the offer. "If it happens again. . . ."

She finished her drink and slowly walked out the back door.

Lucia stood in the cool night air among the young cottonwoods.

"Darlin'?" came a voice from the shadows.

She jumped, and then she almost screamed, which would have brought three murderously angry men pounding from the house.

"Who's that?"

"Me. Tom Beaumont." He was standing by a tree. He looked like part of it.

She approached him. "What are you doing still

here?" She got angry. "Dammit, Tom, if you weren't leaving you should have stayed." She pounded him on his chest. "Why didn't you, damn you?"

Tom caught her hands. He didn't know what to say. He didn't understand her. He was young.

"Was it real bad?"

Lucia nodded, but only because he deserved a response. She'd said all she was going to say; she'd complained enough.

"Do you want to have some fun, Tom?"

That was a peculiar question, thought Tom, considering. And he wasn't sure what she meant. But fun was fun. Maybe they'd roll in the bushes.

"Sure."

"Wait here." And Lucia ran back inside Nellie's. She needed some information.

A minute later she was back outside.

"Come on."

He went with her, without question.

They walked along Walnut to Bridge Avenue and then turned north on Bridge.

"What do you really want to do, Lucia?" Tom asked as they walked. "I don't fancy you want to do this all your life."

"Walk along dark streets?"

"You know what I mean."

"Teach school. Some day I'm going to teach school."

Tom started laughing.

"It's not funny."

"Aw hell, Lucia. You're too young to teach school. You gotta be old and dried up to do that."

"You're wrong, Tom. Maybe back East that's the case, but not out here. I checked, and there are some school-teachers no more than fifteen years old. They finish school themselves and start teaching right away. Most of them are older than fifteen, I'll give you that, but not usually by much, so I'm old enough. I'm almost nineteen." She looked on the dark side. "Heck, I may even be too old."

Tom chuckled. "Well, maybe you are too old."

"How old was your teacher?"

"I didn't have any. My ma taught me, taught us all. In fact—" and then he mumbled on for a while.

"Let's turn here," said Lucia. "Now, what was that you were just mumbling? You have to speak up, darn it."

"I said that down home there's a need for a school—and a teacher."

Lucia thought about it.

"Hell, Lucia, you can't teach here, not in Dodge. You'll have to go somewhere, and down home nobody'll know a thing about—anything."

Lucia couldn't see his face in the dark, but she didn't have to.

"Here we are," she said, grabbing his arm. "Now be quiet."

She led him around to the back of a large house on Spruce Street. Half a block further east, at the corner of First and Spruce, was the Union Church. A real respectable, upstanding neighborhood.

The night was clear, but moonless and dark. A few windows in the back of the house, kitchen windows, glowed yellow but cast no light outside to speak of.

"Give me a hand. You take that side."

They both took hold of a narrow, tall wooden

privy, and, after considerable straining, managed to move it back about four feet.

It wasn't much, thought Lucia, but dammit, it was something. ✑

9

LATER THAT MORNING, nearing midday, Lucia arose and went over to First Avenue just north of Front. There she entered Kate's Artistic Needlework.

It hadn't taken Lucia long to realize she wouldn't have the time to make all the dresses and gowns she was going to need. Kate's was one of the shops where Nellie Pope had an account.

Lucia saw how it worked. The account made it easy for Nellie's girls to get their dresses, but they were soon deeply indebted to Nellie and thereby tied to her.

Nellie had told Lucia to buy everything she wanted, and the fancier the better for Nellie's rising star. Fancier and considerably more expensive. Lucia wondered how much of a kickback Nellie got from the dressmaker. Lucia was determined that Nellie would make as little as possible from her.

Lucia ordered a sufficient number of dresses, skirts, blouses, undergarments, and capes from rich material, but simply cut. Lucia had heard that an elegant gown for one of the hurdy-gurdy dancers, who needed such things, could cost as much as seven hundred dollars. Lucia's entire wardrobe didn't cost nearly that much.

She smiled as she ordered one additional outfit, an especially severe and prim dress. It was sure to please one of the local ministers, one with flesh so weak it couldn't hold his trousers up.

She left Kate's and walked down to Front Street, where she encountered stares from both men and women. She ignored them, her mouth fixed in a sweet smile, and walked over to Henry Sturm's Occident, which she entered.

She was almost a regular by then, and few heads turned as she entered. Those that did turn belonged to men who didn't know who or what she was.

"*Guten tag*, Lucia," said Sturm.

"*Guten tag, mein Herr*."

"Today, *liebchen*, I haff zum new cheese you must try."

"As long as it won't make me smell too bad."

"Neffer, Lucia. You can neffer smell too bad. It is goat's milk cheese."

"Goat?" Lucia stared at the cheese dubiously. "It's brown."

"Z'goat voss brown. No, no, dot voss a joke!"

Lucia came back out carrying a small bag of cheese and sweetmeats, an odd but tasty combination.

She walked west on Front. She saw Brooker come out of a saloon up ahead and quickened her stride. But then he saw her and turned abruptly, and disappeared back into the saloon. She slowed, and seemed to wilt a bit.

Outside the Long Branch she was almost run over by Bat Masterson, Wyatt Earp, and Bat's younger brother, Jim, who, at twenty-three, was not only the co-owner of the Lady Gay, but another member of the Dodge City Police force. The three were laughing too hard to watch where they were going, and Lucia had to dodge out into the street to avoid them.

"Y'all are reeling around like a bunch of drunks," she cried.

They finally steadied. A few passersby, of the town's "better element" sniffed at such carrying on by their men of the law. Bat Masterson wiped the tears from his eyes and focused on Lucia Bone.

"Oh," he said, "it's you."

"Yes, me. What are you all breaking up over?"

Wyatt was his sober self once more, and no one ever looked soberer. Jim Masterson blew his nose on Bat's handkerchief, earning himself a glare, and Bat grinned at Lucia.

"Well, I guess we can tell you, Miss Bone—it's not as if you were one of the ladies."

Lucia could have taken insult, but didn't. She didn't think Bat meant it meanly, he was just stating a fact—as he'd been calmly stating facts that day in her room, when she'd hated him as she'd hated no one else. She was over that hate now. He was just a sheriff doing a job, and it wasn't an easy job.

"We just heard," said Bat to Lucia in a confidential voice, "that along about three o'clock this morning, ol' Roscoe Fraley went stumbling out the back of his house to answer a call of nature and stepped into his own latrine pit." He gurgled with mirth. "He screamed so loud he woke up the neighbors. Someone had moved the latrine!"

He'd explained it to Lucia, that last part, because she was new to Dodge. Wandering latrines, though, were an old joke around Dodge City, and Fraley wasn't the first to have disappeared into a pit.

"You don't think that's funny? You sure don't have much of a sense of humor."

"Sure I do," said Lucia, "but it must have been four o'clock, not three. That sonuvabitch was at Nellie's until three-thirty."

The three lawmen fell silent, exchanging looks. But the Fraley-Pope connection was nothing new. "What was he doing there?" asked Bat.

"What the hell do you think?" she cried, and her response told them a lot more than they'd asked. Bat's eyes softened.

"Yeah," he said, "he's sure an ugly customer. But otherwise, Miss Bone, how's it going?" He remembered the cool way he'd treated her, and then standing outside her door listening to her cry.

Lucia recovered, and shrugged. "Not as good as I expected, not as bad as I feared. But darn, I just had to spend damn near four hundred dollars getting clothes over at Kate's."

"Where'd you get—ah, yes, Nellie's account. You fell into that trap."

"I didn't fall, I was *pushed,* by those goddamned

thieves that you can't catch." She glared accusingly at Bat. "But what the hell? I charged as little as I could, not wanting to make Nellie any richer than she is—yes, I figured out that little game—and it won't take me long to make it good."

Lucia's face was stormy. Bat decided she needed some lightening. "Well, Miss Bone, I'm happy to see you landed on your feet"—he winced as Lucia shot him a look—"so to speak, and some investigating I've done leads me to believe that, ummm, you may have been telling the truth about being robbed, and that I treated you poorly."

A number of expressions flitted over Lucia's face.

"You're a tough little young lady, aren't you? An honest-to-God fighter. I kind of wish your friend could see that."

"What friend?"

"The imbecile, Brooker."

"Oh." She spoke softly and thoughtfully, "He's not such an imbecile, and I've got other friends."

"Indeed," said Bat. "Well, I also wanted to say that I was sorry I hadn't dropped by to see you." He smiled ambiguously. "To pay my respects."

"If you do come by you'd better bring a barrel of money. There are a lot of school kids that are going to need books."

"You're still planning to open a school?"

She nodded.

"Here?"

"I'll open it wherever I damn well please. Don't be surprised to hear about me running a school down in Texas."

"Whereabouts?"

"I'm not sure yet, but I'll find out."

Bat's eyes narrowed. "About those schoolbooks, you can count on me and Wyatt and Jim to put up our share." Wyatt and Jim looked a bit surprised by Bat's largesse. "You just make sure you do what you say you're gonna do."

Lucia came to the end of a 180-degree turnabout, and she was suddenly glad she knew this calm, sleepy-eyed gunman who took life as it came and didn't pass judgment on things that couldn't be helped.

"Thank you, Bat," she said. "Thank you all."

Bat smiled benignly, but Wyatt and Jim started pawing the ground and tugging at their forelocks.

"Oh, cut that out," ordered Lucia, "you're acting like children."

She made ready to continue on to the post office in McCarty's drugstore, but then a thought occurred to her.

"Come here," she said, "gather close."

The three men gathered around her, curious.

"I don't normally tell things like this," she said, "but this one's special. As you might have guessed, that loathsome Fraley came by late last night. I told you that much already, and how he behaved—"

"Well, no," said Wyatt, "you didn't really get into it. You just said—"

"Never mind. What I will tell you is that, well, I've seen a lot of men in my time, if you know what I mean—"

They all nodded solemnly. They knew.

"—and that Fraley has got about the tiniest dick I've ever seen."

Three mouths dropped wide open.

"You make sure you pass it around, you hear,

and tell 'em it comes from a reliable source. You can even tell 'em who the source is."

By then the news had been digested, and the three lawmen were threatening to fall to their knees, shaking with laughter.

Lucia marched off toward McCarty's drugstore.

Before she entered McCarty's she glanced back, and was pleased to see that the three lawmen had split up, each heading for a different saloon to pass the word.

Lucia smiled. Stories defaming one person or another made the rounds constantly, and were often discounted. But when a professional, such as one of Nellie's girls, took the trouble to pronounce words on the size of a certain member, well, that had to be taken seriously.

It wasn't long before the word, carried by fleet-footed if unsteady drunks, had crossed Dodge's plaza to the southside saloons. And in those places lively debates soon sprang up as to just who owned the smallest, and exactly how small the smallest really was.

The girls in Fraley's saloons, some of whom knew very well whereof they spoke, defended their boss, defended his masculine reputation, but they were overwhelmed.

Eddie Foy and Jim Thompson tried to figure out how to get some comment on the subject into their act.

Lucia had not yet finished in McCarty's, sending a progress report to Belle at the orphanage, when a gent went steaming by, heading toward Fraley's Last Stand.

In the time it took him to get there, get Fraley

aside, and give him the news, Lucia had posted her letter and stepped back outside.

She'd missed the messenger whipping by, and the stupendous roar of outrage from the Last Stand came as a surprise. But she quickly divided its meaning and smiled. It sounded like the latrine pit episode all over again.

She'd smiled prematurely, however, for the batwing doors of the Last Stand suddenly exploded outward and Roscoe Fraley surged forth, his head swiveling on his bullneck and his beady, angry eyes finding Lucia.

He was again neatly dressed for the early evening trade. But he'd grabbed his guns and gunbelt—probably figured on justifiable homicide—and they were on his hips, and his pasty face was blotchy red. The sight of Lucia's smile only enraged him more.

"*You!*"

Lucia suddenly thought that perhaps defaming Fraley hadn't been such a good idea, especially if she might end up a corpse. She wondered if slander justified killing.

Fraley started toward her, his hands pawing for his guns. Usually he was sure-handed, but he was so damned mad.

"Hold it, Fraley!"

The command snapped like a whip. Fraley slowed and stopped. Lucia looked back out in the street.

Bat Masterson stood there, coat drawn back. He was wearing the short-barreled Colts with the cutaway trigger guards. He clearly meant business, but

Lucia had trouble believing that the harsh command had come from a man who seemed so mild-mannered.

A corner of her eye caught a movement. She looked and saw Jim Masterson. Jim gave her a smile and inclined his head, requesting her to move back out of his line of fire.

She backed up, wondering where Earp was. She didn't see him, but was sure he was somewhere nearby. He wasn't; he was busy taking money from a gent who was laughing so hard he couldn't play his cards right.

"Get rid of those guns, Roscoe Fraley," said Bat calmly, "or use them."

Fraley's hands edged away from his guns, but he finally found his voice. "She's a goddamn liar!" he roared.

Bat eyed him steadily. "Prove it."

It took a few seconds for the implications of Bat's suggestion to sink in. Roscoe Fraley wasn't about to drop his pants in the middle of Front Street to prove anything. The splotchy face turned a brilliant red.

Bat hoped he wasn't going to lose his man to a heart attack.

Fraley suddenly turned on his heel and marched off.

"Roscoe!" Bat snapped out, stopping him in his tracks. "This is the end of it, Fraley."

Fraley didn't move, but he didn't turn around either.

"She's not going to say another word"—and Lucia realized Bat meant it—"and it's probably not true," he had to smile. "But don't you lay a hand on that girl ever again. If you do, I'll personally plant you on Boot Hill."

Fraley waited for more, but there was no more. He finally started walking again, hesitantly at first, but gaining confidence with every stride, and by the time he disappeared into the Last Stand he was swaggering as much as he ever had.

Bat's eyes found Lucia. "Now see what you went and started? Don't do it again."

That wasn't fair. But it was true, she was the one that had told them to pass the word, so she nodded.

Bat walked off. Lucia wasn't sure she didn't catch a smile.   ∞§

10

"You snubbed me before."

Lucia'd spotted Brooker again and this time, though he hadn't smiled or approached, he hadn't run away, so she went up to him. After what she'd just gone through it was easy.

"I thought you were something special," he said, shaking his head slowly. "Then you disappear, without a word. And then I hear that anyone who wants can go up to Nellie's and slap his money down and st-st-st—"

"Stick it in me, is that what you're trying to say?"

"That's it."

"I'm sorry you think of it that way."

"Well it's true, isn't it? How am I supposed to think of it—as a pat on the back? A handshake? A rare and beautiful love affair, for as long as a brass check lasts?"

"Stop it, Paul, just stop it." She shook her head. "I didn't know you were taking things—taking me —so seriously. I had no idea you were so passionate."

"Passionate. Is that a word you just learned?"

She'd actually wanted to say jealous, but had settled for passionate.

"There's one of your *passionate* admirers staring at you."

Lucia looked. Tom Beaumont was standing outside a saloon trying to hide his longing. And doing a fair job of it, thought Lucia. She was also glad he hadn't been around earlier. He would have tried to kill Fraley, and likely would have lost.

She smiled at Tom, but she wasn't ready for him just then. Paul Brooker, the unexpected romantic, was giving her too much to think about.

Some hard-nosed detective he was.

With a last look and smile for Tom, she took Paul Brooker by the arm.

"Come on, Paul, let's walk and talk. People are watching, and listening. You don't want them thinking you're going soft over a soiled dove."

"I don't give a damn what they think," and he looked around angrily. But he let himself be led away.

Some half-hour later three men, grimy and rawhide-tough, with bony faces and red eyes, reeled from Cattle Annie's. They hooted and hollered as they staggered about, all the time eyeing the north side of Front Street, which, at that quiet time of afternoon, might have been another world entirely.

They strapped on their guns as they approached their horses. Even drunk, their fingers were sure as they fastened the buckles and tied down the holsters. Likely it was instinctive. They could probably tie them on in their sleep.

They mounted their horses without a bobble, too.

Jim Masterson looked out a window of the jail, some forty yards away, and spoke over his shoulder.

"Them gents you spotted, Bat, looks like they're clearing out."

"Good," came from behind him.

"Looks like their holsters got tie-downs," he added.

There was no further response.

By then the three men had started riding, heading east along the south side of Front Street. Once past the depot and Railroad Avenue they swung north, crossed the tracks and then started down the north side of Front, drawing their guns as they kicked their horses into a dead run.

They started firing their guns as they swept past the Dodge House. Normally, when that sort of thing happened, the shots went harmlessly high. These shots, however, were coming in dangerously low, and pedestrians, what few there were, began to duck as windows shattered.

Paul Brooker and Lucia Bone were out in front of the Occident, eating cheese and still arguing. The sound of shots drew Brooker's attention. He started to smile but then saw where the bullets were hitting. He saw a few people freeze and some duck, and he could almost follow the riders' progress as the windows disappeared, one after the other. He watched as if hypnotized.

It wasn't until a slug shattered the window of the butcher shop next to the Occident that Brooker woke up.

Lucia was watching the riders, too, but she had no sense of danger. Both she and Brooker were right in line to take the next few shots.

Brooker grabbed Lucia and flung her down, but he took a slug in the fleshy part of his shoulder. It shook him for a second, and delayed his own descent to ground level, which was lucky for him as two slugs plowed into the wooden sidewalk right beside Lucia and right where he'd been planning to lie.

By then Bat and Jim Masterson were out of their office. Jim snapped a shot at the three riders, but had to be careful because of the people and businesses behind them. As it was, he missed the riders but shot out a window himself.

The three riders picked up the pace again, riding west. They shot out a couple of more windows but then holstered their guns.

Further west on Front Street Tom Beaumont had come out of the Alamo with the first sound of gunfire. With everyone ducking and falling back he'd had a clear line of sight through to Lucia and Paul Brooker. He'd recognized Lucia, and seen how close she'd come to death.

Enraged, he leaped out into the street as the three riders pounded his way. He was vaguely aware of Bat and Jim, off to the side, untying their horses.

Tom was unarmed, but he figured he could delay

them, maybe tackle one; at least make a grab for one of the horses' reins.

The riders swerved their horses, and he missed the first two, but he did manage to hook the reins of the third horse.

The horse twisted about sharply, almost dislodging the rider, who yelled.

The two up front stopped, turned, and rode back. All three started shooting at once.

Tom Beaumont was driven to the sandy soil, where he twitched a few times, and then lay still.

The three riders turned their horses once more and headed west. Their final gesture, before riding out of town, was to whoop and shoot out the windows of Roscoe Fraley's Last Stand.

Bat and Jim Masterson fairly flew down the street on a pair of matched sorrels, passing Tom Beaumont without a hitch.

Wyatt Earp came out of the Long Branch, made a move toward his horse, but then saw he was too late. He headed instead for the jail and his office. Someone had to be there.

Lucia, regaining her feet, looked down the street and saw the body lying in the dust.

"What happened?"

"He tried to stop them," said Brooker, who'd seen the action. "He wasn't armed. He caught hold of one of the horses. They shot him."

What a dumb thing to try, thought Lucia. "Who was it?"

Brooker took a few moments to answer. "I think it was that friend of yours—"

Lucia was puzzled. She had acquired a lot of friends.

"—the one you smiled at."

"I smiled—*Tom?!*"

"I don't know. I don't know his name. A young—"

But Lucia was gone, dashing down the street toward the body.

She skidded to a stop on her knees by the body and heaved it onto its back.

"Tom!"

Tom Beaumont's eyes cracked open.

"Get a doctor!" cried Lucia.

Doc Holliday, standing outside the Lone Star, a bottle in one hand, cards in the other, felt eyes upon him. "I'm a dentist," he muttered. "Besides, it ain't no use." He felt a cough rising and he swigged from the bottle.

Tom Beaumont's mouth opened, and he tried to speak. But no words emerged, only blood. Then his head rolled to the side, and he was dead.

In time Lucia became aware of feet by her side. She wiped at her eyes with a sleeve, and then stood up.

Paul Brooker was there. Lucia showed him a stony face.

Brooker wore an odd expression. Was he jealous of the dead man? Surely he couldn't envy the young man's death.

"He was a good friend?"

Lucia shrugged. "I knew him. I never guessed he was that stupid."

"Come on, I'll get you a drink."

"No. I don't need a drink. I want to go home."

"Home?"

"Nellie's."

Brooker frowned.

"Why not? It's no worse than this." And, without another word, she walked off.

Paul Brooker trailed at a distance, concerned, but feeling helpless. He was sure those men had been trying to kill Lucia. Why, he didn't know, but someone might try again. Hell, hadn't Roscoe Fraley gone after her not two hours earlier?

But he felt helpless because if someone did go after her, he'd not be able to do anything, lacking his guns. He'd have to talk to Masterson. Maybe Bat would deputize him.

Bat and Jim Masterson rode hard, slowly closing the gap. They'd left town about a quarter-mile behind and were now getting into pistol range. Jim's pistol range, though, not Bat's. Bat had been wearing his short-barreled Colts when the trouble started and he still wore them. He'd have to get closer to be certain.

"Hold your fire, Jim. Let's run 'em down. I want to have a word with these bastards."

They drew closer.

The three red-eyed, bony-faced wild gents were trying to make the Ford County line, for whatever good that might do, but they soon realized they wouldn't.

Their horses were beginning to labor. They looked back and were startled to see how close the Mastersons were. What the hell was that blasted Sheriff trying to do? Why weren't they shooting?

They'd reloaded on the run, just out of town, and now they suddenly reined in and vaulted from their horses, clawing at their holstered guns as they went.

The Mastersons, only fifteen yards away at that point, jumped from their horses, too.

Bat was confident. When confronted with opposition, there were a number of things that automatically registered in the mind of a professional gunman. One of them was the type of sidearm he faced.

The three men were packing two guns apiece, and the length of the holsters had told Bat that they were guns with seven- or eight-inch barrels, probably Peacemakers. They came out a hell of a lot slower than Bat's Colts with the four and three-quarter-inch barrels, not to mention the cutaway trigger guards and the filed-down front sight. And at fifteen yards, the greater accuracy the longer barrels afforded wasn't a factor.

The three gunmen were still wrestling the long guns out when Bat's Colts whispered clear and exploded.

He was still moving when he shot, costing accuracy. He had to shoot for the center of his targets.

Jim Masterson, slower than Bat and less skilled, also beat the three gents. Lacking Bat's finesse, he couldn't even consider picking a spot. He just pointed and cut loose.

At first the Mastersons didn't know what had happened. There was no return fire, but the cloud of smoke caused by igniting black powder ten times in three seconds was such that they couldn't see a damn thing.

They crouched and moved to the side until the

Plains wind, always blowing one way or the other, dispersed the smoke.

The three men lay in awkward positions. The Mastersons had been too close for their shots to miss by much, and they hadn't. Eight of the ten shots would have killed.

"Dammit, Jim," muttered Bat. "Didn't you hear me say I wanted to talk to them?"

"Dammit yourself, Bat. I didn't see them wavin' no white flag."

"You know what I mean."

Jim had finished looking over the bodies. "Hell, Bat, you tryin' to say that all these shots are mine? I didn't even *use* my off-gun."

"Do tell," said Bat dryly. "Both of your guns are *off*-guns."

But Bat had known all the time that he was as much more than a kid, thought the twenty-five-year-pect from a twenty-three-year-old like Jim? Not much at fault as Jim. And hell, what could you ex-old Bat Masterson.

An hour later Bat and Jim rode back into town leading three horses, one corpse per horse.

As they passed the Last Stand, Roscoe Fraley came out. He glowered at the Mastersons, then eyed the three bodies apprehensively, as if they might rise up and start shooting again.

"They dead?"

"They're not riding that way by choice," said Bat.

"You see what they did to my windows?" squawked Fraley.

The Mastersons regarded him with a cold lack of sympathy.

"Don't get excited," said Jim. "You ain't the only one."

"Too bad you weren't standing in front of them," added Bat.

The Mastersons rode on, leading their cargo.

As they passed, Fraley's expression changed, satisfaction mixing in with the anger.

He went back into the Last Stand.

"They suspect anything?" asked Maggie.

"Nope," said Fraley. "And dead men tell no tales." He'd heard that somewhere.

"But the sonsuvbitches missed that Bone girl," he went on. "Had her dead to goddamn rights but they missed. If that lousy Brooker hadn't pushed her."

A man entered. "Hey Ros, whaddya suppose got into them gents, besides a whole lot of Bat's lead?"

"Got me, Fuzzy," growled Fraley.

"An' who's gonna pay fer yer windows, Ros?"

Fraley grinned at him. "You are, Fuzz."

"Me?"

"Give him a drink, Maggie, and keep 'em comin' 'til he's paid fer the windows."

"Hee-hee," cackled Fuzzy, thinking that was pretty funny. He didn't realize that Fraley meant exactly what he said.

Fraley headed for the rear storeroom, where he had the replacement windows already cut and ready to be installed, but at the last moment he decided he'd wait until morning. It'd look better that way.

Bat and Jim drew up before the jail.

"Hey Mel," called Bat to a slow-witted handyman who hung around the jail, "go round up some coffins. Might as well get these gents up Boot Hill right away."

"Why coffins?"

"'Cause they're gonna be diggin' that place up soon, and they're not going to want to mess with half-rotted bodies."

Mel paled at the idea. "Reckon I'll be makin' myself scarce when it comes to doin' that." He wasn't that half-witted.

Paul Brooker and Wyatt came out of the jail.

"They say anything, Bat?"

"Never had a chance."

"Brooker here thinks they were gunning for Lucia Bone, deliberate."

"That a fact? Let me get my horse taken care of, Brooker, and we'll talk about it."

"Brooker wants to be deputized, too."

Masterson noticed the hole in Brooker's sleeve, up near the shoulder, and some dried blood around the hole. Apparently Brooker didn't particularly cherish being shot at.

"Well, we'll talk about that, too."   ✑

11

Lucia Bone was sitting in a corner of the downstairs bar when Nellie Pope came to her. Lucia was nibbling on some bread, sipping some wine, and sketching Giovanni and JB, who were behind the bar on the far side of the room. They were supposed to be working, setting up, but were continually striking poses.

"There'll be some supper later," said Nellie.

"I don't like eating in the kitchen."

"Don't you be putting on such airs, Lucia. Not yet. You haven't been here long enough."

Lucia nodded, glanced at her subjects, and completed a line.

Nellie watched silently for a while as the sketch took shape.

"You have talent," she said at length.

"A lot of good it does me," replied Lucia bitterly. "The only talent that counts around this town is with guns."

Nellie didn't quite understand her bitterness. She looked up at Giovanni and JB.

"Go work someplace else," she said. "Lucia's got you down already."

They left and Lucia folded her pad.

"I didn't mean for you to stop."

"I'm finished."

"It didn't look finished."

"Nothing I draw ever looks finished, like nothing I do is ever finished."

That had a disturbingly philosophical sound to Nellie. That was all her house of pleasure needed, a girl pausing in the middle of a quick date to plumb life's meaning.

"What is that supposed to mean?"

Lucia grinned. "Damned if I know. It sounded good, though, didn't it?"

Nellie relaxed. The girl was bright, that was all.

"I want to talk to you, Lucia, in private." She glanced about, checking on privacy. "I must warn you never, never, to repeat, in public or even to the girls here, the kind of thing you said about Roscoe Fraley."

"I won't, but if he ever tries to force himself on me again, I'll kill him."

"I know, I know, you've already said that," Nellie responded wearily, "and don't worry, I'll see that he doesn't. *We'll* see that he doesn't."

Perhaps she'd heard of Red's offer to kill Fraley.

"But Lucia, what you said wasn't even true. Roscoe Fraley may not be a pleasant man, but he's more than adequately equipped."

"I really fixed him, didn't I," said Lucia. "He won't forget."

"That's what I'm afraid of." She seemed to know a lot more than she was saying. "Poor Roscoe—" Lucia made a face.

"—he had such a bad night, after he left here, I mean. You may not have heard, but some pranksters moved his privy and he fell right into—" She caught the expression on Lucia's face. "Oh no, Lucia, you didn't! But how, all by yourself?"

"I had help." And she remembered Tom Beaumont. She'd been trying to forget.

"Someone from here?" Nellie was prepared to laughingly scold any one of her male help.

"No, he's dead now."

Nellie had heard about the shooting on Front Street, and that a cowboy had been shot and killed.

"You're not very lucky, are you, Lucia?" she said quietly.

"Me?" Her voice sounded brittle. "I'm still alive."

Nellie sighed. What would the world do without sarcasm, without its bitter medication?

"You puzzle me, Lucia. You're not anything like the rest of my girls. What are you doing here, what are you looking for?"

"I'm looking for my mother." Lucia opened her pad and sketched a quick likeness. "That's her— looks familiar, doesn't she?"

Nellie Pope scowled at the sketch. "I've heard about the picture you keep showing your dates."

Lucia told her of her quest.

"What are you going to do when you find her?"

"I don't know. She's got a lot of explaining to do. To me, and to the law."

"The law?"

But Lucia didn't want to talk about it. "After that's over I plan to open a school."

Nellie didn't want to talk about it either. "Really? That's quite admirable."

"You don't think I'm crazy? Or too young?"

"Neither; except not in Dodge City, of course. You know as well as I do, Lucia, that there are teachers younger than you, and that the frontier needs all the teachers it can get.

"But Lucia, why stop there? The opportunities for women out here are much, much better than they are back east. A much higher percentage of the female population out here are, well, actresses of course, but also lawyers and doctors and journalists."

"And madams?"

"Yes! Madams, and prostitutes. Look at me, a model of success."

Lucia'd never seen Nellie smile before, really smile. It was nice. "Well, I've been schooled, but *lawyers*. Not *that* schooled."

"You don't have to be. You just have to be willing to try."

"Teaching school's not good enough?"

"It's good enough for some but . . ." Nellie looked as if she wished she'd tried those other things. "Why do you want to find your mother, Lucia? You're grown now. She can't help you any more."

"I just want to find out who I am."

Nellie regarded her sadly. "So you don't know who you are. I know who you are."

Lucia looked at her sharply.

"You're a beautiful young woman with a wonderful life ahead of you, and you're wasting your time digging around in the past."

Lucia looked back down at her sketch and added a few details.

Nellie watched her. Finally she said softly:

"I used to be beautiful, just like you—or almost like you."

"You still are."

Nellie shook her head.

"What happened?"

"Fire. A lamp blew up."

Lucia recalled the Abilene fires. "Can't be all that bad."

Nellie Pope pulled aside the hair that hid the left third of her face. The skin was scarred, red, glassy and ugly.

Lucia stared at it, fascinated. The difference between that part of her face and the rest was like night and day.

"What do you do when you're . . . entertaining?"

"Turn out the light." She kept the hair pulled back, forcing the ugliness on Lucia.

Lucia reached out and gently touched the scar tissue.

"Ugly, isn't it?" said Nellie.

"That's not *real* ugly," said Lucia softly, "the same way the rest of your face isn't *real* beauty. It's just the surface. Real beauty's inside, and so's real ugliness."

Nellie impulsively grabbed her hand and held it tight, just as she held Lucia's eyes with her own.

"If there's ever anything I can do to help, Lucia, just ask."

Lucia felt a trifle uncomfortable. "All I want is not to see that damn Fraley."

Nellie nodded. "I told you, I'll take care of it, but you can make it easier for me."

"How?"

"I know that some of the men who visit you, they're important men in Dodge. But I also know that a lot of those same men have something to hide; some secret. In some cases that's the reason they're here on the frontier. Hiding. Now, if they let slip anything that might be useful—"

"You mean to use against them?"

"Yes. You pass the information on to me. Use your own judgment. If you think there's something you can weasel out of them, go ahead and do it."

"And where does this information go?" asked Lucia, though she had a pretty good idea.

Nellie kept tight hold of her hand. "To Roscoe Fraley. That's one of his sources of power—or will be."

"Do you like Fraley?"

"That doesn't matter. I wouldn't have this place if it wasn't for him. He helps maintain it, and protects it. Not from drunken cowboys but from the town itself; from those holier-than-thous you see on the street whose husbands were here the night before."

Lucia withdrew her hand. Nellie didn't want to let go, but she did. Nellie then rearranged her hair to hide the scar.

"So you owe Fraley," said Lucia. "You must know him then. Where does he come from? And who's that woman that's with him—I think her name's Maggie?"

"It is Maggie. That's his woman."

Lucia's mouth worked for a while as she formed and reformed words, and tried to figure out how much to say.

"I think she may be my mother, and they may both be killers."

"Killers?"

The exclamation was a little forced, but less so than Lucia'd expected. She had surprised Nellie in one way or another.

Lucia knew there'd been three people involved in those old killings; two women and a man. She'd also satisfied herself that Nellie'd been one of those women, Maggie the other, and Roscoe Fraley the man. Nellie's burn-scar, undoubtably from the Abilene fires where they'd supposedly died, had helped to clinch it. It wasn't absolutely certain, of course, but anything else was asking an awful lot of coincidence. Maggie's resemblance to the mother she'd been tracking, Fraley's ugly, homicidal character, Nellie's scar, all three of them in cahoots working for who knows what. . . .

The only problem was that Lucia had grown fond of Nellie. She was sure that Nellie was incapable of really hurting anyone. Lucia could have told Nellie that there were three killers; Roscoe, Maggie and . . . , but she just couldn't bring herself to say anything that would scare this woman, that would hurt her. The scars Nellie carried were painful enough.

So dammit, she'd leave Nellie out of it. Completely.

In the meantime, Nellie was also wrestling with the same thoughts, the same memories, and also with a curious refusal to place her own safety and security ahead of Lucia's.

If Lucia knew that Roscoe and Maggie were killers, then she must know. . . .

But Nellie was so far from drawing that obvious conclusion it was pitiful.

"I did think I saw some resemblance," Nellie muttered, "but killers? Lucia, you must never mention that to anyone. I can't believe it's true, but I wouldn't put anything past Roscoe. Do you understand what I'm saying?"

"Yes. I'll look out for myself."

"You have to do more than that. You have to be quiet as a mouse."

"Gol-leee, Nellie, I can't do that. A mouse?" She smiled reassuringly at Nellie. "Don't worry, I'll be all right. I'm lucky. I've already been shot at once, but they missed."

"Shot at? You were shot at?" That was something she hadn't heard. "When was that?"

They met soon after dark.

"Leave her alone, Roscoe, I'm warning you."

"Dammit, Nell, she'll ruin everything, and get us hung besides."

"I'll take care of her. She won't say anything. She's going to gather a lot of dirt for you."

"Huh?"

"She said she would, and she will. That girl is going to be your stepping-stone to real power."

"Well."

"Trust me. She and I, we're very close now. She'll do what I say. And besides, she doesn't really belong at the house, or even here in Dodge. She'll soon be gone."

"The hell she will. She's got that picture, and it looks like Maggie, of all people."

"She'll realize it's a mistake. That was just unlucky."

"Maybe so, maybe so, but unlucky ain't the word for it. She musta made that unlucky mistake real early on, got onto our trail, or blasted Maggie's trail, way back." Even though it was dark and there was no one around, Fraley's voice fell to a hoarse whisper. "She knows about you-know-where."

"No, I don't know where."

"Hannibal!"

"Then say it," said Nellie crisply. "I told you not to worry. I've got her under control." Nellie saw he still needed convincing. "That shooting on Front Street may not have scared her then," she lied, "but it's scaring her plenty now."

"Oh yeah?" Fraley brightened in the dark. "Then it worked, huh? Good."

"Yes. It worked." And Nellie's suspicions were confirmed.

Lucia was downstairs in the reception room, perched on the edge of a sofa by the door. It was where she always sat; if she didn't like the look of a customer, whoosh, she was gone.

There was a knock on the front door and Cassie went to answer.

Moments later a compact, mustachioed, well-dressed man entered the reception room. Lucia was so startled she almost lit out for upstairs.

"Sheriff Masterson, what are you doing here?"

Bat smiled and touched his derby, canting it even more.

"I told you I was going to drop by and pay my respects."

"Oh. Do you—ummm—want to—"

"With you? No, I have another little sweetie I favor from time to time." He regarded Lucia, trying to see if she was disappointed or not. "And I'm sorry, I didn't bring that barrel of money you asked for."

Lucia looked at him, sorrow etched on her features, making her suddenly older. "That's all right, Sheriff. That school down in Texas? I guess I won't be teaching there. That school died on the street today."

Bat nodded. So that was the reason for that young man's madness. Bat let the silence stretch.

"Beaumont's father rode into town tonight to pick up his son's body. Guess he didn't know about you," Bat said finally.

Lucia's eyes were wet. "What was there to know?"

Bat Masterson pursed his lips, then touched his derby again. "I'll be going now. If you see Kippie tell her I'll try to get by later."

Kippie was a cute little black-haired girl, a little chunky but always laughing. "I'll tell her. But why don't you wait? Maybe she's—"

"No. I'll be back later."

And he would. But not just for Kippie, whom he liked and was only eight years his junior. He'd also listened to Brooker, and checked the wooden side-walk outside the Occident. He agreed that the riders had tried to kill Lucia.

He wondered why, and meant to find out. In the meantime, he was going to keep an eye on the girl.

Lucia did that to people: inspired love, inspired loyalty.

But she also inspired feelings that were considerably different.

The clerk from Zimmerman's Hardware made a damn poor indian. True, he was wearing a full war bonnet, the moth-eaten bonnet of a long-deceased minor chief, and he did wear a loincloth, which only got in the way, but his raised behind was fragile, pale and pimply, and his skinny torso was splotched with some kind of rash.

The girl on the bed was on her hands and knees. Her client, the quick date, the "hostile," was presumably raping her from behind.

The indian leaned over his victim, resting on her back, arms around her body clutching her full breasts, his bony behind rising and falling.

"Oh Lucy, Lucy, Lucy," he moaned. "Lu-*cia*!"

The girl craned her head around, much like a milking cow would in response to icy fingers. "What the hell are you groaning about, Harry? I'm not Lucia."

"Hell. Don't you think I know that? Lucia didn't want to do this."

"I don't blame her. I'm getting tired, Harry."

"Just take it easy," he instructed, readjusting his loincloth—how the hell did those indians do it? "Lucy, Lucy, Lucy . . ."

"Goddammit, Harry, don't call me that. I don't like it. I'm *not* Lucia."

"So what? I'm not Harry."

Paul Brooker entered Nellie Pope's. It was his first visit. He was well-experienced as far as bordellos went, but in other cities, not in Dodge.

He wasn't sure why he'd come. To see Lucia, of course. But he'd hesitated. He certainly didn't approve of this life, and was afraid his coming might send her the wrong signal.

But then, she had a right to run her own life. And if he couldn't take it he knew he could simply stay away.

But in the end he couldn't—couldn't take it and couldn't stay away. It was a very upsetting situation.

Fortunately, Lucia was not immediately available when he got there. He was glad for that. It gave him time to compose himself.

On the other hand, her absence got him to thinking about what she must be doing, and why she wasn't available. He knew she was popular, but he'd never really nailed down exactly what that meant in visual terms. Now he did, and he started losing his recently acquired composure.

He examined the room. The luxurious trappings, while not standard, were not that unusual for such places. The deep sofas, the heavy drapes, the tall, ornately hand-carved liquor cabinet, the red parlor lamps that made everything look rosy. "Denver Modern."

Two young girls wearing full-length, off-the-shoulder gowns lounged on the sofas, eyeing him.

They were fleshy. They would eventually be fat,
but their youth was, for the time being, holding
their excess flesh in check. They rather resembled
the overstuffed but firm sofas. They were not his
type. He smiled at them, simply as a friendly gesture, and then studied the ceiling.

After awhile he walked over to the liquor cabinet. A green canister sat atop the cabinet and he
examined its contents. Belladonna leaves.

In excess, belladonna was a poison, but in mod-
eration it served as a pain killer, as did morphine.
Both of them, and opium, and cocaine, were readily
available over the counter.

Paul Brooker wondered what the painkiller was
used for. That room was the last place he expected
to see pain on display.

Just then Lucia entered the room, trailed by
Nellie Pope.

"Paul!"

Brooker looked at her, but couldn't find the
proper words.

Lucia smiled and waited, and waited. Finally she
said, "Bat Masterson was by."

"What'd he want?" burst from Paul.

Lucia widened her eyes in all innocence. "Just
came by to say hello."

Paul's doubt showed, though it was possible the
Sheriff was taking the alleged threats on Lucia's
life seriously and was just keeping an eye on her.

"Bat likes another girl here," said Lucia. "Kippie."

Oh really? Brooker suddenly had an urge to see
what Kippie looked like.

His eyes moved to rest on Nellie Pope.

"This is Nellie," said Lucia, "Nellie Pope." She assumed Paul knew who Nellie Pope was.

Paul had heard the name and may have passed her on the street, but had never been introduced to her. He studied her closely, wondering what the fall of hair hid.

Nellie began to grow restive under his scrutiny, which seemed to grow harder with each passing moment. Possibly he was trying to avoid looking at Lucia.

Paul registered the chin, the mouth, the nose, all of which had the confident, upraised look of breeding, if not the fine lines. And he noted the green eyes. Looking into them reminded him of looking into clear water that took its color from the green vegetation beneath the surface. In the eyes, as in the water, some invisible current seemed to disturb the greenery, making it come alive.

"Your friend certainly does inspect things closely," Nellie said, resisting an edgy impulse to toss her hair back.

"He finds things out," explained Lucia, quoting him. "He's—"

"Just a traveler," Brooker inserted forcefully, "a businessman, always got my eye peeled for something new and different; something saleable." He smiled engagingly.

Lucia realized Brooker didn't want everyone knowing that he was a detective. It would make his job all the harder.

"Well then," asked Nellie, "what's your opinion of my merchandise?"

His eyes dropped to her bosom.

Nellie laughed. "I meant my girls."

"They don't amount to much compared to you, what few I've seen—excepting Lucia, of course."

"Of course. But what *about* Lucia?" She was ready to deal, ready to barter, but was still bothered by Brooker's gaze.

"Well," began Paul, "I . . ." Once again he had trouble finding words. "Actually," he finally managed, "I just came by to see how she is, how she is getting along."

Lucia's lips compressed, but Nellie thought she understood his problem. She smiled. He'd overcome his reluctance within the week, she was sure. "Well then, just make yourself comfortable. Perhaps you and Lucia can chat until—"

Until some rowdy gent came in and grabbed Lucia and hauled her off upstairs? The hell he would. "No, I think I'd better be going. I've got things to do."

"Just what have you got to do?" demanded Lucia.

"They're waiting a game for me at the Long Branch."

"Earp?"

"Uh, no. I might go down to the Lady Gay."

"Who plays down there?"

"Bat does, sometimes."

Lucia scowled. "Some friend you are." She glanced at Nellie. "This is supposed to be my *friend.*"

Paul Brooker realized that Lucia had a slightly different concept of friendship than he had. He started bobbing from the waist, smiling, and backing out of the room.

Out in the foyer, he grabbed hold of the door and yanked it open. And yanked Sheriff Masterson inside, Bat still hanging onto the outside knocker.

"Hey," cried Bat, "take it easy. This here place is supposed to steady you."

Paul Brooker glared at Masterson. "That Kippie," he said, "she's a real nice girl."

Bat's heavy eyes narrowed. Paul Brooker bounced on out the door, for the moment feeling better, and he vanished into the night.

Bat closed the door, a thoughtful look on his face.   ◄§

12

PAUL BROOKER went directly to the railroad depot, where he composed a long telegram. It wasn't in any code, but it wouldn't make sense to anyone who didn't know what he was writing about.

The telegraph operator gave him a fishy look.

"Just send it," Paul said.

Once the telegram was sent, Brooker started thinking about Lucia again, thinking how foolish, how childish he must have seemed to her. He became exceedingly depressed. He thought he'd better do some serious drinking, and do it where the surroundings might take his mind off his misery.

He crossed the tracks and entered one of south Front's hurdy-gurdys, Colonel Major's Saloon and Dance Hall, situated between the Varieties Dance

Hall and Ham Bell's Elephant Livery. He found a table toward the back. He studied the women, but they only reminded him of Lucia, though God knows they didn't look like her. These gals looked dangerous (and were, Colonel Major's attracting the same low-life crowd as Cattle Annie's and the Crazy Hors).

A number of soldiers from Fort Dodge were playing cards and, as far as Paul could see, getting steadily whipped by the house. It didn't help that they were drunk.

Paul overheard, "Ever go snipe-hunting?"

He twisted around. At a table, three plains veterans were sitting with a youngster who had the look of a greenhorn.

The youngster frowned and said cautiously, "No." He'd heard of snipe but never seen any.

"You hunt 'em at night, in marshy places. There's one real close to here, where the Arkansas kinda overflows."

"That so?" Still dubious.

"Yep. An' it's 'bout as delicious a bird as you'll ever sink yer choppers into. Now us three, we been thinkin' mebbe we'd mount us a snipe hunt. Wanta come?"

"Now?"

"Now's the best time. Oh, you kin hunt 'em during the day, but it's real easy at night. All you do is wait at the edge of a marsh with a sack, holdin' the sack wide open. You put a lantern out in front of the sack. The light attracts the snipe. 'Course, it helps if some of yuh circle around in back of the snipe and scare 'em toward the light.

But anyways, the snipe sees the light and he runs to it—"

"Runs?"

"Runs, flies, who cares—but he zooms right intuh the sack, a whole bunch, an' you quick tie the sack closed."

"Sounds easy."

"It *is*. All you need is patience; 'cause they don't come that fast. So how about it—wanta take a crack at it?"

"Gee, sure."

The entire table, now a snipe-hunting party, got up and left.

Brooker downed a couple of more drinks and was working on another when trouble broke out between the soldiers and the house dealers.

The soldiers claimed they'd been deliberately cheated, overcharged for their drinks, and dealt dirty.

They were quite right. They'd been very efficiently and thoroughly cleaned out.

The soldiers weren't leaving without a fight.

They didn't. They had the fight and then they left, all of them carried out the door and pitched onto the dirt and manure of Front Street.

Brooker had another drink, and then another . . . the dance-hall gals were looking better and better.

Three-quarters of the snipe hunting party returned; the three plains veterans, laughing their heads off.

Apparently the greenhorn was still out there with his lamp and his sack, crouched at the edge of the marsh, waiting for the run of snipe.

The three men had first tried to get the green-horn to go off and drive the snipe toward the sack. But the greenhorn wasn't, he claimed, that big a fool. They'd catch the snipe and go off and leave him out in the marsh.

So they reluctantly agreed to let the greenhorn hold the sack while they did the chasing, which they did. They left the kid holding the sack and returned directly to the dance hall.

Brooker had another drink.

A greasy, bewhiskered old fellow sat down at his table.

"Last time soldiers was cheated and beaten up and thrown out, you know what happened?"

Brooker began to worry. "What?"

"Nothing. But it almost happened. Commander at Ford Dodge formed up a platoon, marched 'em into town, and was about to level the pertickler s'loon when, jes' in time, somebody made peace. But it could happen again, an' this time they might not stop."

Brooker figured he'd better get out of there while he could still walk. He left the old man cackling in anticipation.

Brooker stumbled north, for ages it seemed, until he finally wandered into the Occident.

Not being totally competent, he let Sturm talk him into a chunk of Limburger. He hardly noticed the pungent odor, but the combination of his alcoholic breath and the cheese cleared a circle around his table.

Sturm found it all very amusing.

After finishing off the Limburger and a few more drinks, Brooker heaved himself to his feet and weaved his way over to the depot.

"Did I get a reply yet?" he asked the telegraph operator.

The operator stared at him. "I only just now sent it, mister."

"Oh." What time was it? What *day* was it? "Well, keep trying."

Brooker made it back outside and started walking, to clear his head.

After awhile, he thought he was in much better shape. As a test he decided to walk along a railroad track. If he could balance himself on that . . .

It took him a good bit of time to master that balancing feat, which, once mastered, only lasted for five seconds anyway. During that time some pranksters had snuck up behind him and made a noise like the whistle of an onrushing train. He'd nearly sprained his ankle jumping clear.

The next time they tried it he didn't go for it— and almost got run down by a real train.

Also during that hour, the snipe-hunting greenhorn had almost run him down, crossing the tracks from north to south, headed for Colonel Major's. He was carrying an empty sack and his doused lantern in one hand, and a rifle in the other. He hardly noticed Brooker's high-wire act as he charged by.

Reckon he's gonna hunt him some snipe-hunters, Brooker figured.

After he'd damn near teetered all the way west out of town, he headed for the nearest resting place, which happened to be the Last Stand.

He stumbled to a table and flopped down.

Time passed.

"Looks like you really tied one on tonight, fella."

A hard voice. Brooker tried to focus. "Yeshhh . . . shoooor did. . . ."

"Have another one, on me. Hair of the dog."

"Dog? *Dog?*! Sumbitch, feelsh like I awready shwallered a whole damn packa dogsh."

"Here," said Fraley. "This'll cure what ails yuh."

Brooker slowly raised the shot of rotgut to his lips and held it there. Then he slowly tilted his head back. Couldn't miss. He belched, and then smiled foolishly.

"You and that Lucia gal are real close, ain'tcha?"

"Looosh. Looosha? Yesh, shooor am—but she'sh doin' *bad,* bad bad bad—sheeeeet! But not for mush longer, no shurreee. . . ."

"Whaddya mean?"

"Eh?"

"I said, what do you mean?"

"She been chayshun after her muvver."

"Her what?"

"Her *muvver*—muvver muvver muvver!"

"Mother!"

"Yesh, shtupid shumbitch."

Fraley almost strangled him. "So? So what?"

"Sho, she'sh found her."

"What?!" Raw shock was written on Roscoe's face.

Brooker tried to glare at him. His eyes almost fell from their sockets. "Now lishun, you shtupid shumbitch, I doan wanna hafta r'peat myshelf—"

"I heard you, I heard you. Where'd she find her?"

"A-rouuuund." The word started high, swooped

low and ended on the rise again. "Uh-rouuuuund."

"Where?"

Brooker raised his head and rolled his eyes around, trying to figure out where he was. "Dunno," he finally said. "She worksh inna sh'loon. Name'sh Patty."

"Patty?"

Brooker's eyebrows did a crazy dance. "Shumpin' like that."

"Maggie?"

"There you go."

Fraley's fists clenched.

"Maggie'sh bad too," said Brooker, tilting forward confidentially. "She'sh a killer!"

Fraley almost jumped from his seat.

"Looosh's gonna turn her in, too, shumday." Brooker felt like curling up on the floor and sleeping it off. "But she better do it fasht. Shumwun's tryin' to kill her!"

Fraley jumped again, but not as much as the first time. He was getting used to Brooker's drunken pranks. "Reeeee-ly?"

Brooker nodded slowly, exaggeratedly, the more so since Lucia had told him nothing of her plans. He was guessing all the way; jumping to conclusions, which wasn't bad if he'd only keep his mouth shut. "Reeeeee-leee. But doan worry, ol' Bat-sh gonna watch out fer 'er, ol' Bat Mashtershun. I tole Batshurshun thash shumbody'sh tryin' t' kill her." Why didn't he jump? Brooker was disappointed. "To KILL her!"

The next thing Paul Brooker knew, or would have known were he any more alert, was that he was rocketing through the doors of the Last Stand to pitch face down on the street.

He curled up and made himself comfortable.

He was still lying on the ground a few hours later, at about three a.m., when a man rode into town and tied up at the hitching rail outside of the Last Stand.

He looked down at Brooker, but might have been studying an ant for all the emotion he showed. He looked up the street, at the rest of Dodge's red-hot pleasure palaces which were, by that hour, reduced to glowing embers. There was an occasional sputter and flare-up, but that was all.

His face was weathered, lined, and rugged, which somehow made his small pink eyes and knobby nose less ugly. Several days' growth of hair covered his lower face. Spittle was dried white on his lips, except for a corner of his mouth where tobacco juice exited.

His wide-brimmed hat had once been white, but was now grey with grease and grime. His duster overcoat, full length, was fawn-colored and seemed fairly new, but the rest of his outfit, including his vest, shirt, twill trousers, and his once fancy boots were old, worn, and also grimy. Not so his spurs, though—brutal-looking things—nor the brace of pistols strapped around his hips. The leather of his gunbelt looked like it had been worked on recently, and his pistols, Peacemakers, positively sparkled.

He tied up his horse, removed his saddlebags and rifle, and walked into the Last Stand.

The place was pretty much empty. The north

side of Front Street closed down earlier than the south, but Roscoe Fraley was there, and he hustled toward the newcomer.

There were just a few customers still there, and none were in any condition to notice anything, but Roscoe still kept his voice down.

"Get the hell out of here, Jim. Go find yerself a room and steer clear of me and my places. When the rest get here, head 'em off. I don't wanta have nuthin' t'do with them. And stow them guns. There's a gun law here."

"So I unnerstan'."

"I'll find a way to get in touch."

"Yer the boss. We want the money up front, though."

"You'll get it."

Jim turned to leave.

"Hold it. Lemme turn the lights out before you go. Don't wanta take a chance on no one seein' you."

Jim nodded. "Who's the fancy dresser lying out in the street?"

"Who the hell knows? Some jerk. Been hangin' around for a month or so."

"Where's he belong?"

"Dodge House. Why?"

"You threw him out?"

Fraley nodded.

"Don't figger it'd be a good idea havin' him wake up and start sparkin' trouble."

"Hell, don't worry about him. Stupid bastard's lovesick, that's all. But he does blab a lot, some real interestin' stuff. Kinda makes yer visit worthwhile."

Fraley turned out all the lights.

"Hey, what the hell!" cried a drunk.

Jim sauntered out of the Last Stand.

Outside, after resecuring his saddlebags and rifle, and dropping his guns into his saddlebags, Jim Chappelle picked up Paul Brooker and slung him over his horse.

Brooker groaned and wheezed and dribbled from the mouth, but stayed put. Chappelle mounted, half-sitting on Brooker, and rode east along Front, staying well out in the center of the Plaza, in the dark area.

There was only a single, weak light glowing in the jail and city offices. As he rode by, he paused long enough to discern and recognize the profile of Jim Masterson. Then, smiling, he rode on.

He dumped Brooker on the desk of the Dodge House and walked back out before the clerk showed up to take delivery.

Chappelle then rode over to the Great Western and booked himself a room.

As the clerk let him in the room, Jim Chappelle looked at the door.

"How come the door's all shot up?"

"The lock's been fixed."

"I asked, how come it's shot up?"

The clerk thought fast. "Feller locked himself out."

"You don't got no pass-keys?"

"He was in a hurry."

Over the next few days five more men drifted into Dodge City—hard-looking men that went by such names as Abel, Fiore, Bloomer, Gooch, and Swifty. They arrived separately, lodged separately, stowed their pistols—all of which were well-cared for, several with filed-down sights, and most sporting either ivory or mother-of-pearl handles—and kept low profiles.

Jim Chappelle was their contact, and he drifted slowly around town, casually counting heads and passing the word.

One morning, one of them, Bloomer, the one lodged furthest north, heard some distant gunshots. He was tempted to go see what was happening, but didn't, which may have been a mistake.

Just outside the city limits, north, Bat Masterson was putting on his show. He did it frequently, and the public, among them potential opponents, was invited.

He'd set up cans and spend hour after hour shooting holes in them. He called it "sweetening" his guns. As he explained it, "We file the notch of the hammer till the trigger pulls sweet, which means the blamed thing'll damn near go off if you just look at it."

Bat was usually the only one practicing. Sometimes Wyatt, if he could drag himself from the sack, would join him. But never Jim Masterson. Jim, despite having had his older brother killed, would still rather out-talk his adversaries than out-shoot them. Of course, if he had to, he could give a pretty fair account of himself.

Bat Masterson, though, whether practicing, or in deadly earnest, was in a class by himself.

Bloomer and the rest, down from the Dakota Territory, had heard tell of Masterson and his friends, but that was all. They had no real understanding of what might be in store. Which isn't to say they hadn't earned the notches on their guns.

They had. And they'd heard about Ed Masterson buying it, which meant that a Masterson was just as human as the next gent.

They should have checked out Masterson's practice session.

But they didn't, and they'd pay for it.

There was yet another new face in Dodge City, a seventh man. He would play a part in the upcoming events but he was harder to figure.

He alone arrived by train, from the east. He wore no guns, but he was tall and straight, and had an air about him that suggested he was no stranger to guns and gunplay.

He was nicely but quietly dressed, wearing a grey pin-stripe suit with a black velvet vest, white collared shirt, and a grey velvet tie. He appeared to be in his mid- to late thirties. He wore a narrow-brimmed, cream-colored hat and his hair, combed, was blondish and shoulder-length.

His face was thin, almost delicate, but, on closer inspection, delicate in the manner of a bowed, slender slip of steel, or in the manner of a finely-wrought crossbow. The latter analogy was especially apropos seeing how his eyebrows bent down around his eyes and his long nose was like the drawn shaft of an arrow. His mustache was full but trimmed, not a handlebar. It was a mature growth, while the hair on his cheeks and chin seemed barely a week old.

He carried his two bags to the Dodge House and registered.

If he'd signed the register honestly, he would have written Brewster Lowell, Major, U.S. Army,

Retired (albeit prematurely). Instead, he wrote Benjamin Lloyd, which was consistent with the B.L. initials on his clothing and expensive baggage.

He was given a room two doors down from Paul Brooker's room and five from Doc Holliday's.

Late on the afternoon of the day he moved in, he heard a door open and close loudly in the hall. He stuck his head out and saw Doc Holliday heading his way, towards the stairs.

Holliday, as was usual upon his awakening and before his first drinks had taken effect, looked like death.

The Major, or Benjamin Lloyd, wondered who he was. He knew the air in those parts was good for whatever ailed you, but the man looked far gone.

Curious as to Holliday's identity, he started knocking on doors that neighbored his.

Paul Brooker, his gun practice interrupted, opened his door and stared at the Major.

"Benjamin Lloyd, your new neighbor," the Major announced at parade-ground volume, and thrust out his hand.

Brooker frowned, his mouth dropping open a crack, and then he stared down at the hand.

Jim Chappelle had arrived late on Monday. By Saturday the rest of his gang had arrived and taken their places. It was on Sunday that the man calling himself Ben Lloyd had arrived.

Interestingly enough, late Sunday night all seven men converged on Nellie Pope's. The Major, repeating his new name over and over to himself, had probably gone there at the suggestion of Paul

Brooker. It was considered the best way to get the rigors of a long trip out of your bones. The rest, though, Chappelle and his six, they had their own reasons.   ⋙

13

BEN LLOYD had discarded the suit, and showed up at Nellie's wearing an ordinary vest, shirt, string tie, and trousers. The clothing material wasn't ordinary, to be sure, but he didn't want to look too common, and it would have taken a knowledgeable tailor to accurately value the garments.

He mussed up his hair before actually stepping into the house.

He looked over the two girls in the reception room and wasn't impressed. Nellie Pope entered and he stared hard at her. She asked his pleasure and he replied that the two girls weren't it, but he was willing to wait.

Nellie nodded coolly, not displeased. His voice sounded nice and he was well-spoken, and she didn't mind his resting there, engaging her in idle conversation.

More clients came in, among them Fiore, Bloomer, and Gooch, and they were taken care of.

Ben Lloyd remained seated, unusually fussy for a person that was not very unusual in other respects. Nellie took him to be a moderately well-off businessman, probably just passing through.

Abel, Swifty and then Jim Chappelle himself eventually showed up, and Nellie Pope summoned some more of her girls, among them Lucia Bone.

Ben Lloyd's eyes lit up briefly upon seeing Lucia, but they dulled quickly and he passed on her.

Abel, however, didn't pass. He was short and wiry and not very good-looking, but he was neat and clean and made a passable impression. He was also known to be a neat, clean killer. He and Lucia soon disappeared.

"That girl that just left," said Lloyd to Nellie, "I thought at first . . ."

When he didn't complete his statement Nellie said, "I declare, Mister Lloyd, your stay in Dodge City is going to be rather dull if nothing you've yet seen comes up to your standards."

Lloyd smiled, and Nellie liked the smile. She was getting used to this man's thin face, which would be a lot better looking, she surmised, without all that scruffy hair.

"You may be right, Madam. I have frequently suffered at the hands of my own demanding taste, but, as a matter of simple fact, my high standards were met soon after I stepped through the door."

"Then why didn't you do something? Say something?"

He didn't answer but simply looked at her.

She slowly realized what the look meant. "Oh come now, Mister Lloyd—"

"Ben, please."

"You can't be serious. I run this place, I don't—"

"Never?"

"Rarely, and only then with people I know."

"Make an exception."

Nellie took a deep breath.

"Truthfully, Nellie Pope," Lloyd went on, "I may be unusual but I am not that fond of children. These girls of yours, they're terribly young. I, myself, am negotiating my middle years."

"You make it sound like an adventure."

"It is; and you, unless I'm badly mistaken, have entered yours, if only barely. You are?"

"Goodness!" Nellie found herself almost blushing. "A—a lady does not reveal her age, sir."

"Please accept my apologies for being so forward. I—"

"Thirty-five."

"Thirty-eight," he responded promptly.

Nellie fingered the sleeve of her blouse, dropping her eyes. "You know the—fare?"

"I know what a date with the girls costs," he said. "You should come much higher. But I'm quite willing to pay, whatever the cost."

"Dammit, sir," said Nellie, "if you maintain that approach, that relentless flattery, you'll be getting it for nothing." She smiled sort of helplessly, or as helplessly as Nellie Pope could ever become. "Then what would happen to my business?"

They went to Nellie's room.

The walls were covered with various pictures.

Some were sketches, and they were good and bad. The good were recent acquisitions, samples of Lucia's work which Lucia didn't know that Nellie had. The bad were products of Nellie's own hand, though she never identified them as such.

There were two framed pictures, one a landscape, the other a horse. Presumably both held some significance for Nellie.

There were also numerous cut-outs from journals and magazines; illustrations, both in color and black-and-white; some photographs, crude and not very clear, for the most part military portraits, stiff and formal. The illustrations seemed to concentrate on an earlier period in American life when glamour, romance, and aristocracy reigned; a period that seemed to end just after the Civil War. Or was it just before? In any case, a certain young man and woman appeared in many of the pictures, as if different artists were using the same models.

"The girl in these pictures," said Lloyd, "she wouldn't be you, would she?"

"Of course not. She is light-haired, as you can see."

Ben smiled. "Women's hair has been known to change color."

"Not mine."

He pretended to inspect her hair carefully.

"That life," she said, "the setting you see depicted in those pictures. . . ."

"That was the life you came from?"

She lifted her chin perceptibly, proudly.

"Yes." But there was a certain sorrow in her eyes.

"Lost forever." Ben shook his head. "It's funny. If I'd met you anywhere but here I would have recognized breeding—and did recognize it. But I told myself, no, not here."

She smiled and breathed deeply, and her eyes seemed to fill with the glory of yesteryear. She slowly exhaled.

"I'll turn the light out."

"No. Don't."

"I must. I . . . it is better."

Ben quickly stepped to her. "I must know you," he said. He reached out, running his fingers into the heavy fall of brunette hair. He pushed the hair back as his hand reached around to cup her head.

Her scars were exposed and she gasped, but he drew her face, her lips, toward his. "Ben," she began, but then his mouth closed over hers.

She slowly relaxed into his arms.

The man called Abel handed Lucia the brass check and undressed carefully, folding his clothes neatly and draping them over one of the room's two carved wooden chairs.

Lucia hoped that he wouldn't remain quite so careful and neat, that he would ignite into a flurry of fire and emotion and get it over with fast. Lucia got no particular pleasure from her work. Not because she was blue-nosed, as odd as that might sound, but rather because pleasure for her demanded romance, or at the very least excitement, and at Nellie's, both of those were in very short supply—especially since her so-called friends, those who might have had the ability to stir her sleeping passion, were all trying to avoid her.

Lucia stepped behind the hand-painted dressing screen to disrobe. She didn't do that normally, but

since her client was being so sober and dignified.
. . . A sober and dignified weasel, that's what Abel
reminded her of.

The dressing screen was painted with flowers on
two panels, and the third showed a young girl with
an angelic face carrying a basket of kittens.

Lucia stepped out from behind the screen.

Abel looked her over slowly and nodded his approval. Then he turned toward the bed.

Lucia's eyebrows rose in gentle exasperation and
she walked over to the bed herself, and crawled up
onto it.

"You sure are an excitable fellow. This must
mean a lot to you."

Abel shook his head. "Doesn't mean that much,
not to me."

Lucia frowned. To whom, then? she wondered.

"Would you mind getting in position?" Abel
asked.

Golly, wasn't this going to be fun. "On my back?"

Abel looked vaguely shocked. "Of course."

Lucia was disappointed. She'd begun to experi-
ment. It lessened the boredom. Although if "Indian
Harry" showed up. . . .

She assumed the position and Abel crawled up
onto her.

He stared down into her face. "Well?" he said.

Jesus, can't he do anything? What in the world
is he doing here in the first place? But she reached
down and tried her best to excite the strange,
weasel-like creature.

Boy, she thought, this is the last time I pick
someone for neatness.

She then concentrated on what she was doing

and something like a small, surprised smile slowly creased Abel's lips.

What the hell, is he some kind of virgin? "All right," she said, "it's ready."

A little while later, as he sprawled atop her, she was compelled to say, "Come on, goddamn it, I don't want to do all the work."

"I thought they called you the school-marm," he whispered hoarsely in her ear.

"Some do," she replied. "School-marms curse, too."

He raised the upper part of his torso off her slowly and began to do his part.

She relaxed, closing her eyes.

She felt him move. He'd been supporting himself with his arms, hands resting on the bed by her shoulders. Now he moved his hands to her chest, near her neck.

Lucia, her head propped up on the pillow, frowned. That was a hell of a place to rest his weight. It made breathing hard.

"You've got a real nice town here, girlie," gasped Abel, picking up the beat, "a real nice town."

What the hell was this? wondered Lucia and she opened her eyes.

Abel hung over her, lips parted in a mirthless grin, breathing hard, his eyes closed.

"Too bad it's gonna need a new sheriff," Abel went on, his smile widening, "and too bad you ain't gonna be around to see him."

It definitely sounded strange, but Lucia couldn't think that clearly because of the pressure on her chest.

Abel moved his hands to her neck. They closed around it and tightened.

This couldn't be happening, not to her. Lucia tried to object but found she couldn't speak, couldn't even breathe.

Darn it, this gent had one hell of a way of making love. She pounded on his back. But his smile widened even more and his breathing came quicker and his eyes remained squeezed shut.

Lucia reached in back of her head.

Abel stepped up his pace. It wouldn't be long now. He'd done this before. With luck she'd die and relax just as he hit that incredible peak and released.

He felt something hard poking him in the chest, poking him hard and insistently. He'd expected to feel her fists, not her finger. He opened his eyes and looked down at Lucia.

Lucia was staring pop-eyed back up at him, face red, about to die, but there was anger in her expression.

There was more prodding and he looked down. Lucia's Remington was poking him in the chest. He blinked. If she pulled the trigger she'd blow away his nipple and everything behind it. And her knuckles were whitening.

He let go of her neck, and felt himself going soft.

Damn! He was a bloody all-around loser.

He inched backward and crawled off the bed. Lucia, though still on her back and sucking air like crazy, followed him with the gun. Her hand was rock-steady.

He stepped slowly to where his clothes were folded and draped.

"Goddamn," he complained, "can't you take a goddamn joke?"

Lucia sat up slowly, the blood slowly draining from her face and restoring its normal, creamy complexion. There would be bruise marks around her neck, though.

She knew she should kill him. She wanted to kill him.

Abel dressed quickly, cursing to himself. What a hell of a situation, he thought. She's got a gun and I don't. What kind of town is this where the whores pack iron and the men can't.

Lucia, her mind a riot of thoughts and emotions, was still trying to decide whether or not to kill him when Abel escaped out the door.

Afterward, Lucia tried to remember what it was that Abel had been prattling about. A real nice town? A new sheriff?

It occurred to her then that the rude, unpleasant visit from Roscoe Fraley had, in a sense, paid off. If it wasn't for him she never would have thought to keep the gun under her pillow.

Maybe one day she'd thank the sonuvabitch.

Meanwhile, outside Nellie's house, Abel was also trying to remember what he'd said as he was pumping away. He couldn't remember exactly, couldn't separate what he'd said from what he'd only thought, and he finally decided not to worry about it. Rather he tried to think of a good explanation for his failure.

"You let Abel take a crack at her? Why Abel? I've heard he once climbed on his sister, and she was dead at the time. He's crazy!"

"That's why it would have been perfect," replied Chappelle. "He's slick. He's left dead girls in more towns'n you can count. He woulda made it seem almost natural."

Fraley and Chappelle were standing in the dark behind the Last Stand.

"So?" demanded Fraley. "Why didn't he?"

"Because that little bitch keeps a gun under her pillow—" Abel had opted for the truth "—that's why. Whoever heard of a whore keepin' one of them handy?"

Fraley almost smiled, but he just made grunting noises instead. "Well hell, it don't matter. We'll get her later. Afterwards. Your boys ready?"

"Always."

"Then let's do it. I'm tired of waiting."

Ben Lloyd sat on the edge of the bed, feet dangling, a slight bulge of flesh around his waist. The bulge was fairly recent, but since he was neither a fitness fanatic nor, for the past few years, terribly active, he was surprised the bulge hadn't shown up sooner.

Nellie Pope lay back in the bed, her hair spread over the pillow. Her scar was plainly visible but she'd lost her self-consciousness. Ben Lloyd didn't seem to care about it, so why should she?

"Were you ever married, Nellie?"

Oh my God, thought Nellie, he's not going to propose, is he? "No," she said. "You?"

He nodded shortly. "Why didn't you marry?"

"I was raised poorly."

"Eh?"

She smiled. "That's right. I became accustomed

early on to a type of man that, well, there just aren't many of them around."

"You're saying you never met a man you wanted to marry."

"Not never, but none that I could marry." She hadn't thought about this for years, and had never talked about it, not to anyone.

"You'll have to explain that."

"Not on your life. A woman needs to keep some secrets."

Ben Lloyd laughed. This playful creature was very unlike the woman he'd met downstairs. "Well, it's not too late for you to marry."

"Oh yes it is," she responded quickly. Then, after she'd thought about it, she repeated slowly, "Yes, it is."

"There's something you're hiding."

"For good reason," she confirmed ominously, but then she switched to a lighter vein. "I told you, Ben, a woman needs to keep her deep, dark secrets deep and dark."

"Ever have a child?"

She sat bolt upright, as if shocked.

"I said, did you ever have a child?" He seemed serious.

She fell back. "Yes," she said. "In this business it's a risk. I had one long, long ago. I gave her up for adoption."

Lloyd's eyes widened. "Adoption? Really?"

"I was young, and wanted to make something of my life." She looked the room over. "Not this something, I hasten to add."

"Then how did this happen?"

She tried to remember. "It just happened."

Lloyd let that pass. "This baby you had, did you ever learn what became of her?"

"Yes."

"What?"

"She was adopted; she grew up. She's alive, somewhere."

Lloyd nodded.

"Are you still married, Ben?"

"No. She died."

"You loved her?"

"Of course."

"I mean really." The sound of a cynic.

"Ye-e-esss, but we had a hard time. She fell sick early on. It made her unable to have children. Made her bitter.

"She began to complain of pain. I think it was to get attention. I gave her attention but she wanted more, needed more. But I had my work.

"She took painkillers. One day she took too much, and died. It was called an accident, but I think it may have been deliberate.

"She was a girl, or a woman, who might have flourished in a softer, better life, but couldn't stand up to hard times, or to things not going her way—"

"Spoiled."

"Possibly, or just fragile; but with her illness, and no children, and not getting the attention she needed, nothing went her way."

"Lacking a child must have hurt you, too."

"Yes, but I had work."

"What kind of work?"

"First the army; there was a war, you may recall —and then the family business."

"What kind of business?"

"It's not important."

"Now you're being mysterious."

"I've got a right."

She conceded that. Then she stroked his cheek. "You should shave. The beard, at any rate."

"I just started growing it."

"I can see that. But I'd like to see what you look like. You've seen what I look like, and I've got more to hide than you."

"You've got nothing to hide," he said, fondling her breast.

"I meant this," she said, touching her scarred face.

"That's nothing," he said, smiling.

She regarded him thoughtfully. "You remind me of a boy I once knew."

"Oh?"

"Something about the voice . . . the eyes . . . That's probably why I like you."

"The man you couldn't marry?" he asked with difficulty.

She didn't answer directly. "He died in the war."

Lloyd nodded understandingly. Then he looked around. "Who did the drawings?"

"I did some, the bad ones. One of my girls did the rest."

He reflected that drawing was one thing that women could do as well as men, and also as badly. He himself had some flair for drawing, though military sketches were all he had to show for it. It was his wife who had turned out a mass of expert drawings, which became increasingly morbid as the years passed.

Thinking of morbid, he remembered the wartime news bulletins that had reported him dead.

He studied Nellie's "bad" drawings.

He remembered that Nellie had always tried to draw, liked to draw, thought it made her more refined, but had never shown any talent.

Some things don't improve with age.   ◄§

14

Lucia had taken some time to compose herself, gather her wits, and then, although it was barely midnight, she decided she'd had all the "dates" she wanted that night.

She dressed for town and walked down the hall to Nellie Pope's room. She was about to knock when she heard voices.

She was not surprised. She knew that Nellie entertained selected clients. She decided not to interrupt her.

Paul Brooker was sitting in Colonel Major's Saloon and Dance Hall. He had decided to spend the evening as far from Nellie Pope's bordello as possible, and the rowdy Colonel Major's was about as far as he could get.

The crowd was about the same as on his previous visit. He recognized the plains veteran snipe-hunters and wondered what had become of the greenhorn. He vaguely remembered the greenhorn passing him in the street toting a rifle. My God, that was nearly a week ago. It was said that time flew when you were having fun, but Brooker reflected that it also flew when one was spending several miserable days recovering from alcohol poisoning.

He looked around. He couldn't tell if the dance-hall girls were the same, but they sure didn't look any different, or any more tempting.

He saw that there were no soldiers. Apparently they'd learned their lesson.

Just then, over the hurly-burly and the music, he thought he heard the sound of tramping feet. That was funny. He searched the room for whoever was making the noise, but in vain.

Then the tramping sound stopped.

Within moments, though, there came to his ears the sound of a peremptory command. He frowned.

He frowned even more when he saw people toward the front of the saloon beginning to hit the wooden floor.

That behavior spread toward the back of the saloon, like a wave running to shore. Brooker decided it was the better part of discretion to get down next to the floor himself.

There came next a thunderous crash from outside the saloon, and immediately the front windows disappeared, and many of the overhanging lamps shattered.

There was absolute silence within the saloon,

until the coal oil dripping from the shattered lamps caught fire and dripped flames onto those crouching below.

That caused a lot of excitement.

Brooker stood up. The table he'd been sitting at was collecting a pool of burning oil. He seized a cloth from the bar and succeeded in smothering the flames. Then he stood on the table and took down what was left of the lamp.

He set it on the table and then, from his high vantage point, he looked once again toward the front.

Out in the street was a line of soldiers, some with rifles still at their shoulders.

"That should teach you a lesson," said a voice from their ranks. "You'd best think twice before trying to cheat and assault members of the United States Army again."

Brooker wondered why they'd taken a week to retaliate—perhaps they had just run out of indians to fight.

"Right face! For'rd, march!" Off went the soldiers, back to Fort Dodge.

It was a long march. No wonder they were in a nasty mood.

Bat Masterson stood outside the Lady Gay and watched them march off, and then he reentered the Lady Gay.

Jim Masterson, standing outside the jail, tipped his hat as the column marched by.

Brooker was still atop the table, trying to decide whether to stay at Colonel Major's or proceed to another, calmer habitat, when Lucia Bone spotted him through the shattered front windows.

"Paul!"

Brooker rapidly made his way outside.

"What happened?" she asked.

"Nothing much. An army massacre, that's all."

"I haven't seen you. I thought you'd left. I thought—" She was surprised at how happy she was to see him, somebody safe and sane. "I thought you'd abandoned me to my awful fate."

"I've been sick."

"You have? With what? Why didn't you tell me? I could have taken care of you, or brought you things, anyway."

He planned to get sick more often.

"Actually, all I needed was a stomach pump. I—ummm—drank too much."

Lucia blinked. "Why Paul, how unlike you. I thought you were a terribly sober type."

"So did I."

"When did this happen?"

"Ummm, that night. The, uhh, last night I saw you."

"Darn it, Paul, I told you not to get upset about that. I'm not worth it."

Lucia saw that Paul was preparing an indignant response to that bit of self-deprecation and she said quickly, "Not now, anyway, or not yet. Darn it, Paul, you don't know me."

Paul Brooker frowned so hard his brow began to hurt.

"Let's talk about that later. Do you know where the Sheriff is? I glanced in his office—"

"I think he's in the Lady Gay, dealing a game."

"I've got to talk to him."

Paul nodded.

"Well come on, a lady can't go in there *alone*."

Brooker smiled in weary resignation. Lucia seemed to have a very weird idea of what was proper and what wasn't. Or else she had a very individual sense of humor. He gave her his arm.

Outside the Lady Gay Lucia paused.

"Perhaps I should wait out here." Her eyes crinkled in amusement. "You'd better go get him."

Brooker stared at her in disbelief. Then he turned and disappeared into the Lady Gay.

Fortunately, Bat Masterson was just finishing a game when Brooker approached his table.

"There's a lady outside, Sheriff," said Brooker with a blank face. "She says she'd like to speak with you."

"A lady? On south Front?"

Masterson got up and following Brooker eased on out of the saloon.

Outside, he glanced at Lucia, and then made a great show of looking around for the *lady*. Lucia continued to stare at him innocently.

Bat finally acknowledged her with a smile. "Yes, miss, what can I do for you?"

Lucia scanned those within earshot. Then she smiled brightly.

"I have a proposition for you, Sheriff. I think you'll be interested."

Someone laughed. Bat glared and Lucia continued.

"But I have to tell you in private." Such was the nature of the secret proposition, apparently, that Lucia could barely restrain her merriment.

Bat glanced at Brooker, but there was no hint of an answer there. He then looked at Lucia, and happened to catch her face between one merry spasm and the next.

"By all means, young lady, why don't we go someplace private?" He managed a dirty chuckle.

All three stepped off down the street until they were alone in comparative blackness.

"What's going on, Lucia?"

Lucia told them of her experience that night with the murderous Abel. By the light of a match she showed them the bruises on her neck. Brooker started to react but Bat gripped his arm hard. "Go on, Miss Bone."

She told them of Abel's words as he was trying to strangle her.

"New sheriff, huh?"

Masterson thought about it as Lucia and Paul watched him.

"What do you think, Sheriff?" Lucia finally asked.

"Do you want to go find this gent?" queried Brooker.

"I think you'd better keep that gun under your pillow," said Bat. "I've had my eye on some suspicious characters. Strangers. Five or six. Going after one of them wouldn't do much good."

"This one looked mean," said Lucia. "And he *was* mean."

Bat nodded. "None of them have been seen together, but they wouldn't be if they'd been brought in to do a job. If we discount coincidence, it's probably the same party that's been trying to nail you—probably Fraley—and he wouldn't have anything to do with them, not openly; couldn't risk it.

"If Roscoe gets rid of me, then that will give the other side, those sober, strait-laced residents, a chance to run their own man for office again. They almost made it last time. This time. . . .

"Damn. They've already managed to get one of their kids on the force. Brisbane's kid, Tom. Nice looking kid, but cold."

Lucia and Brooker wondered what Bat was mumbling about.

"But I still can't see how that's going to benefit Roscoe Fraley, though maybe—"

"You said he might flip-flop and join the respectable folk," Brooker reminded him.

"And he's got dirt on all those *good* citizens," said Lucia.

"From Nellie's," muttered Bat. "So maybe he's ready to make his move. Well, can't say I'm surprised. It's about time."

Masterson seemed suddenly charged up.

"Well, thank you, Lucia. You've been a big help. As for you, Brooker, you've been complaining about not being armed; about how being a licensed detective qualifies you. How'd you like to become a deputy? Temporarily?"

The next day passed peacefully enough.

In the morning Bat went off and practiced by himself, for a change.

And in the afternoon, Brooker headed south of the Arkansas, found a secluded draw, and almost raised blisters honing his skill. He made no effort, though, to "sweeten" his gun. He was damn good and damn fast, but he didn't want his gun going off unexpectedly; he'd leave sweetening to the rare artist.

Come evening, Masterson pinned a badge on Brooker and told him to stay at the jail.

"When do you think it will happen?" asked Paul.

"Tonight," answered Bat, "or tomorrow night, or the night after. It'll be late. They'll make believe they're drunk. And it'll happen on the south side, in any one of the dance halls."

Brooker looked disappointed. It seemed cut and dried.

"Just relax. When Jim finishes his rounds maybe you can take a walk around, let folks see you, see the badge."

"Where will you be?"

"Lady Gay, if you need me. I asked Wyatt if he wanted to do some dealing there."

"For a cut of the house winnings?"

Bat Masterson smiled. "Now don't get carried away, Paul. I asked him as a friend. I didn't hire him. Nor did Jim."

"And he'll be there?"

"I think he's still trying to make up his mind."

Bat left.

Jim Masterson took a leisurely tour of the town, as did Paul Brooker. Paul was tempted to drop by Nellie Pope's to flaunt his new authority, but didn't; he was really too mature and experienced in his work for Flaherty Investigations to do anything so childish.

He returned and Jim took another tour, accompanied by an assistant marshal.

One of Bat's off-duty undersheriffs, Tom Brisbane, looked in, then went his way.

Paul Brooker relaxed. Dusk had begun to settle. Nothing would happen for at least another three or four hours.

"Where's Bat?"

Paul Brooker looked up. A young man in dirty workclothes stood in the doorway. Paul recognized him as a swamper from one of the saloons, but he couldn't remember which one.

"Who wants him?"

"Who're you?"

Paul Brooker hooked a thumb at the badge on his chest. "Bat's not here. He'll be in later. What's the trouble?"

"Where is he?"

"Dealing at the Lady Gay. If you want to interrupt a hot streak, you go right ahead."

"Awwww. . . ."

"What's the trouble?"

"Ruckus at the Occident."

Yes, that was where Brooker'd seen him, cleaning tables.

"Sturm sent you?"

"Didn't have to. Another fella did. Get the Sheriff, he said, this man's bad news."

Paul laughed. Sturm's Limburger would do that to anybody.

"How bad is bad?"

"Says he's gonna shoot the place up."

Jim Masterson and the assistant marshal entered then.

"What's up?" Jim asked.

"Sturm's having some trouble at the Occident," said Paul. "They sent this fella for Bat, but I don't see no sense in bothering him. I figure I can handle it. After all, it's Sturm's place. Not likely to be a shoot-out there. Besides, it's too early." He took his guns out, spun the cylinders for show, and dropped

them back home. "I'll be right back. Warm up one
of the cells."

Paul Brooker strolled out the door. Once outside,
he cocked his ear for the sound of trouble. Hearing
nothing, he strolled unhurriedly toward the Occident, some one-hundred and fifty yards distant.

It occurred to him to check out the depot telegraph office for messages. It wasn't until he was
about to step through the door that he remembered
it was no longer necessary.

He stopped short and shook his head. Damn. Was
he still feeling the effects of that drinking bout? He
resumed his stroll toward the Occident.

After pausing again to check his guns and polish
his badge with his sleeve, Brooker mounted the
sidewalk in front of the Occident.

A gun went off and one of the Occident's windows disappeared—one that Sturm had replaced
not two weeks earlier.

Paul Brooker pursed his lips. He knew he should
enter the saloon with his gun drawn and extended,
but he'd look silly if it was just some foolish drunk
waving a gun around, shooting at lamps and windows. So he settled for resting his hand on his gun
butt, and he entered.

Most of the saloon's occupants were frozen in
place, only their eyes moving, watching a tall gent
in greasy clothing weave drunkenly around toward
the rear of the saloon.

"I ain't about to pay fer thet stinking cheese you
gimme," he roared at Sturm, who frowned at him
from behind his glass cheese cabinet, "and I ain't
payin' fer nuthin' else, neither!" Another shot took
out a mirror.

"Hold it!" Brooker commanded, his voice echoing through the saloon.

"It's the law!" someone shouted.

"The hell it is! That ain't Bat!"

The reeling drunk at the rear slowly came to a standstill and peered toward the front, trying to focus on Brooker.

Actually, he was able to focus quite well. Jim Chappelle had been putting on quite a drunken performance, but he wasn't drunk at all. He'd only had a few shots of whiskey, which tended to relax him and improve his coordination.

"Where's Bat?" cried someone.

"Yeah," another joined in, "where's Bat?"

One of the gang, Fiore, had been the first one to ask where Bat was. Abel had been the second. Both were seated with their backs to the wall toward the front of the saloon.

Bloomer, who'd sent the swamper for Bat Masterson, was at the bar.

Gooch and Swifty were near Chappelle. Gooch was standing by the billiard table, ready to drop the cue from his left hand, and Swifty sat at a table holding a card hand in his left hand and a gun under the table in his right. Anyone entering the saloon faced a crossfire from about five different points.

Jim Chappelle cursed to himself. He didn't want this fool with a badge. He didn't even recognize him, but he figured he'd have to take him out and then the rest would come running.

But Paul Brooker, for all his youthful mooning about, for all the trouble he had dealing with the fair sex, was no man's fool; not when it came to gunplay.

He'd quickly registered the rapidity with which the drunk appeared to sober, but that didn't surprise him at all. Nor did he wonder where the guns had come from in this no-guns town; why no one had sounded the alarm.

Rather, he paid close attention to a scent he'd picked up, a whiff of the outcast, the outlaw. An acrid, intangible scent that made his flesh crawl. Not all men could sense such things, nor as quickly, but he could. It was his job.

As the short silence stretched—this was all happening over a period of about fifteen seconds—he registered other phenomena.

He noticed that most of the saloon's occupants were, perhaps unconsciously, shrinking in size, making themselves smaller targets—*except* for two, three, four . . . Jesus, *five*, not counting the drunk.

They all had to have guns; he knew it in his bones. This was the killing bunch, the men who had come to town to gun down Masterson.

This wasn't supposed to happen now, thought Brooker. It was supposed to be later, and on Front Street's south side.

Bat had been right about one thing; that it'd be a drunken display that baited the trap, but about the rest he'd been wrong, very wrong.

Damn. One out of three was one hell of a percentage for a man like Masterson. How in the world had he lived so long?

Brooker eyed Chappelle, who now stood as still as a poised rattler.

Paul Brooker saw his situation clearly, but he wasn't going to back off, wasn't going to try to crawl out of it, even though he knew he was a goner. He cursed his own pride.

He also thought about how the legendary gunslingers were always supposed to give their opponents a fair break, if not the edge. Paul knew it was a crock, but that was indeed the legend.

Well, he muttered to himself, I'm no legend. So to hell with it.

He yanked one gun clear and his left hand grabbed for the other.

15

CHAPPELLE WAS SURPRISED. About the most he had expected was for the lawman to tell him to put the gun away, and then he would have cursed drunkenly and shot the lawman dead. It was kind of a shock to see the bastard's eyes harden, and then see him bringin' a gun up.

The moment lost on surprise cost Chappelle dearly. He'd been waving his gun over his head. He brought it down and desperately triggered a shot, but he shot before the gun was level and the slug whined high, just nicking Paul Brooker's hat.

Brooker paused a split-second just to be sure, and then split Chappelle's breastbone with his first shot.

Chappelle was pitching backward, his eyes already starting to glaze over, when Paul tried to twist and crouch—he knew that a hell of a lot more slugs would be coming his way.

He wasn't quite fast enough. Bloomer, stepping away from the bar, sent a slug into him. It didn't catch him square, but it hit him, and Brooker was knocked to the floor.

Then a blast from somewhere stood Bloomer up straight.

Fiore, Abel, Swifty, and Gooch wondered where the hell the lead was coming from.

Doc Holliday came through the front doors, his face twisted in a confident smirk.

He threw shots at Fiore and Abel as they shot at him. All missed.

Fiore happened to glance toward the rear, and saw Jim Masterson and Wyatt Earp coming in the back way. "Watch it!" he screamed.

Swifty and Gooch spun around.

Jim Masterson, when pressed, could shoot and kill, but, as previously pointed out, his first instincts were to talk, to debate, to argue.

Earp's weren't, which made a split-second difference. Both Earp's guns were out, a short-barreled Colt and the longer Scoff, and he was squeezing the triggers while Jim was still selecting his targets. Both guns thundered.

"Jesus," croaked Fiore as he and Abel watched Earp make their pards dance, the impact of the heavy .45 slugs seeming to keep them jerkily suspended.

Both men made the same quick decision, and threw shots toward the bar to keep Holliday down. Then they quickly ducked out the front doors.

Bat Masterson was waiting for them.

Six slugs, sounding like one long blast, drove them right back in the doorway.

They died before the doors stopped swinging.

They carried Paul Brooker back to the Dodge House, where Doc Holliday and Doctor Thomas Stearns fought over him. Fortunately for Brooker, Stearns won, and Holliday went back to his card game and his bottle.

The wound wasn't bad, but blood had been lost. Once the extent of damage had been determined, Brooker was bandaged up, given some booze and left to recover by himself.

The next morning Masterson dropped by the Dodge House to look in on Paul Brooker. He knocked on the door, just by way of a warning.

Bat was surprised when the door was opened by Lucia Bone.

"You're up early," Bat commented quietly.

"This wasn't supposed to happen."

"Don't blame me, blame him," said Bat, stepping past her.

Paul Brooker lay in bed grinning foolishly.

"I came over as soon as I heard," said Lucia. "I've been here all night."

"So, Brooker, you finally spent a night with Miss Bone."

Brooker nodded glumly. "It wasn't all I had hoped it might be."

Lucia smiled. Such bland innuendoes didn't bother her at all.

Bat noticed a third person in the room, the ex-Major Brewster Lowell, presently passing himself off as Ben Lloyd. Bat had seen him around town.

"This is Ben Lloyd, Bat," said Brooker. "Ben's a couple of rooms down. He knocked on my door as soon as he moved in to ask me who the dead man was that'd just walked down the stairs."

Bat frowned.

"He'd just seen Doc," explained Brooker. "It was early."

"Ah," said Bat, "Doc does tend to look a mite corpse-like in the full light of day."

"Ben heard I was hurt and dropped by."

Bat regarded the well-dressed man. "Where're you from, Lloyd?"

"Lately from San Francisco. Originally from the east."

"What are you doing here?"

"I'm connected with the railroad," said Lloyd.

Bat nodded. He wondered what that might mean. He decided that he'd find out. "Connected" was a funny word. Frank and Jesse had connected with one or two railroads. "Well, how are you feeling, Brooker?"

"Fine. A little stiff, but that's it. I'm getting up later today."

"You are not," said Lucia.

"Nonsense. I may dress like a sissy sometimes, but I'm tougher'n you think."

Bat remarked quietly, "I rather thought you dressed like me."

"And not quite as well as me," muttered Lloyd.

Brooker laughed. "You know what I mean."

"I'm not sure I do," said Bat, implacable.

Brooker eyed both men. "You're not going to let me forget that, are you?"

"No," said Bat.

"With difficulty," said Lloyd.

"By the way, Brooker," said Bat, "just so you don't feel you have to leap out of bed and report for duty, why don't you let me have that deputy's badge?"

"With pleasure. My vest's over there. I don't think any blood got splattered on it."

Bat smiled as he retrieved the badge. "I'll be running along now. Good to see you're healing up. And, since I haven't had a chance to tell you, thanks for the help."

Brooker suddenly sat up. "There's something no one's told me. How the hell did you get there?"

"Soon's you went sashayin' off to get yourself blown away, Jim ran down to get me. Me and Wyatt. Doc was there, too. That kid? The swamper? He told Jim it was a stranger that'd sent him running for me, me specifically. Jim thought it sounded funny. I did, too."

"I should have guessed it was a trap."

"Nope. We're paid to guess those things. We're professionals."

"I'm a professional, too."

Bat smiled indulgently. "You just keep right on thinking that. Just don't try to *professional* the wrong men." He looked around. "Well, I'm off." He gave Lucia Bone an extra long look before he left the room.

"I'll be right back," Lucia said to Brooker, and she hustled out after Bat.

Bat was waiting for her down the hall.

"Who is that man? Do you know anything about him?"

"Nothing, except that I think he's spent the last couple of nights with Nellie."

"With one of the girls, or with all of them?"

"No. With Nellie."

"No kidding." He looked thoughtful for a second. Then he snapped out of it. "What I wanted to do alone was thank you for the tip. You may have saved our lives."

"So now you owe me," asserted Lucia.

"Still don't know for sure who was behind it," mused Bat. "I'm dead certain it was Fraley, but with all of those men dead. . . ."

"You owe me," Lucia repeated.

"Yes, I guess I do. What do you want?"

"I still want to start that school."

Bat cursed beneath his breath. "For God's sake, why?"

"I want to teach, I like to teach, the West needs teachers—and I want to be respectable."

Bat regarded Lucia in the dim light of the hall. The shadows softened her face considerably. At that moment she was much more a very young woman than a prostitute. She was vulnerable, and she was damned attractive.

She had some romantic notions about teaching, decided Bat, notions that ignored the hard work involved, and she was dreaming if she thought it would bring respectability. It wouldn't, not in Dodge. Never. Once a whore, always a whore. Bat knew his citizenry.

But there was only one way that she'd find that out, and he did owe her.

"All right, Lucia, I'll do what I can."

"Really?"

"Yes, but I can't promise anything. In fact, I doubt if I'll get anywhere. But I'll give it an honest shot."

"That's all I ask, Sheriff."

"No, Lucia," he said kindly, "you're asking for more, for a lot, lot more."

He touched the brim of his derby and departed.

Bat dropped by the depot, where he telegraphed an inquiry to the home offices of the Atchison, Topeka & Santa Fe. He asked if they knew a Ben Lloyd and he described the man. He didn't expect much, but it was a start.

Later, at the McCarty drugstore post office, Bat stood behind a familiar figure.

"You missed all the fun last night, Roscoe. I was looking for you."

Fraley stiffened, but didn't look around.

"Why me?"

"One of them talked before he died."

Fraley knew for a fact that was untrue. He relaxed.

"Well now," he said, turning and grinning, "that's a real break, ain't it? What'd he say?"

He smiled back at Roscoe. "Asked to be remembered to his mother."

"Ain't that sweet?" His grin started to get stiff.

"Can I help you, Mister Fraley?" asked the clerk.

Once back at the Last Stand, however, Roscoe Fraley quickly came to a boil.

"The more I think about it, someone tipped him off, it hadda be. There was no way he shouldn't have been suckered into it. It was perfect."

"How could he have found out?" asked Maggie.

"I told you, he was tipped off. Don't you listen?"

"Who coulda done that?"

"If I knew. . . ."

"Maybe Nellie told 'em."

"Yeah, she might've, that bitch, if she'd known about it. She's been gettin' awful uppity lately. I'm sorry now I didn't tell her. At least then I'd have someone t' blame."

"Lookit it this way, Ros. Maybe Masterson's just too smart for you."

Fraley shot her a look.

"Awww hell," said Maggie, "I'm thirsty. Let's forget about it and get drunk."

Roscoe Fraley regarded her balefully. "Lay off that stuff, Maggie. You're drinking too damn much. You're getting sloppy."

"So poo! Who the hell cares?"

Nellie Pope looked down at Ben Lloyd. His eyes were closed but he wasn't asleep, just resting.

She got off the bed, walked to one of her dressers, opened a box, and took out a long, slender cigar. She lit it, drew on it, and then sent a narrow stream of smoke toward a corner of the ceiling.

"Come over here and smoke that, Nel," said Lloyd softly. "I like the smell."

Nellie smiled. "Not on your life. If I come over there we'll start wrestling around and the next thing you know the bed'll be on fire."

"So what? We set the bed on fire anyway, don't we?"

Damn near, thought Nellie, damn near.

Ben closed his eyes again, and Nellie wandered

over by where he'd folded his clothes over a chair. She felt the material. Nice, expensive. She glanced at the labels. Then she folded the clothes carefully again and stepped back to the dresser.

"Ben, did you say you came from Philadelphia?"

"Very tricky. I didn't say," Ben said with a smile. "But what the hell, why shouldn't I say? Yes, as it happens, I started out in Philadelphia, then Chicago, now San Francisco." He pulled the sheet up to his nose. "Satisfied?"

"Yes. I won't ask you any more questions."

But the labels in the clothes had said Boston, and she'd recognized the tailor's name. The more she thought about it the chillier she got.

She looked at the bed, at Ben Lloyd.

The sheets covered his beard and mustache, leaving only his long, straight nose, eyes and brow exposed. The head was angled away slightly.

It was a familiar angle, suddenly very familiar.

Was such a coincidence possible? Was the world that small?

But why a phony name? Why the make-believe?

Because he was still married, that was why. Because he'd made up that elaborate tragedy involving his wife. Hell, she'd known his wife, and Alice Longstreet was about as delicate as a buggy whip.

No, his wife was alive and healthy and caring for twenty damn kids and would probably go screaming for lawyers if she knew he was staying with a whore, especially a whore that used to be a friend to them both.

Maybe she was jumping to conclusions, silly conclusions. She ground out the cigar in an ashtray and returned to the bed. She got in with Ben, who responded immediately, and they wrapped themselves around each other.

She nibbled his right ear.

Behind the ear were three little black specks, clustered together.

Dammit, Brew. Why the hell didn't you stay in Boston where you belonged? ◄§

16

It was several days later when Lucia Bone walked out the back of Nellie Pope's wearing a neat new suit, a new bonnet, and armed with a list.

The list was of houses in Dodge that might be available for rent. Lucia intended to see if any of them might make a satisfactory schoolhouse.

At the corner of Bridge and Walnut she eyed the Drover's Rest Hotel owned by Roscoe Fraley. It would be perfect. You could pack two or three schools in there and have room left over, but it wasn't on her list, and wouldn't be unless Roscoe suddenly passed away.

She wondered how the hell she could arrange that.

Lucia walked on over to First Avenue, where she checked out the already existing school. It didn't look like much, but all a school needed was space, books, and a teacher.

She smiled, thinking that back in '72 a nineteen-year-old subcontractor named Masterson had probably volunteered his help in building the simple structure. It'd be like Bat to do that.

She glanced back along Walnut and saw a man walking slowly toward her.

She checked her list, then glanced back at the man again.

"Paul! What are you doing up?"

"I've been up a lot the past few days. I've missed you."

"You didn't need me. As soon as I figured out you weren't going to die. . . ."

"Sorry to disappoint you."

"I see you're wearing your sissy clothes again."

"Don't you start up on that. It's enough that Masterson can't seem to forget I said that. What are you doing?"

"Looking over houses."

"Ah. Planning to go into real estate with all the money you're making?"

Lucia looked at him crossly. "Why yes, Mister Brooker. I expect you'd be surprised by the generosity of my . . . dates."

Paul was angered. "No, I wouldn't," he snapped. "Favors beget favors."

"I've never asked you to approve my life," Lucia snapped right back. "I don't need your blessing."

"Good."

"In fact, your blessing would make me damned nervous."

It was getting out of hand. Brooker waited until Lucia was breathing evenly again.

"So what are you doing?" he asked.

"Checking out houses for my new school, seeing if any are appropriate."

"When are you going to quit dreaming?" Brooker asked. "When are you going to call it off as a bad idea and pack up and come to Denver?"

"Come to Denver?" repeated Lucia while she thought about it.

She'd known Paul was serious, but hadn't known how serious. It was suddenly tempting, but she couldn't give up her quest, not when she was this close. "I'll have to think about that, Paul," she said, "a lot . . . I need time. But there's no hurry, you're not going anyplace."

"Yes I am," he said. "I've been called back, as soon as I recover."

"You've done what you were supposed to do?"

He made a sort of dismissive gesture.

"Well, gol-lee, Paul, hurry up and get yourself shot again. I've got my gun with me. I can shoot you in the leg."

Paul Brooker didn't think it was that funny.

"It's no joke, Lucia," he said, "but I've got to go now, and meet a gent. I'll see you later?"

She frowned, studying her list, and nodded shortly.

He turned abruptly and walked away.

She watched him go with a trace of sadness on her face.

"Oh, fiddle-dee-dee," she finally said. "I'll think about him later."

* * *

Lucia stood on Spruce Street trying to choose among three houses. One of them was for rent, and one of them was Fraley's, behind which he'd stepped into his latrine pit. It had been dark that night and she'd been guided by the house lights. Now, in the daylight, she wasn't sure which house was his.

She decided to pick at random. Even if she picked Fraley's he wouldn't be there. He'd be at work.

She knocked and the door was opened by Fraley's woman, Maggie.

She wore an old robe. Her hair was a tangle, her eyes bleary as they blinked in the light, and her complexion splotchy. She was unsteady on her feet.

"What the hell do you want?"

Lucia was about to turn away, but then decided not to.

"I'm here on business, Maggie."

"Business?" Maggie tried to narrow her eyes suspiciously, but instead closed them and almost went to sleep on the spot.

Lucia seized the initiative and stepped forward, taking Maggie by the arm and turning her around.

"You need to sit down," Lucia said.

She smelled her then, and realized that Maggie also needed another drink, and another, and. . . .

Which was true. Three days earlier Roscoe Fraley had told Maggie to sober up or stay inside, out of sight. She'd tried to sober up, but unsuccessfully. The shakes would have to set in before she'd go on the wagon. It had happened before, just that way, several times.

Lucia was paradoxically pleased to learn that this woman, who might be her mother, was a hopeless drunk. It was God's punishment.

Lucia led Maggie into the living room, but as soon as Maggie saw her bottle she shook free.

"Lemme go, I don't need your help. I jus'—I jus' been losin' sleep."

She poured herself a drink, but didn't offer Lucia one.

"You said you were here on business—what kind of business?"

"I'm going to open a school," Lucia said matter-of-factly.

Maggie's bleary red eyes opened wide and she laughed harshly.

Lucia saw that Maggie still had good teeth. At least that was something Lucia could look forward to.

"Why do you laugh?" she asked.

"Why? 'Cause you ain't gonna be around long enough to open no school," Maggie said.

Lucia didn't think that sounded very promising.

"An' what the hell makes you think the re-spectable folks here in town are gonna let you open a school? Huh?"

Lucia wished the woman didn't sound so stupid. Uneducated was one thing, but dumb was another. She certainly wasn't going to waste valuable time arguing the school question with her.

Lucia studied Maggie. This was probably the only time she'd catch Maggie so alone, so vulnerable, so out of control.

"You know," she said quietly, "I've been follow-

ing you. You and your friends. All the way across
the country."

Maggie blinked at her. "I know you have," she
said. "How come?"

Lucia took a deep breath. "Because I think you're
my mother."

Maggie belched, and inside her skull molecules
of alcohol wrestled with brain cells as she tried to
comprehend.

"What makes you think that?"

"Because you look like the woman who left me
at the Fairmont Orphanage. There's a woman there
who remembered my mother and described her.
Because my mother left a trail to Illinois, to Chicago, where you said you were—and I followed
the trail to Peoria, to Hannibal, to Abilene. I know
my mother was in Abilene."

Maggie drained her glass and poured another
while her soggy brain slogged down memory lane.
A grotesque look of cunning contorted her features.
"So?"

"*So?* Well, are you or aren't you? Did you leave
me at Fairmont or not?"

"Maybe. Maybe so, maybe no." She grinned,
showing her good teeth. "What's in it for me if I am
yer ma?"

"What's . . . ?" Lucia was appalled by the display
of motherly love. The end of a rope, she thought
savagely, that's what. "I'm not sure what you mean."

"Well, darling daughter, Dodge City's darling,
you say you been followin' me, followin' us. Maybe
you learned some things along the way, huh?"

"Yes."

"Some things that ain't so nice?"

Lucia paused a beat. "Yessss. I told you I'd been through Hannibal."

Maggie concentrated. Was that where it had happened?

"So? What do you think?"

Lucia appeared to be confused. "Well, if you were really my mother. . . ."

Maggie reached out and patted her hand. She was happy. She hadn't liked the idea of killing this girl. Now. . . .

She took hold of Lucia's hand and gripped it powerfully. "That's my little girl."

Lucia, unwilling just then to face up to her discovery, or the confirmation of her suspicions, looked around the room. After a while she asked, "Can you draw?"

"Can I . . . what?"

"Draw."

"Draw?" She followed Lucia's gaze. "Draw pitchers? Not hardly."

"Not at all?"

Maggie shook her head, grinning.

"Then who did those?" asked Lucia, pointing to a couple of framed line drawings on the wall. "Or did they come with the house?"

Maggie had never noticed them. They must have come with the house. "Them? Hell, Roscoe did them. Roscoe kin do a whole hell of a lot of things."

Lucia stared at her, thunderstruck. Roscoe? Was it possible that Roscoe and this woman had known each other long before Chicago, that maybe she'd followed him out there, that Roscoe might be Lucia's . . . ? Oh Jesus, it was so probable, so obvious, but the thought had never crossed her mind. Roscoe Fraley, the monster that had forced himself on her. . . .

Lucia could have asked Maggie directly, but she couldn't summon the nerve. If Maggie were to confirm these awful suspicions, Lucia would have just died, died right on that spot.

"What's the matter, luv?" asked Maggie. "You suddenly don't look so good. Here, havva drink."

Lucia knocked on Nellie Pope's door.

Nellie opened it a crack. "Yes?"

"Are you busy?"

"No. What do you want?"

"Talk. Just talk."

"Just a minute." Nellie closed the door. A few minutes later she opened it wide enough to slip out. "Let's go downstairs."

"Can't we talk in your room?"

"Downstairs," insisted Nellie.

In the bar, which was empty that afternoon, Lucia told Nellie about her travels around town, her finding Maggie, her bracing Maggie with her suspicions of motherhood—

"She as much as admitted she was my mother."

"She did?"

"Yes, and now I'm almost sorry I ever started looking. But what's worse is that now I have a hunch that Roscoe Fraley may be my father."

Nellie's glass almost dropped from her hand. She controlled her voice. "What makes you think that? I can't say you look that much like either one of them."

"Thank God. But you know how I can draw. I

figured I got it from my parents, or from one of them anyway. Maggie can't draw worth a lick."

"I know that. Neither can Roscoe."

"But he can."

"What makes you think that?" Nellie asked coolly.

"There're some pictures in their house. Landscapes, from out here somewheres. I thought Maggie'd done 'em, but it turned out Roscoe had." Lucia's shoulders slumped. "It had simply never occurred to me to put those two together."

"Those pictures—" began Nellie, but then she broke it off.

"The two of them, it's so obvious."

Nellie looked utterly confounded.

"It's about the worst news I've ever had," concluded Lucia.

"I don't doubt it," murmured Nellie, "I don't doubt it, but now let's talk about something else. Let's talk about this school of yours. You're really serious about it, aren't you?"

"Yeah, I guess so," but she didn't sound it.

"And whom do you plan to teach? The respectable people of this community aren't going to be very anxious to have their children taught by a prostitute."

"So I'll teach other kids. Whores have kids, don't they? And just plain poor people have kids."

"As a matter of fact—" Nellie tried to interject, but was cut off by Lucia.

"Maybe I'll open a school on the south side of Front. It'll give the people a real choice of where to send their kids."

"Indeed it would. I was about to tell you that the

first child born in Dodge City was an illegitimate child, born to a prostitute and delivered in a house of prostitution."

"Started the town off right, didn't it?" groused Lucia. "The kid's probably working the streets already."

"Not yet. The girl's only six. Those women don't put their girls to work until they're at least twelve or thirteen."

Lucia was honestly shocked. "Here? In Dodge City?"

"I know of one girl who's fourteen who's helping support her family that way." Nellie enjoyed the idea as little as Lucia. Sixteen was about as young as she'd go; in the rare instance, fifteen. "Nobody likes it. They've tried to stop it."

"And have they stopped it?"

"No." Nellie was sorry she'd brought it up. "I'll tell you what, Lucia. I respect your ambition. And you don't really like this life, do you? Of course not—"

"It's honest."

"In a sense, perhaps. In most places it's an honest circumvention of the law, like refusing to enforce prohibition laws."

"What prohibition laws?"

"I realize you'd like to be a lady, an independent lady—" She noted Lucia's scowl. "An independent woman. Well, I'll see what I can do."

"What can you do, Nellie?"

Nellie was about to tell her when Ben Lloyd entered the bar. "I looked for you upstairs."

Nellie spoke to Lucia. "Get along now, Lucia, go

to your room and get ready. We'll talk later." She looked up at Lloyd.

"Ben. Come sit and keep me company."

Lloyd glanced at Lucia, rising from her chair.

"Aren't you going to introduce me to this lovely young thing?"

"Run along, Lucia. Sit, Ben."

Lucia paused.

"Lucia, I said run along." God, she thought, everything was unraveling, getting out of control. If she could only be honest with Lucia, but that might set in motion. . . . She didn't like to think about it. The consequences could be terrible. Everything she'd worked for, lived for—

Ben Lloyd sat. "My, my, you're in another one of your moods, aren't you?"

Maybe she could swear them all to secrecy, make a secret pact. It was all so frightening. She never thought it would come to this.

"I wish you'd tell me what's happened," pursued Lloyd.

Nellie looked at him. The years had changed him. He'd lost all the weight he'd had, especially in the face. Now he truly looked "to the manor born."

She forced a smile.

Actually, she didn't really force it—but it was a long time getting there.   ঙ৽

17

Lucia didn't go to her room. Heavens, it was only three in the afternoon. What could Nellie have been thinking?

She simply didn't want to share her man with anyone, decided Lucia, also deciding that Nellie didn't have anything to fear from Lucia, not on that score—even though the tall man, Ben, was unusually good-looking.

Lucia contented herself with being happy for Nellie's sake.

She left the house and headed for the center of town, for the Sheriff's office.

Bat was behind his desk, feet up, chair tipped back. When he saw Lucia, the feet came down and he sat bolt upright.

"Uh-oh."

"Hello, Sheriff," said Lucia.

Bat Masterson searched his desktop for a good explanation.

"I said *hello*, Sheriff."

Masterson looked up, fingers twisting the end of his mustache.

"You're gonna pull that thing off."

"I've tried, Miss Bone."

"And?"

"You have to understand, Lucia, that I am not in good favor with those in Dodge who are most concerned with schools, churches, and matters of high culture. I am—or was—the candidate of what's called the "Dodge City Gang," those that profit from the wild visits of our Texas cowboy friends. And most of *them* couldn't give a tinker's damn about a new school. And when I mention you, and the fact that you want to teach, they practically fall down laughing."

Lucia Bone regarded Bat with sympathy. She knew he was an intelligent man who, though he approached life calmly and seriously, could also see the comic side of life. But that didn't necessarily mean that he saw, or could appreciate, himself as one of the comedians.

"I'm sorry, Sheriff," she said softly.

"For what?"

"For making a fool out of you."

"Well, it wasn't quite that bad. It'll pass, as soon as they want someone arrested or killed."

"Well, I appreciate your efforts."

As she left the Sheriff's office, Lucia saw Paul Brooker moving swiftly along the wooden sidewalks.

He saw her and his wound suddenly acted up, and he began to stagger.

She shook her head slowly, smiling.

"I think it's getting better," he shouted to her. "Then it acts up, just like that." He grimaced. "Maybe it'll be better by tonight."

"Your bosses are going to have to send a man to track *you* down," cried Lucia.

Paul Brooker nodded grimly. That was no joke.

Since his bosses weren't looking for him yet, the wound showed miraculous improvement by the time night rolled around, just as he'd hoped it might.

Paul Brooker nodded at Cassie as she let him into Nellie Pope's. He was aware that Cassie was an uncommonly good-looking young girl. She could probably make a fortune down at one of the colored dance halls. That she chose to do menial work for considerably less at Nellie's said something about Nellie Pope. He wasn't sure just what.

What he didn't know was that JB, the mulatto bouncer, wasn't about to let Cassie work anywhere else.

Brooker waited patiently for Lucia to make an appearance.

Nellie Pope came in and saw him, but knew who he was waiting for and didn't bother him.

An hour later, though, she noticed he was still there.

She called one of the girls over to her.

"Does Lucia have an all-nighter?"

"I haven't seen Lucia all night, Nellie."

Brooker didn't hear Nellie's question, but he

heard the girl's response. He frowned, and Nellie glanced quickly his way before leaving the room.

She returned a few minutes later and went right up to Paul Brooker.

"She's not in her room. No one's seen her for a while."

"Don't you—ummm—check on them?"

"Not as a rule." She smiled. "They don't sign in and sign out. We're like a big family here."

Brooker resisted comment. "Do you know where she might be?"

"She's been preoccupied these past several days."

"I know. That damned school."

"You don't approve?"

"I'm realistic, that's all."

"I am, too, Mr. Brooker. But while there's realism that recognizes conventional rules, there's also realism that recognizes the strength of individual will."

"Very well said, Miss Pope, but what the hell does it mean?"

Nellie only smiled.

"Well, I guess I'll go look for her. Damn, I hope she's all right." Nellie gripped his arm. "What do you mean?"

Brooker looked at her, surprised, and then said in a lowered voice, "Someone's been trying to kill her. Didn't you know that?"

"What are you talking about?"

Brooker described the near-miss a few weeks earlier on Front Street, and then the session with Abel right there in Nellie's own place.

"Lucia got out of that one just barely, but something that gent said made her think a bunch was gunning for Masterson, and she tipped Bat off. That was what that shoot-out in the Occident was all about, where I damn near got killed."

Nellie was staring at him. All the terrible consequences she'd anticipated—that she'd been trying to avert—they were happening!

"Of course, what I figure is. . . ." Brooker had to unbutton, confide in someone, and he guessed that this woman, considering her profession and apparent fondness for Lucia, could respect a confidence.

"Lucia's been searching for her mother. She thinks she's found her. The problem is, this mother was involved in something bad—something she and her friends are trying to hide from, changing their names, stuff like that. . . ." His voice dribbled away as he belatedly recalled that this woman, to whom he was confiding, just might be one of those fugitives.

"And you think that her mother," prompted Nellie, "and her friends, might be trying to kill her to keep her quiet?" Nellie had herself under full control. The news of Lucia's quest for her mother was no surprise, of course, but that someone was trying to kill her because of it was a surprise.

"Yes," conceded Brooker with some reluctance.

"And you think that the attempts on Lucia's life and her tipping off Masterson and the attempt on Bat's life, you think they all may be connected?"

"I think it looks that way." Brooker couldn't see what further harm he was doing telling her. Maybe if her friends—if it was her friends that were responsible—maybe if they knew he was on to them, they'd call it quits.

"Who does Lucia think is her mother?" She knew, but Brooker didn't know that.

"That woman, Maggie, down at Fraley's Last Stand."

"Mmmm. I thought she might resemble Lucia's picture. And that would mean that Roscoe Fraley was behind it." She shook her head. "Roscoe hates Bat, everyone knows that. Does she think that Roscoe's her father?"

Brooker's eyes widened in horror. "Good Lord, no!"

Good. Nellie knew something that Brooker didn't. She also knew she was going to have to start coming up with some answers. It would be hard, but she wasn't going to ask anyone for help. She'd never asked for help before and it was too late to start.

"Well, Mr. Brooker, you've certainly given me something to think about."

Right, thought Paul. You run and tell Fraley the jig's up, and to lay off Lucia.

"Guess there's no reason for me to stay here," he said. "Maybe I'll run into Lucia somewhere."

Nellie Pope's expression never wavered, and she was still looking steadily at Brooker, or through him, as he stepped out the door.

Paul moved along Chestnut Street at a brisk pace. He had to. If he lingered it would give the cool night air a chance to get to his wound and his side would stiffen. Then he'd have to drink the stiffness away.

"Brooker!"

Brooker jumped. When he came down a man stepped from the darkness. It was Ben Lloyd.

"Good evening, Major."

"Have you been in touch with the home office?"

"Yeah. But I couldn't wire specifics. That'll have to wait until I get back there."

"When will that be?"

"Soon."

"How soon? Time is money, Brooker. I've been a patient man for a long time, but this has been so frustrating. I thought this was the break we'd been waiting for; now there's a lot of backtracking that'll have to be done."

"What about Nellie?"

"What about her? She's suddenly, for some reason, gotten a little cool, a little distant. I seem to have lost my charm."

"Maybe—"

"No. Not a chance. I know her. If she'd recognized me she would have said something. Since she hasn't, it means she doesn't know who I am, or she's chalked the resemblance up to coincidence."

"I can't see her going for a coincidence, or not even mentioning it."

"I can. She always believed what she wanted to believe. She was very simple that way. She's still the same simple kid, unless she's changed a lot more than I think."

"I thought you said she had changed."

"I think we've had this conversation before; been over this same ground. You know where I stand."

"Then you'll be leaving yourself, as long as this is a dead end?"

The Major didn't answer.

"Or have you changed your mind? You said you were drawn to Nellie. Are you and she—"

"That's enough, Brooker, quite enough," the Major cut in.

"If you say so."

"Where are you going now, Brooker?"

"I'm going to have a drink or two, then go back to my rooms to nurse this wound. It's acting up. That's one of the reasons I'm still here—"

"Don't shit me, Brooker," snapped the Major. "I may wear sissy clothes—"

"Dammit, Major."

"But I've commanded. I know men, and you're drooling after that Lucia girl."

"I wouldn't call it drooling."

"I would. Not that I blame you. She's a fine specimen of young womanhood, her profession notwithstanding, but—"

"Good night, Major."

Brooker abruptly turned and walked off.

The fire in the Major's eyes slowly died.

Brooker didn't settle for a drink or two. He settled for several, and several more that he never touched as he visited practically every establishment in Dodge City.

But it was all in vain, and it was nearing midnight as he entered Dodge House and slowly mounted the stairs.

The lamp was glowing faintly in a corner of his room. He couldn't remember if he'd turned it on before he left, or—

"It's about time you showed up."

Lucia Bone lay in his bed, her head propped up on the pillow, the covers drawn up to her chin.

Paul was about to mumble something inane, or

try a sophisticated remark, when he suddenly came to terms with his own true feelings, with his desires.

"I went to Nellie's," he said softly. "I wanted you. If I'd known you were here I'd have been back hours ago."

A small smile played on her lips. "You won't feel dirty? Or ashamed?"

"With you? Never."

"Or think less of me?" she asked. She was confident of his reply, but wanted it on record.

Paul Brooker scratched his head. "Funny you should ask, Lucia, because I've been asking myself the same question, and the more I ask it the more I realize that it is a question of almost philosophic proportions.

"There is no easy answer, no simple yes or no. Nor is it simply a matter of morality. After all, what is morality—"

"Jesus God!" exploded Lucia. "Paul, the night's not going to last forever, and I'm about as fidgety right now as I'm going to get, so—"

"Care for some laudanum?"

"Paul!" she wailed, and sat upright in bed. The covers fell to her waist.

He stood gaping at her breasts, alabaster-white and as beautiful as anything he'd ever seen.

"Are you just going to *stare*?"

18

SEVERAL OF DODGE CITY's most upright citizens, the distaff portion, met the following afternoon at the home of Mrs. Abigail Forester.

"I hesitate to bring this up, ladies," said one of the women. "It's such a seamy matter."

"You'd better anyway," said another, anxious to hear what it was.

"It can't be any worse than what we see on the streets every day," said a third, also anxious.

"It's a scandal," said the fourth.

"What's a scandal, dear? What have you seen now?"

"Myra's always the one to see the most awful things. Poor Myra."

"What I wanted to talk about," said the first

woman before Myra could get started, "was this matter of a new school."

"What new school?" asked one.

"I thought we'd settled that," said another. "It'll be built next year. I've already volunteered to teach decorum and etiquette."

"No, I don't mean *that* school. I mean the school that a girl from one of the—God save us—bordellos wants to establish."

"Samantha! You must be *joking!*"

"Would that I were, ladies."

"What kind of school?"

"A regular school, I imagine."

"Rather a school for scandal," said Mrs. Abigail Forester archly, eliciting giggles.

The five ladies then fell to thrashing over the idea of Lucia Bone's proposed school, and gave the idea a damn good thrashing.

Toward the end of their discussion, when each was scaling new heights of disparagement, Mr. Aaron Forester returned home and inclined an ear.

He didn't normally involve himself in the ladies' discussions, which were as politically meaningless as they were frequent—Kansas wasn't Wyoming, where women had the right to vote—but this time he stood in the doorway from the hall to the living room and cleared his throat several times.

"Is that awful dust bothering your throat, dear?" asked his wife.

"Not this time, my dear," said Aaron Forester. "Rather I thought I might seize this opportunity to introduce a word of wisdom to your conversation."

A pompous remark, but the men of Kansas were determined not to let their women get out of hand, to keep them in their place, and, in that respect, those men were a far cry from their Wyoming brethren. As legend had it, upon the occasion of their women becoming the first in all the United States to get the vote, those men proposed a toast: *"Lovely ladies, once our superiors, now our equals."*

The ladies of Dodge had heard of that legend, that toast, but judiciously never quoted it, save among themselves.

On this occasion, Abigail Forester's eyes merely narrowed as she calmly waited to hear what "wisdom" her ass of a husband might bray this time.

"I think," he brayed, "that you are blinding yourselves to the merits of this proposed school."

The sounds of astonishment pleased him.

"You must consider this. There is a large proportion of our younger population that is not well-bred nor well-behaved. Far from it, in fact. Should those children wish to attend school, or should their parents, whoever they might be, desire it for them, then those mongrelized urchins—"

A gasp from the ladies. *Mongrelized urchins!* How awful, and how true.

"—would be seated cheek-by-jowl with our own fair offspring. Your polite and well-behaved Raymond, Myra, for instance. Think what an advantage it would be having another school, possibly even south of the tracks, where those children might be sent."

Polly Griffin's eyes widened. "My God. I've seen some nigra children running around down there. If they ever went to school with my Pauline. . . ."

It'd serve her right, thought Aaron Forester.

"Well, that needn't worry you," Aaron continued.

"Nigra children schooling with whites? Never! But that still leaves quite a number of unsavory little boys and girls."

Abigail Forester eyed her husband with grudging respect, fighting the revulsion she also felt. The ass made sense for a change.

Aaron Forester, for his part, tried to remember Nellie Pope's instructions, thinking there was something else she'd wanted him to say. He smiled, thinking of the gentle treatment he'd receive when he reported back.

This had to be Nellie Pope's doing, correctly divined Abigail Forester, watching her husband delight in the flattery the other ladies were bestowing on him. He'd saved their children from a ghastly fate. Abigail wondered what Nellie Pope saw in him.

Abigail felt no animosity for Nellie, whom she saw as a successful woman. Abigail had married a foolish, plain, but well-placed man in order to be near the seat of power. She wondered if Nellie Pope had not chosen the better means.

Ben Lloyd recalled a conversation he'd had with Brooker. Not the recent one, when that ass had pretended to be still crippled, but an earlier one.

"Why don't you just tell her the truth, Major?"

"Because I'm not sure I want her to know who I am, ever. I . . . I didn't treat her well, back then. And what might have happened, compared to what really did happen, then and afterward—it would surprise me if she didn't resent the hell out of it, and resent me."

"She was young then," Brooker had said.

"Weren't we all. But I can't take the chance. What if she's lying? What if she knows where the girl is? After all, that's who we're looking for. She might use that against me, to hurt me, and I'd never find her."

"It might not help, but we wouldn't be any worse off."

"Maybe"—he'd given Brooker a glimpse of his anguish—"maybe I'm just afraid to tell her."

"Don't you think you might like Nellie for herself?"

"And what if I did? Should I propose marriage? To a madam? I'm not the man you think I am, Brooker, unfortunately.

"I do find that I am drawn to her; it surprises me. But there is no place that it can go. Believe me, Brooker, I know myself. I'm not the callow youth I once was; I'm a callow man."

"Not that bad, I'm sure."

"No, possibly not that bad, but I'm still waiting to grow up. You see, Brooker, I loved her, and I hurt her as badly as a man can hurt a woman. I regret it, and will to my dying day, but I am still the same man that hurt her, and if I were in the same position today, I'd do it again—I'd hurt her again. A person may get wiser, Paul, but he doesn't necessarily get better."

Damn, thought the Major, he'd been near lachrymose on the occasion of that conversation with Paul Brooker.

He raised his hand to the door knocker. Cassie opened the door and let the Major in.

Nellie Pope had just shown a proud and demanding Aaron Forester out a side door when Cassie came to her.

"That gentleman friend of yours is here, ma'm."

"Oh God." She knew she'd been treating him badly, this *Lloyd*. Not that he didn't deserve it, but. . . .

If he'd only be honest, tell her his real name, tell her all about his wife and children and all the rest of it and, well, then maybe they could really talk to each other. And she'd give him a surprise that would knock him for a loop. But until then. . . .

"You'd better tell him that I'm too tired, Cassie. Possibly tomorrow."

Cassie brought the word back to the Major, who was naturally unhappy.

At that moment Lucia entered the room.

The Major looked at her and saw her for the first time; the fine face, to say nothing of the rest of her.

"You're the Dodge City Darling, aren't you?"

Lucia recognized him and smiled. "Is Nellie coming down?"

Damn. Her voice reminded him of Alice. And, now that he was on that track, her looks did, too.

"No. Not tonight. I'm free." He'd spoken without thinking.

"Well," laughed Lucia, an edge to her voice, "I'm not." She, too, had spoken without thinking.

"Are you busy at the moment?" he inquired.

"Nellie—"

"It's all right. Nellie and I are just friends." But apparently not even that. This'll teach her.

A man came in then; a slender, dapper man of

less than medium height. Not bad-looking, but cold-eyed.

Those cold eyes studied Lucia. "What's your name?" he asked, his voice almost rude.

"Lucia," she said, and the man immediately lost interest.

"Where are the rest?" he asked.

Lucia went to the door and summoned Cassie. "Bring down anyone you can find, Cassie. This man seems to be in a hurry."

Lucia stepped aside, and the Major held his tongue as the girls appeared. The dapper man went from one to the next, looking each over and inquiring her name. There were five girls, and after he'd examined and questioned all five, he returned to the third and followed her. He kept his right hand in his jacket pocket the entire time, holding the clasp-knife that Roscoe Fraley had supplied him with.

"Well?" asked the Major of Lucia.

Lucia looked at him. What could be wrong? "Wait until I take care of this."

She meant the money that she'd taken it upon herself to collect from the dapper, cold-eyed man. She went to the door and called for Cassie again and gave her the money. "Take this on up to Nellie. I'll be with the gentleman if anyone should ask for me."

She turned back toward the Major and offered her arm.

"Shall we?"

Nellie opened the door a crack, afraid that in spite of everything she'd see the so-called Lloyd.

But there was only Cassie, who gave her the money and explained where it had come from.

Nellie nodded, took the money, and closed the door. She returned to her dresser, where she'd been preparing a dose of laudanum. She rarely used opium, but there was a time for everything. The pressure that this Ben Llo—no!—that Brewster Lowell was putting on her, and the danger to Lucia, and. . . .

Why hadn't Lucia told her about the attempts on her life, one of them mounted right there in Nellie's house? Could it be she thought Nellie was somehow involved? Impossible. Lucia trusted her, she was sure of it. But. . . .

She went to her door and pulled on a velvet strap that rang a bell downstairs. A minute or so later Cassie knocked on her door.

"Cassie, can you ask Lucia to meet me in the bar?"

"She's busy, ma'am."

"Well then, afterward. Who's she with, one of her regulars?"

"No, ma'am." Cassie appeared reluctant to speak.

An alarm went off in Nellie's head. "Then who? Is it someone I know?"

Cassie nodded her head.

"Speak, dammit."

"It's your friend. Your special friend." She watched Nellie's eyes widen with shock. "The one you didn't want to see."

Nellie Pope almost bowled Cassie over going by.

Cassie recovered and, as Nellie dashed down the hall, Cassie smiled.

*   *   *

"This is a very nice room," said the Major. "Are they all like this?"

Lucia smiled. "I think so."

"Porcelain spitoons. It's really very classy. Do you spit much yourself?"

Lucia laughed. "Oh no. That's strictly for the men. Some dates come in chewing tobacco and never stop."

"Dates," repeated the Major, amused.

They heard a distant yelp and footsteps.

"You know, Lucia, it's funny, but you remind me of my wife."

Well. That was a new one, thought Lucia.

"She's dead, of course."

That was more like it. "Of course," said Lucia.

He stared at her harder. "Damn. It's positively eerie. How long have you been with Nellie?"

"Only about a month. Why?"

The door suddenly crashed open and a wild-eyed Nellie, her hair askew, slammed into the room, her eyes darting to the bed, which of course was empty.

Her eyes found the startled Lucia and the confused Major, who'd been concentrating heavily, possibly on the brink of revelation, and who'd been severely disoriented by Nellie's crashing arrival.

Nellie struggled to control her breathing.

"Ben. How could you?"

The Major was at something of a loss for words. Going with this girl may not have been the best of ideas but Nellie had only herself to blame.

"I'm disappointed in you, Lucia," said Nellie.

"I didn't think—"

"Then try thinking for once," snapped Nellie. "I won't have this."

"You won't have what?" wondered the Major.

"*This!*"

Since both he and Lucia were still fully dressed the Major was tempted to argue the point, just for the hell of it, claiming that he and Lucia had only meant to chat. But the Major correctly guessed that there was something more going on. He wondered what it was.

"If I'm not good enough for you, Lloyd, then you can just stay away." Whatever her motivation, Nellie was playing the spurned lover to the hilt.

The Major thought it defied rational understanding.

"Why don't we all go downstairs, have a drink, calm down, and talk this over? There's something strange going on."

Nellie blinked rapidly, eyes darting from one to the other. She realized that what she'd been saying hadn't made much sense.

"All right," she said, "we'll go downstairs and have a drink."

Five minutes later they were settling down at a corner table in the bar. Nellie ordered a bottle delivered to the table. She sounded crisp and once more in control, but she hadn't the foggiest idea of what she was going to say; how she was going to explain her words and actions. She considered the truth, but that would be complicated. She was also surprised to discover that the resentment she harbored for this man was stronger than she'd thought. The bastard didn't deserve the truth.

She'd always thought she'd loved him, and she had, but now she also hated him. Like a cancer it had grown, undetected, over the years.

So to hell with him! She'd come up with *some* explanation, and she'd take care of the whole damn mess, all by herself.

But she didn't have to, didn't get a chance to.

There was suddenly a series of shrieks from above, muffled but distinct, toward the front.

"Oh God," cried Nellie, "we've got one of *those.*"

She shot to her feet and headed for the front stairs. She was joined by the big colored man, JB, and followed by the Major and Lucia.

They bounded up the stairs, and then went toward the front, throwing open one door after another.

At length they came to a door that was already open.

A naked figure lay huddled on the bed, a bloody shape. The room was a shambles. There'd been one hell of a fight.

There came the sound of shots.

"He went down the back. Red must've gotten him. Go see, JB."

JB took off while Nellie, Lucia, and the Major entered the room.

Nellie looked the girl over quickly. "She's still breathing—Lucia, go get Cassie and send her for a doctor. Ben, go get the Sheriff. I'll—I'll do what I can here."

Ten minutes later Doc Stearns, nightshirt stuffed into his trousers, came bounding up the front stairs, satchel in hand.

Five minutes later Sheriff Masterson showed up, his usual composure askew. Nellie wouldn't have sent for him unless. . . .

"Customer roughed her up, Bat. She's barely hanging on."

"Who are you talking about?" Bat asked impatiently.

"Kippie."

Bat Masterson's entire face tightened and grew extremely pale in the dim light.

"Who did it?" The Major had fetched him, that was all. Bat had moved so fast, in fact, the Major'd had trouble keeping up, much less telling him anything.

"I don't know," said Nellie.

Lucia wasn't there but the Major, who'd seen a lot of bloody victims in his day, had had no trouble recognizing Kippie. "I do," he said. He described the dapper little man.

"At first we thought Red got him," Nellie said. "There was firing."

"Red tried, but he was the one who got shot," Lucia added.

"Bad?"

"A lot of bleeding, but he'll be all right."

"Major," said Bat to Lloyd, "go find brother Jim and some deputies. Set them to finding this gent—you can describe him. If he rode out of town I want to know which way."

Bat Masterson calling him "Major" had shocked him, but Lloyd left before the Sheriff could say it again.

Nellie Pope, still bending over Kippie, had also heard the "Major", but only half-heard it, and it wasn't until afterward that she'd realized whom Bat had been addressing.

As for Masterson's intelligence, it was easily explained. He'd received a reply to the query he'd telegraphed the Atchison, Topeka & Santa Fe home office. A bit of luck there.

An hour later Bat Masterson and Undersheriff Tom Brisbane rode south out of Dodge on what were probably the two best horses in town. They thundered over the toll bridge and disappeared down the trail to Texas.

Two hours later Kippie Russell died.

"What should I do with her, Miss Nellie?" asked Cassie.

"Clean her up," said Nellie, her voice dull and wearied. What a night it had been.

"Do you think he'll catch the man?" asked Lucia.

"He'll catch him," said Nellie, "or we've seen the last of Bat Masterson. He'll never quit. Kippie was. . . ."

"Kip was only sixteen," said Giovanni, who'd left the bar to visit his dead little friend. "She was just a little girl."

Nellie nodded. Nellie looked old, and felt old. "And to some of us Bat's just a boy. Not a little boy, but a boy. He's only twenty-five, and there's still some sentiment left in him."

And in Giovanni. She watched the tears stream down the bartender's face.

"Let's put her downstairs," Nellie said, "where it's cool." She took a deep breath. "Then we'll have to look after business."

Giovanni turned his head to look at her.

"Oh hell," she said, "let's close it up for the night."

Giovanni nodded slowly, then turned and bent down to pick up Kippie.

* * *

Roscoe Fraley leaned across the bar and snarled at Maggie. "That oughta teach that bastard Masterson a thing or two."

"You'd better hope the Sheriff doesn't catch him," said Maggie. "He could talk."

"There ain't nuthin' t'worry about, Mag. Trust me."

19

MASTERSON RODE HARD, Brisbane in his wake. Bat had wanted to go alone, for personal reasons and because he didn't want to leave Dodge unattended. But Brisbane had badly wanted to come. Very badly.

Tom was a real good-looking boy, clean-cut, and from one of the town's better families. He was young, and Bat had seen him hanging around for the past five years. Bat had never thought much of him, though; the boy had never done anything particularly noteworthy.

The kid's job with the police force was a political pay-off, Bat was sure, but he didn't know who had paid whom, and didn't care.

What he did mind was that he didn't know what Tom Brisbane could do. Tom had gotten by so far on his good looks and a ready smile. This would be a good opportunity for Bat to take his measure.

So far Bat had learned that he could ride. They followed the cattle trail, angling slightly southwest toward Texas.

"Why don't we slow up some?" called Tom. "We'll prob'ly find him camped sooner or later."

"He won't camp," replied Bat. "Wasn't dressed for it."

They rode some more. A half-moon dipped toward the west.

"You can turn back if you want," said Bat.

Tom Brisbane didn't.

Along about four in the morning Bat angled off to the left. Brisbane caught up to him. "What's goin' on?"

"He's headed for Redoubt."

"Gee, I woulda thought he'd keep on south, get as far away as possible."

"I don't figure he thinks anyone's chasing him. Redoubt's the closest town. He'll go there."

"I dunno," said Brisbane. "Hope you're right."

They rode into Redoubt as dawn was breaking.

The liveryman wasn't up yet, but they found a well-lathered horse tied up outside with a note pinned to the saddle instructing the liveryman to feed and take care of the animal.

Redoubt was a small town, with one hotel which was also a saloon and restaurant. Bat reached over the hotel desk and shook the clerk awake.

"Damn. What the hell's goin' on?" The clerk stammered. "Sure is awful busy all of a sudden."

"You're the night clerk, you oughta stay awake."

"I'm the *only* clerk. Whaddya think this is, Chicago?"

"Where'd you put the man that just came in?"

"Who wants to know?"

Bat flipped back his jacket and tapped his badge with the snout of his gun.

"Oh. Dint see that. Upstairs. Eight. Front room."

"Lemme go get 'im, Sheriff," said Brisbane eagerly.

Bat decided Brisbane was unusually stupid.

"This is mine, Tom, all mine."

He saw that Tom was unusually jumpy. Maybe it was because this was his first action as a lawman. "Go around front, Tom. Cover the window, in case he makes a run for it."

Tom Brisbane practically sprinted from the building.

Bat smiled sadly. He didn't plan to let their man make a run for anything.

He slowly, silently, mounted the stairs. The floors weren't carpeted so he had to move carefully.

Eventually he stood just outside the door to room eight, just off to the side. He reached out and tried the handle.

The handle turned but the door didn't budge. Locked.

Should he knock on the door and say he was the night clerk? Or shoot the lock to pieces?

Just then he heard distinctly, through the door, the sound of glass tinkling. That was followed immediately by a shout: "Raise 'em, you sonuvabitch!"

Bat cursed and kicked at the door.

Shots thundered.

Bat shot the lock and kicked again. The door slammed open.

Bat leaped into the room.

A man was on the bed, the blood from his chest wounds beginning to stain the sheets.

A bitter taste was in Bat's mouth as he stepped to the bed.

The man was dead. There was a chair by the bed. The man's dapper clothes were neatly folded over the back of the chair. His gunbelt, empty, hung from it.

Bat turned slowly to face the window. His gun was still level.

Tom Brisbane crouched outside, looking in.

He was still as good-looking, but his eyes were cold. He was barely nineteen and he'd killed a man and his eyes didn't show a thing.

"I warned him," said Brisbane. "He didn't listen." There was no doubt in his voice, no question, no second guesses. Just the first notch on his gun.

His eyes, as they rested on Bat, did not ask for understanding.

Bat had seen eyes like that before, and in men younger than Tom Brisbane. There was no age limit.

Bat holstered his gun.

Tom Brisbane seemed to relax. The nose of his gun dipped.

"Why'd you shoot?"

"He was reaching for his guns, or I thought he was."

"Well? Was he or wasn't he?"

"Yeah. He was."

Silly fool didn't even know where the guns were.

They weren't in his holster so they had to be under his pillow.

If he'd been awake enough to reach for his guns, Tom Brisbane would be dead.

Bat reached under the pillow and his hand closed around the handle of a .45. He drew it out. It was loaded. He carefully but quickly examined its action.

Just as he'd thought; the gun was almost as sweet as his own.

He looked down at the man in the bed.

"Good God! Tom! He's still alive!"

As he bent down over the once-dapper man he heard behind him the click of a hammer being drawn back.

He stepped to the side, turning as he went.

The slug went into the wall as the crash of the shot nearly deafened him.

He saw a shadowy outline through the gunsmoke. He put three quick bullets into it.

The dapper man's guns were good.

When the smoke had cleared, Bat looked at the body of Tom Brisbane. A playing card would have covered the three holes in the boy's chest.

He decided he just might keep the guns.

Bat explained to the sleepy-eyed local law that the dapper man had killed in Dodge and had shot Bat's assistant before Bat could get to him.

"What'd he do, get there five minutes before you did?"

Bat looked at the marshal questioningly.

"I was awake," said the marshal. "Heard the whole thing. Insomnia."

"You should do something for it," said Bat.

The marshal nodded.

"Like go back to sleep," suggested Bat.

"C'mon, Sheriff, no need to bully me. This fella been your assistant long?"

"Not long."

"Known him long?"

"Not long. Not long enough. Or well enough."

The marshal nodded and scratched his ass for a while. "Well," he finally said, "have a nice ride back."

Bat touched his derby. "Will do."

He loaded both bodies up onto their horses and rode north with them.

He wished he hadn't had to force Brisbane's hand, but he'd had to. The possibility of lingering life in the dapper man was the only leverage he'd had.

He knew now what he'd suspected; that not only was the kid's job a result of political pay-off, but that the kid had been paid to kill Kippie's murderer. But that was all he knew. Who had done the buying and the paying off was still a mystery.

It was probably Fraley calling in his markers.

Bat felt weary. It was always Fraley.

Bat rode into Dodge late that night. It had taken him eight hours to get to Redoubt; eighteen hours to return. And it'd been about thirty hours since he'd slept.

"She's dead, Bat," said his brother Jim.

Bat only nodded.

"You gonna have her buried at Fort Dodge?"

Bat shook his head. "Boot Hill."

"I kinda figured—"

"You figured wrong, Jim. I had time to think. I knew she was as good as dead. That gent was a professional. She was Kippie; now she's just a dead girl."

"I only thought—"

"Don't! Just get this sonuvabitch buried off in a corner. We'll bury Kippie later." He tried to rub the weariness from his eyes. "She'll like the view. We probably should have buried Ed there."

"They're gonna move it, Bat. It won't last."

It would be a year before they got Boot Hill moved.

"Nothing lasts forever. Now I've got to take Brisbane to his folks and listen to them yell about how us Mastersons are too fast with our guns."

"They're not happy with the law, and they're less happy without it. It's too bad about Tom."

Bat looked at his brother. "I shot him, Jim."

Jim only looked at him.

"Had my reasons, which don't have to be repeated, but give an ear around town; see if you can find out whose muscle got Tom the job."

Jim nodded.

"There's poison in this town, Jim, and we're gonna have to get rid of it."

Jim Masterson looked up sharply. "How about waiting until we get these folks buried, all right?"

Bat laughed shortly and rode off, taking Tom Brisbane home.

"Masterson's back!"

Roscoe Fraley's hand tightened around his glass. "He got that bastard, too."

Fraley held his breath.

"Must've been one hell of a shoot-out. The feller they was chasin' nailed young Brisbane—"

"Who?" asked someone.

"The kid. The new assistant, or undersheriff, or whatever they called him. Hell, you remember him, he used to hang around here."

"The hell he did!" snarled Fraley. "He never came around here."

"Hey, sure he did, Ros—"

"He was never in here, you got that?"

"All right, I got it—ya don't hafta bite my head off."

There was silence.

Fraley, after his explosion, had commenced holding his breath again. He was going to have to breathe soon, or faint, or—

"So? How bad was Brisbane hurt?"

"How bad? 'Bout as bad as you kin be hurt. The boy's dead."

The air slowly seeped out of Fraley.

Maggie leaned close. "For Christ's sake, quit grinning."

Apparently that was impossible, but Fraley knew it was inappropriate to leave his grin on display, so he grabbed Maggie and hustled her into the rear office, growling about how terrible it was all the way.

Once the door was closed, though, he let his true feelings out.

"It couldna worked out slicker iffen I'd planned it that way. Dammit, Mag, I'm a goddam genius!"

Maggie's agreement was less than wholehearted.

"Whaddya mean? Didn't I fix Masterson up proper? Hit him where it really hurts?"

"Too bad he doesn't know it was you that did
it."

Fraley was brought down. "Yeah. That's right."

"Do you want me to tell him?"

"Are you crazy?" He felt like wringing her neck.
"Oh, you're joking. Some joke. Still, look at it this
way. At the moment we're safe; no one can pin anything on us, and I'm just about ready to make my
move. Nellie's got a lot of valuable dirt on all the
"good" people in this town." He bit off the end of
a cigar and spat the piece on the floor. "Masterson
may be a problem for now, but the next election
will take care of him. Hell, now the Brisbane family
don't just disapprove of him, they hate him. We'll
get rid of him and his brother and Earp."

He lit the cigar and blew a cloud of smoke at the
ceiling.

"You know," said Maggie after a while, "that
Lucia girl, it looks like she's going to get that school.
You'd think the ladies'd scream bloody murder,
but—"

"There you go, that's what I mean," crowed
Fraley. "Of course they'd scream bloody murder,
and the reason they ain't is Nellie's doin'. She's got
their hubbies under her little thumb. If she can
force the town to let a whore open a school,
well. . . ."

"That reminds me. That little bitch Lucia. She's
still alive. I don't like that. She kin blow the whistle
on us." He puffed savagely, but soon began to take
longer, deeper drags.

"Of course, if she ain't tried to do nuthin' yet
about thinkin' yer her mother, and about that old
killin', maybe she ain't gonna do nuthin' after all.

If she's decided you ain't her mother, and she ain't dumb, then she's prob'ly forgotten all about it. Or it could be that she was blowin' smoke all the time."

"She still thinks I'm her mother."

"Yeah? Well, so what? You're not. If she thinks she's gonna use that to tie us in with that Hannibal—"

"I told her I was."

Fraley's face got as red as the tip of his cigar. "You what?!" he roared.

"She caught me up at the house. I'd had a little bit to drink. It sounded like a good idea at the time. I figured that if she thought I was her ma she wouldn't bother us about Hannibal. Mother love, y'know."

"I don't believe it."

"Well, it's true, ain't it?"

"I do not be-lieve it."

"She ain't been runnin' around with those pitchers of hers tellin' everyone how this gal's a deadly killer. She thinks I'm her pore ol' ma, and no one wants to string up their own ma."

Fraley was chewing his cigar to pieces.

"And I kinda suspect," said Maggie, "that she thinks you're her pa. She likes to draw. She figures her folks could draw, too. I told her the pitchers at the house were yours, and she knows how close we been, you'n me."

Fraley ground his cigar out. "So the next thing you know she's gonna want me to draw her pitcher. Dammit, Mag, yer dangerous!"

Maggie took that as a compliment.

Fraley lit another cigar and puffed it down a full third before he spoke again.

"All right, that does it," said Fraley. "Thanks to you and your big mouth I've had all of Miss Lucia Bone that I'm gonna take. She's too goddamn dangerous." He ground out the cigar. "I want you to get her down here—tonight. If she thinks yer her lovin' ma that shouldn't be too difficult."

"She works."

"Afterward. The later the better. That little bitch has reached the end of her rope."

"What are you gonna do, Ross?"

"Me? Nuthin'. But it's a nice night for a swim, ain't it?"

"Swim? In the river? There's alligators in that river, Ross."

"Who told you that?"

"Everybody knows that."

"Yeah, well, Miss Lucia Bone don't."

"She won't come here, Ros. She don't like you."

"I'm her 'pa', remember?"

"She still don't like you. She thinks you deserted her."

Fraley controlled himself with difficulty. "So have her come to the house. That'll be just as good. Tell 'er I won't be there."

"I dunno, Ros. If yer gonna hurt her, an' she's my daughter—"

"If she's—what the hell are you talkin' about? You said she wasn't your daughter, that you didn't have any kids."

"Maybe I lied," said Maggie, sullen and stubborn.

Fraley glared at her. He'd seen what alcohol could do to brains. Hell, with all his saloons he'd gotten rich off it.

"Just get her there, Maggie. She's the only one that can connect us with that Missouri business— her and Nellie."

"But Nellie was with us."

"I know that, but she's been actin' strange."

"I'll tell yuh, Ros, Nellie's one I wouldn't mind kissin' good-bye, she's gotten so high and mighty, but Lucia. . . ."

"Nothing's gonna happen to her, Mag, nothing. Just get her there. For drinks and an old-fashioned mother-and-daughter talk."

"What'll we talk about?"

"I'll let you know later. I'll have drinks there ready for you, t'loosen her up."

"I thought you didn't want me drinkin'."

"Just this once. Now go take care of it. Make the arrangements."

They came out of the office into the saloon proper.

"What about settin' up here?" asked Maggie.

"Hattie can handle it," Fraley said. Hattie was a lean, dark-haired, hatchet-faced woman. Maggie might have recognized her heir-apparent if her brain hadn't been numbed by alcohol. "You just run along."

Maggie stumbled off, and Hattie sidled up to Roscoe Fraley. He was seated, and she bent over so he could look down her dress as long and as far as he liked.

"What've you got in mind, Ros?" Hattie asked.

"Got me a brainstorm, Hat. An' you kin start cuttin' Maggie's dresses down to size."

Hattie smiled coldly as Fraley reached out and squeezed her rump.

Then Fraley went back into his office, where he started spiking a bottle of his finest whiskey with laudanum. He planned to prepare some tea, too, just in case the little bitch didn't feel like boozing. He was also prepared to physically force it down her throat, if necessary. That girl was going to be so doped up she would hardly be able to stand, much less swim.

He had a further inspiration. He emerged from his office and called Hattie.

"Let the word out around town that Maggie is Lucia's mother, but be careful. I don't want Lucia or Maggie hearing it."

Maggie had no trouble finding Lucia at Nellie Pope's. She arranged to meet her late that night at Fraley's home.

Maggie was happy at the prospect of being able to get drunk, and her obvious happiness was enough to quell any suspicions Lucia might have had. ✺

20

THE THREE SNIPE-HUNTING plains veterans had hooked another sucker, another greenhorn.

It had taken awhile, and a lot of drinking, but by three a.m. the greenhorn was primed for the hunt.

By four a.m. they'd found an appropriate spot, a place along the banks of the Arkansas where the bank was separated from the main body of the river by about one hundred yards of marsh.

The lamp was lit and the sucker was positioned with the bag.

"Now me'n my buddies, we'll circle around to the far side and drive the snipes towards yuh. It means wadin' through a lot of goddamn muck, but it don't figger that we'll do any good here, an' we don't wanna stay out here all night any more'n you do, so we'll roust 'em out and send 'em headin' yer way. Don't get antsy; it takes awhile to get them tasty beauties movin'.'"

With that they headed upstream.

It was a dark, moonless night, and they picked their way carefully. They had a-ways to go. As long as they could still see the sucker and his light, then it figured that the sucker might be able to see them.

After they'd gone a good way they stopped.

"This is far enough. That kid couldn't see this far in broad daylight."

"All right. We'll—"

"Shhhh!!!!"

"Whass up?"

"Somebody's comin'."

"What the hell. Some more hunters?"

"Shhh. They're comin' this way."

The three snipe-hunters had passed just beyond the marsh area and were standing on the bank of the Arkansas, no more than five feet from the gently lapping river itself.

The noises grew louder, slowly turning into voices; urgent voices.

"C'mon, dammit, walk by yerself. You kin walk! Hey, Emery, gimme a hand, she's about fallin' down."

"So carry her."

"T' hell with you. She weighs about a ton. You fellers got the light one."

Threaded among that heavy male conversation was some barely distinguishable, sing-song female vocalizing.

The heavy voices and the lighter ones got closer.

The snipe-hunters crouched, their mouths sealed.

In time the voices told them that the new arrivals were damn near close enough for them to touch.

"Awright, let's get their clothes off."

"All right!"

"Control yerself, Birdy."

"Strike a match."

"No lights, dammit!"

"Aw c'mon, I wanna see what this here Dodge City Darlin' looks like in th' raw. I never got a chance up at Nellie's."

The snipe-hunters nudged one another. There was only one Dodge City Darlin' they'd heard of, and only at Nellie's.

"That's just too goddamn bad, Birdy. No lights."

"Then how about lettin' me put it in her jes' once."

"Goddammit, Birdy, keep yer goddamn pants on and help me get hers off—an' let's get 'em into the water."

"What's the hurry?"

"'Cause somebody might come by. You know how them sneaky bastards like t'fish real early. An' this here gal is a friend of Masterson's. Masterson gets wind of this he'll shoot you so fulla holes there won't be nuthin' left to fall down."

"Oh. Well then, gimme a few more secs."

"Hurry. Clay, you stay here and hang onto our guns. If yuh see anythin', start blastin'."

"All right, all right," Birdy said. "She's ready."

"Then let's get 'em into the water."

"How far?"

"We're gonna have to take 'em out a-ways. They

sure as hell ain't apt t'drown in shallow water."

The snipe-hunters, unarmed, hearing that these men had guns, were scared witless. They didn't want to end up full of holes, either. But they were when it came to the crunch, fair men. Practical jokers—but fair men.

One of them reached out to his closest buddy and started to unbutton the buddy's shirt. The buddy got the idea. Soon all three were shedding clothes —shedding enough so that they wouldn't drown themselves.

Then, as they heard the other men slipping into the water they slithered into the water, too.

"Max!"

"Goddammit, Birdy, what is it?"

"I saw an alligator."

"You stupid—"

"I did, I seen one."

"Jesus wept. There ain't no goddamn alligators, yuh got that? None. Now you keep yer mouth shut or I'll shut it fer yuh."

The killers wrestled their burdens out into deep water.

The snipe-hunters went with them.

"All right, let 'em go. G'night, ladies, swim yer little ol' hearts out. Now let's get th' hell outa here."

The snipe-hunters waited a few moments before moving toward where they thought the women had been let loose, feeling beneath the water with their hands and feet and trying not to make much noise.

Paul Brooker was preparing for bed when the knock came at his door.

When he opened it, he was confronted by the sight of three soggy men, one carrying the limp but living Lucia Bone. She'd been wrapped, or covered, with one of their shirts, but just barely.

"Goddammit, don't jes' stand there, let us in."

Brooker almost fell down leaping backward, and the men entered.

"Jim told us t'bring her here. He went t'get Bat."

He laid Lucia on the bed and reclaimed his shirt. "Mighty purty filly," he said.

Paul Brooker harrumphed and quickly covered her with the sheet and quilt. "What happened?"

The man was about to explain, when boots clumped on the stairs, and he waited until Bat and Jim Masterson entered. Bat looked terrible. He'd only had about four hours sleep.

The snipe-hunter explained what had happened. "I thought maybe she was drunk, but I never seen no one this drunk."

Bat studied Lucia with an experienced, if bleary eye, and listened to the fragmented pips and squeaks that were coming from her, and to the moans.

"Jim. See if Doc's home," Bat said. "Doc's been trying to kill himself for years. He knows about every way there is."

They waited, helpless, while Jim went down the hall and knocked on Doc's door.

"There was another one, another victim," said one of the snipe-hunters, and he almost cringed as Bat and Paul looked sharply at him. "I guess it was the one they said weighed a ton. Dammit, we tried, Sheriff, but it was too dark to see a damn thing.

This one here we caught pretty quick, but the other, she musta gone down fast, or drifted in th' wrong direction."

Bat looked at Paul. "Weighed a ton?" he repeated, puzzled.

"He might have been a little guy," suggested the snipe-hunter. "But anyway, we're sorry we didn't get her, too."

"Forget it," said Bat. "It's a miracle you got Lucia. Half is better than none."

Doc Holliday stumbled in. He hung over the bed like a vulture, bent down and lifted Lucia's eyelids, smelled her breath.

"Sure as hell isn't drunk," Doc said. "But she's been doped."

"What can we do?"

"Nothing. It's already in her system."

"Will she live?"

"Depends on what was used. Morphine'll kill, but usually faster'n this. Belladonna will, too. How'd this happen?"

Brooker condensed the snipe-hunters' story for him while Bat Masterson yawned.

"If they were trying to make it look like a drowning," Doc said, "cocaine or laudanum would do the trick. They'd die happy as clams, 'bout as painless as you kin get."

They all stared down at Lucia.

"I wouldn't be surprised if the other one wasn't her mother," Doc said.

"Who?"

"Well, the word around town is that ol' Maggie down at the Last Stand is—or was—her mother.

It'd look like her an' her mother was celebrating, decided to go for a midnight swim, maybe to sober up—I understand people actually do that."

"Who the hell would want to fake something like that?"

"Fraley?"

"If it was just Lucia, but him and Maggie were real close."

"Still, I wouldn't put anything past him," said Brooker, as if he was telling the Mastersons something new. "And Lucia had something on him, I think."

"What was it?" demanded Bat.

"I don't know," said Paul, "but it was serious."

"Mind if I go back to bed?" asked Doc Holliday. "She won't die?"

"I doubt it. Might sleep forever—I've seen that happen sometimes—but I don't think she'll die."

The gathering broke up then. It was agreed not to mention a word to anyone of what had happened.

A half-hour later, as Brooker was preparing to make himself comfortable on the floor, there was another knock on his door. He opened it, expecting to find someone bent beneath the weight of Maggie.

But it was the Major.

"Mind if I come in?"

The next morning, Bat and Jim Masterson discreetly checked along the banks of the Arkansas, but to no avail.

"Might've drifted into the marsh, and got tangled up in roots.

"Then she'll never come up."

"Probably not."

"You and Jim couldn't have covered too much ground," said Brooker. "Perhaps if you sent the entire police force out looking. . . ."

"Don't want anyone else knowing about it," said Bat. "People who kill by "accident" are apt to make noise if the bodies aren't discovered."

Paul Brooker didn't argue. Instead he headed for the Last Stand.

Maggie was nowhere in sight, as expected.

"Maggie off getting drunk again?" asked Brooker. "She sure drinks a lot, that woman."

Fraley eyed him suspiciously. He wasn't aware that Brooker even knew Maggie.

"Dunno," Roscoe growled. "Ain't seen 'er since last night. An' I don't appreciate her leavin' me in a hole. Hattie here's had to fill in for her."

Hattie looked like she could fill in for a wolf, too.

"How's that girl of yers, Brooker, that Lucia gal? Maggie's been seein' a lot of her lately. Wouldn't be surprised if them two went off an' got drunk last night. Celebratin'. I'm sure you've heard the word around town, 'bout her and Lucia bein' related. Coulda knocked me over with a feather. Maggie's even got an idee that I coulda been the father! I dunno about that—bein' a father—but I must say, I've gotten kinda fond of that Lucia gal."

Paul Brooker could scarcely believe his ears. The man was preposterous. He thought he might be able to shake him up some.

"Lucia's disappeared, too, it seems."

"I told yuh, they went off drinkin'."

"It's awfully suspicious."

Fraley nodded, as if in accord.

"Lucia told me a lot about her search all across the country, some of the things she found out— things about her mother and her friends. I'm not sure I'd want her thinking I was her ma, or even her pa."

Fraley had quit nodding..

"Well," concluded Brooker, "if Maggie shows up, ask her if she's seen Lucia. It might be important." He rode heavily on the word "important", and he was pleased by the way Fraley stiffened, his fists clenching.

Brooker walked out.

Fraley made another mental entry on his list of people to be eliminated. Goddammit, how many people had that little bitch babbled to?

That evening, Bat Masterson and Paul Brooker sat talking in the Sheriff's office.

"We'd better take her up to Nellie's," Bat said.

"Why?" asked Brooker.

"Because Nellie came by my office in what was, for her, a state of excitement. She said Lucia'd disappeared, wanted me to turn the town inside out looking for her."

Brooker frowned. "I thought she and Fraley were kind of partners. Distant partners, at any rate."

"It's been getting a little more distant as of late," Bat said. "Don't know why. Maybe Nellie's thinking she doesn't need Fraley. She's the one digging up the dirt.

"At the same time, remember, we're not dead certain it was Fraley behind the drowning. Emery and Birdy are his, all right, but drowning Maggie makes it hard to figure."

"He's got Maggie's replacement," said Brooker. "Someone called Hattie."

"Hattie," said Bat. "That woman gives me the chills, but any way you look at it, I still think we'd better sneak Lucia up to Nellie's. That'll keep Nellie quiet, and give us time to do some quiet investigating.

"We've put Emery and Birdy and Clay and another gent I don't know, put them four with a Max Probst who's just the right sort for that kind of thing. We've got them together at the right time."

Brooker decided it was just a matter of time before Masterson had those five hanging. "All right then, let's move her."

"Wait a while. It's not dark enough."

A voice came from the doorway. "I'll bring a wagon around to the back."

Brooker and Masterson turned to see Brewster "Ben Lloyd" Lowell standing in the doorway.

"Might as well lend a hand, as long as I'm here," said Lowell.

"You're a quiet one," said Bat.

"When I have to be."

"Uhhh, Bat," said Paul Brooker, "he knows all about what's going on. He's Major Brewster Lowell."

Bat nodded. "I know."

Brooker was startled.

"You've hung onto that brevet rank a good long while," Bat continued.

Lowell smiled. "It's convenient in my business."

"How did you know?" asked Brooker.

"It wasn't that strenuous a deception," said the Major.

"That new growth on your face made it a little tricky."

"Deliberately so," said Lowell.

"You working for him, Paul?"

Again Brooker looked startled.

"Dammit, Paul," said Bat, "how dumb do you think I am? I've got people around town that tell me everything; who talks to whom and so on. This is my town." He saw that they understood what he meant. "I've also got contacts in a lot of other places. Lawmen tend to hang together, and they know things. The Major hired your agency to find someone—a mother and daughter. I reckon that someone, that mother, is Nellie Pope. It'd be real convenient if Lucia Bone, who's looking for her mother, was the daughter."

"Except—" began the Major.

"Except Nellie Pope doesn't look like the picture Lucia likes to draw—"

"Nor does my wife," the Major inserted mysteriously.

"—but Maggie does," completed Bat.

"All the pieces seem to be there," said Brooker, "but they don't fit. Too bad. It'd wrap things up very neatly."

Bat was puzzling over the Major's terse insertion.

"But Sheriff," said Brooker, "could you keep all this to yourself for a while? Nellie still doesn't know the Major's who he is. We're afraid she'll panic, or just shut up tight."

Masterson silently regarded both men. "It's dark enough now. Let's go move her."

* * *

Jim Masterson opened the door to Brooker's room where Lucia lay. They wrapped her and carried her down the back way, loading her onto the wagon the Major had brought around.

At Nellie's, they went in the back way. Masterson went in first and made sure there was no one around who couldn't be kept quiet. Then he came back out, trailed by Red, his arm in a sling, and the hulking JB. The colored man plucked Lucia from the wagon and carried her back in and upstairs.

Red had gone ahead to warn Nellie, who had her door open and her bed turned down. JB laid Lucia down gently.

"Is she dying?" asked Nellie.

"Doped," said Bat. "She'll come out of it sooner or later, we hope. Soon, maybe. She was babbling a lot on the way up. I wasn't listening, but she was talking up a storm."

Just then Lucia started tossing on the bed and talking. It was hard to understand, at first, the words and phrases uttered in her delirium, but after awhile, as they became used to the speech rhythms and slurred pronunciations, she seemed more coherent.

What her unconscious released, in jigsaw fashion, was the story of her search for her parents. It included bits and pieces about the orphanage, the Crowleys, Chicago, Peoria, the bloody events in Hannibal, Abilene, and finally Dodge. Roscoe Fraley, Maggie, and Nellie Pope had brief but unmistakably starring roles all along the way.

It also included the late-night tête-à-tête with Maggie, which ended, with startling clarity, with

Fraley's appearing at the house and giving orders to his men.

The last part had the sound of being lifted off her brain, pure and whole, as her brain had recorded it. It had neither been digested nor understood; nor had any judgment been made.

When what she was saying was finally clear, attention shifted to Nellie Pope.

"He killed Maggie?" she said in a voice little above a whisper. She was pale with shock. "It's all true—about Roscoe, Maggie, and myself." She told them what had happened, when, and where.

"There's a trunk full of circulars back in the office," Bat said. "I don't know how far back they go. This happened when—ten, eleven years ago? They may be there. If not, I can wire for information." He looked at Nellie, Paul Brooker and the Major. "Guess I'll go do that. I could use some help."

"I'll come," said Paul.

The Major, after studying Nellie's drained, drawn face, decided to go along as well.

Bat hesitated.

"She'll be safe, Sheriff," said Nellie Pope quietly.

"Damn right she will," said Red with a snort.

Bat, Paul and the Major left.

Nellie silently regarded the sleeping girl. Lucia had quit tossing and talking. Now only her eyes moved restlessly beneath her closed lids.

"Wait outside the door, boys," she said to Red and JB.

After they were gone she took out a sketch pad and tried to draw Lucia. As usual, she did a bad job.

She shook her head slowly. It had all been doomed, right from the beginning.

She turned the page of the pad and began to write.

Ten minutes later she'd finished. She tore the sheet out, folded it, lit a candle, and sealed it with sealing wax. On the outside she wrote, "Brewster Lowell."

She opened the door and handed the sealed letter to Red.

"Hold this for me, Red."

He glanced at the name and didn't recognize it.

"For how long?" Red asked.

Nellie hesitated a second. "Until tomorrow, or give it to my friend."

"Lloyd?"

She nodded.

Red tugged at the lobe of his right ear.   ক§

21

"Are you sure you sank those two?" asked Roscoe Fraley. "How come no one's found their bodies?"

"Dunno," said Probst. "Musta sunk 'em too good. Musta gotten tangled up in that marsh."

Probst, who'd commanded the drowning, Birdy, Emery, Clay, and the fifth man were in the Last Stand. Fraley had summoned them there to try to find out what the hell had gone wrong.

"All right," growled Roscoe, "I guess they'll turn up sooner or later, or jes' be clean forgot, but we got more trouble."

"We?"

"I got it, so you got it. There's this nosy gent, name's Paul Brooker; we may have to get rid of him, fast. But he's close with Masterson, so. . . ."

"Aw hell, boss," said Birdy, "gimme a shot at Bat's back and I'll take it."

"You may have to," said Roscoe, "or we'll have to outnumber them, and I think I've got enough men around town to do just that. But that's still in the future. First we got to get this Brooker aside and—"

He broke off as a small man known as "Weasel" entered the Last Stand at a run.

"I been keepin' my eyes open, boss, like you tol' me," said Weasel, arriving at Fraley's table and pulling a chair up for himself. "I seen Brooker, Masterson, and some other gent walk from the jail to the Dodge House. The other gent brought a wagon around back and they loaded someone onto it. They took the wagon to Nellie's and unloaded. I ain't dead sure but I think it was that Bone girl. Anyway, 'bout a half-hour later, the Sheriff, Brooker, and the other gent come dashin' back out and ride the wagon like hell back to the jail.

"I tried to get me a peek. They's goin' through piles of 'wanted' circulars like crazy."

It took Roscoe less than five seconds to realize that time was running out. He told Weasel to head for Cattle Annie's and the Crazy Hors and bring back certain men.

"An' Birdy, you head up t'the Drovers Rest. There're some dudes stayin' there—" He named them. "Bring 'em back, armed."

Birdy left on Weasel's heels. The other four prepared to leave also. "Where the hell do you think you're going?"

"Hell, boss, we gotta get some guns, too."

"Ferget it. I got some in the office. Come on—"

Fraley had half-risen from his seat and was looking toward the front of the saloon. His mouth dropped open.

"Here it is!" cried Paul Brooker. "'Magine that. After all that time they were still sending them out. They must've really wanted them."

"Not enough to go lookin' for them," said Bat as he snatched the yellowing sheet of paper from him. "Descriptions fit. Nathan Budde. Maggie Franklin. Hell, Maggie didn't even bother changing her first name. Jenny Parker—that must be Nellie; she didn't say what her name had been."

"Can I see that, please?" asked the Major. He took the sheet and looked at it. His lips tightened. "She'd already changed it once. Her name was Porter, Jennifer Porter, when I knew her."

"I don't care about her," said Masterson. "It's Fraley I want, and now I've got him." He snatched the sheet back. "Guess he's put on some weight Figures. So have I."

"At your age?" asked the Major dubiously.

"Brooker," said Bat, "grab yourself a badge and help yourself to the guns. Major, I'll deputize you, if you want."

"I'd like that."

"It's done. There're guns in the drawer."

"I wouldn't be any good with them. I have handled a Henry, though."

"There're a couple there," said Bat, pointing to the rifle rack, "and some Winchesters. Ammo in the drawer. Grab it and let's go."

As they left the jail, Weasel was sprinting across

the plaza not far from them, but they didn't pay him any heed.

"We'll drop by the Long Branch and pick up Wyatt. Maybe Doc'll be there, too."

Bat spotted Jim Masterson on the north side of Front, making his rounds, and waved for him to join them.

Bat had just entered the Long Branch, leaving the rest outside, when there came the sound of gunfire from down the street.

"Where's that coming from?"

"It's way down, in the next block. It's gotta be Roscoe's place."

The Major had been thinking of Nellie. He remembered her face, her expression, the way she'd looked at Lucia. "Oh God!" he cried, and he started sprinting.

Paul Brooker took off after him just as Bat came out of the Long Branch. Bat started running, too.

Jim Masterson brought up the rear until Earp came out of the Long Branch and tried to run and strap on his guns at the same time.

Roscoe Fraley looked up as Nellie Pope strode into the Last Stand, a long-barreled Colt Peacemaker held down by her side.

As Roscoe's mouth dropped open she walked toward him.

"Watch out, Roscoe," yelped Hattie from behind the bar.

Nellie started to bring the gun up.

Roscoe didn't waste any time arguing. He twisted out of his seat and made a run for the back room.

If Nellie had had a lighter gun, she might have gotten it up in time to nail Roscoe. But as it was, she was just bringing it level when she caught movement from the corner of her eye.

Hattie had ducked down behind the bar and come back up with a sawed-off shotgun.

Nellie squeezed a round off toward Roscoe, missing, and then swung the Colt toward Hattie.

Her first shot glanced off the barrel of the shotgun, knocking it off-line.

The shotgun went off, bringing a shower of glass and plaster down from above to fall through the billowing gunsmoke.

Nellie's next shot, when she got the rearing Colt back down again, plowed into the bar and through it, punching Hattie in the belly, not hurting her, but making her blink. The shotgun went off again, once more making harmless holes somewhere.

Nellie cursed. "What's wrong with this blasted gun?"

She took more time with her third shot, and shot Hattie through the neck.

"Now for that damned—"

But by then Roscoe and his four men had made the office. Roscoe's guns were hanging from a peg. He and Probst each grabbed one of them. Emery and the other two men grabbed some other guns from the desk.

Roscoe looked back out just as Nellie finished shooting Hattie. The saloon was fast filling with acrid gunsmoke.

Roscoe fired once, staggering Nellie, and then he fired again. Nellie fell to the floor.

Roscoe advanced slowly toward the prone figure, his mind flooding with curses.

Probst, Emery, and the two other men followed him out of his office, fanning out and trying to peer through the gunsmoke that was dissipating very slowly.

"Somebody'll prob'ly check to see what it was all about, boss," ventured Probst.

"Yeah, but not right away," said Roscoe. "Weasel'n Birdy'll be back with the boys by then. We've got time."

But they didn't. As the gunsmoke dispersed, five figures took shape at the front end of the saloon: the Major, Brooker, the two Mastersons, and Earp.

They'd been peering into the gunsmoke just as hard as had Fraley and his crowd.

The Major saw the form on the floor and gasped.

"I want Roscoe," said Bat Masterson quietly. Then he raised his voice. "Roscoe Fraley, you're under arrest for murder."

"What the hell, Sheriff. She came in here gunning for me."

Bat smiled coldly. "For Missouri, Fraley. Hannibal, Missouri."

Fraley and his boys had their guns in hand. The Major gripped the Henry so hard his knuckles were white. Brooker and Jim Masterson had their guns out, but held down by their sides. The confident pair, Bat Masterson and Wyatt Earp, stood with their guns still holstered.

If Fraley and his boys had made their move quickly, aiming and shooting, they might have had a chance, but Fraley wasted that edge with an explosive curse, and while that curse was still riding the air waves Bat Masterson's guns, "sweetened" to a fine deliciousness, were sweeping up.

Eighteen shots were fired in the space of three seconds, fourteen by Bat and his men. Then it was impossible to see a damn thing.

Bat and his men crouched low, just in case, and waited for the gunsmoke to clear.

A dozen unlucky, awestruck customers, caught in the opening gunplay and subsequent crossfire, lay flat on the floor, scarcely daring to breathe. At length the saloon cleared sufficiently for Bat to conclude that the fight was over.

He stood up. "Any of you that can still move, get the hell out of here."

The twelve customers sprang up and got the hell out.

Bat advanced slowly, his guns holstered.

He bent down over Roscoe Fraley and rolled him over.

The Major went to his knees by Nellie Pope, trying to hold back his tears.

Paul Brooker stood by Bat. "What's that, only one hole? I figured you'd empty your gun into him."

Bat gave him a look that made him sorry he'd said it. He turned and retraced his steps to where the Major was cradling Nellie Pope in his arms. He heard Nellie whisper, "Brewster—I knew it was you."

Then she said something that only the Major heard.

The Major turned his face to Brooker.

"Go . . . go see if the girl's awake," Major Brewster Lowell croaked.

As Brooker left, Bat Masterson came over to stand by the Major and Nellie Pope.

Bat knelt down and gently stroked Nellie's cheek.

Lucia Bone had regained consciousness soon after Nellie Pope had left on her ill-considered mission of vengeance.

She'd slowly figured out where she was, and the setting, with the many sketches on the wall—hers and, she assumed, Nellie's—had fascinated her, and filled her with wonder.

The photographs, the illustrations, the wedding pictures, the—good grief, that awful photo of the Crowley family, including Lucia, so terribly stiff. . . .

She began to claw through Nellie's belongings, emptying out her dresser, her desk.

At length she came upon the box that contained the correspondence between Nellie and Belle at the orphanage.

The door opened and Paul Brooker stood in the doorway.

Red and JB peered past him.

Lucia slowly raised her face to Paul Brooker, a smile of wonderful relief breaking over her face. "She's my mother, Paul. Nellie's my mother!"

Paul Brooker visibly winced. He was speechless. He felt an inexpressable sadness.

Lucia sensed it. "Where is she? Where'd she go?"

"She's dying, Lucia."

Brewster Lowell, Brevet Major, U.S. Army, Ret., was still cradling Nellie Pope when Lucia Bone burst in the back door of the Last Stand.

The Major's face was ashen as he stared down at Nellie.

He seemed to take no notice as Lucia fell to her knees beside Nellie and reached out to gently touch the scarred face. Nellie's eyes opened and she fought to smile.

"Mother," Lucia whispered.

Nellie's eyes closed. Then they opened and rolled up, with great effort, searching for the Major.

But the Major was in some world of his own. His tears had dried but the paths they'd made down his cheeks, through the dust and gunsmoke grime, were still visible.

"Mother," Lucia pleaded, "don't go!"

Nellie shook her head feebly.

Paul Brooker had finally caught up, and he watched silently, helplessly.

Bat Masterson, after listening to and comforting Nellie, had seen to the removal of Fraley and his henchmen. Now he moved slowly back toward the trio of Nellie, the Major, and Lucia.

A hiss escaped Nellie. It sounded like "Bat."

Masterson said quietly, "She wasn't your mother, Lucia."

"She *was!*"

"No."

"But she did this for me, was shot for me. What more? She's the only mother I'll ever want." With that fierce statement her grip on Nellie tightened.

The Major seemed to emerge from his reverie. "Your natural mother is dead, Lucia," he said softly.

"No." It was a moan more than a cry.

The Major nodded slowly, just once.

Lucia looked down at Nellie who, eyes closed, also nodded.

"But who . . . why did . . . Nellie . . . she wrote to the orphanage about me."

"You'd been entrusted to her. She cared about you. Nellie was a dear, dear friend," said the Major, "to your mother, and to me."

"To you?"

"Yes. I'm your father."

Lucia Bone stared at him.

Paul Brooker stared at him, too. He'd seen it coming, but still he stared.

Lucia Bone couldn't handle it. She moaned as she bent to clutch Nellie Pope to her.

She held Nellie tight until she died—and for some time thereafter.

22

THE STORY, as Lucia Bone finally came to understand it, was this:

Nellie Pope, whose real name was Jennifer Porter, had been a resident in the Massachusetts home of Grover Longstreet, his wife Mary, and daughter Alice. Nellie, who was the same age as Alice, had been the daughter of Alice's governess and tutor. The governess had died in '55, but Nellie, by that time a close companion of Alice's, had remained with the family.

In constant attendance at the Longstreet home was young Brewster Lowell, scion of a wealthy, patrician Boston family. He was obviously in love with the lovely Alice Longstreet, and she with him. They seemed meant for each other. Overlooked, though, were the healthy appetites of young Lowell and the appeal of the comely and earthy young Nellie.

While young Lowell courted Alice, in the manner of the times, he made love to Nellie.

There sprang up within young Lowell a sore conflict: the cultured and distilled beauty and temperament of Alice, versus the raw intelligence, gusto, and sensual beauty of Nellie.

In time, and given space to breathe, young Lowell might eventually have chosen Nellie, but circumstances intervened.

Young Lowell had been selected to attend West Point, and he still had a few years to go there.

The Civil War was brewing, casting all futures in doubt, especially any future involving the son of an aristocratic family and the daughter of a common governess.

Finally, Alice Longstreet had apparently recognized the enemy, and decided to take matters into her own hands. In late May of 1859, she'd gone off with her family to summer on the Maine coast. Nellie, unaccountably, had been left behind.

When Alice returned during the first days of fall, she had with her a baby girl.

Brewster Lowell was surprised and distressed. He'd known nothing of it, and he was not permitted to claim parentage, which would have brought shame to himself and to the Longstreet family.

The baby was declared the offspring of Nellie Pope and was given to Nellie to care for and raise.

Up until then, the situation was under control, but after Brewster Lowell had returned to West Point, Nellie was given money and told to go else-where—to stay in touch, if she liked, but not to

otherwise intrude in the lives of the Longstreet
family.

Nellie left with the baby, hurt and resentful, but
cherishing the baby for what, or whom, it represented—Brewster Lowell.

But Nellie soon ran out of money and, being
young, healthy, good looking, and vigorous, she
began to resent the burden the baby represented.
She tried, for better than three years, to both
raise the child and make a life for herself, all within
the environs of Philadelphia, but in the end she
gave up. She turned the baby over to the orphanage and set out across the country.

She kept in touch with the orphanage; knew what
had happened to Lucia, and even convinced the
orphanage to supply Lucia with a phony description—that of her traveling mate, Maggie Franklin
—should Lucia ever come looking.

The argument can be made that by staying in
such close touch she fully intended that Lucia
would someday come looking for her.

In any case, she never entirely forgot Lucia, or
the man she represented, and thought that maybe,
someday. . . .

In the meantime, with Nellie out of the way,
Alice Longstreet had the field to herself. Whatever
regret Lowell might have had, with the war a
reality he was preoccupied. He did marry Alice
Longstreet, but they did not live together until the
war's end, by which time Alice had fallen ill and
lost the ability to bear children.

They'd adopted a few children, who were presently in their teens and living in San Francisco, but
that had failed to compensate for Alice's sense of

loss and failure, and failed to arrest her gradual decline. She'd never mentioned her one natural child, and neither had he, but she could never have been far from their thoughts.

During that time their lives had changed greatly, environmentally if not stylistically.

Brewster Lowell, who'd risen to Captain by the end of the war—but had a temporary brevet rank of Major, and thus was called Major—retired as soon as the conflict was over, and took over the conduct of his family business. Those interests included shipping, ship-building, textiles and railroading.

A sorrow ate at Brewster Lowell and, as the years passed, he found himself concentrating on the westward-pushing railroads. He himself followed them west, at first to Chicago, and finally to San Francisco. He was putting distance between himself and that Massachusetts Longstreet mansion where life, at one time, had seemed so wonderful and promising.

With Alice's death in San Francisco, something was released in Brewster Lowell, and he hired the Flaherty Agency to track down Jennifer Porter and his daughter, who had been named, but not baptized, Elizabeth Anne.

That search by the Flaherty Agency had ended in Dodge City.

Major Brewster Lowell stared at the limburger. He had yet to develop a taste for it.

He, Paul Brooker, Bat Masterson, and Lucia were in the Occident one week after the death of Nellie Pope.

Nellie Pope, over many protests, had been buried, complete with religious service, at Fort Dodge. Major Lowell and Lucia had wanted it. And all those wishing to physically protest the event had been advised to address themselves to the Masterson brothers and Earp. The ceremony went off without a hitch.

Lucia finally emerged from her mourning, and had listened to, and finally understood, the truth of her parentage.

Neither she nor her father mentioned the time that the Major had almost bedded his daughter. Both, however, remembered, and fully appreciated Nellie Pope's agitation at the time.

"Well, young lady," said Bat Masterson, "what are you going to do now?"

"I don't know."

"You can do whatever you want," said the Major. "Money's no problem."

Lucia laughed nervously. "That'll be a change."

Paul Brooker, just a poor, working stiff compared to the Lowell family, wondered what kind of change.

Lucia read his expression, gave him a quick smile, and winked.

"Paul may have some plans, but it will take a while for me—for us—to get things straightened out.

"Nellie had some good thoughts on what women could do. Women as doctors and lawyers. Maybe I'll go back to school, to a college—"

"College!?" exclaimed both Brooker and Lowell.

"Or maybe I'll open that school after all—"

"Don't," said Bat.

"What?"

"This town's only got a few more years until the farmers and Texas fever writes an end to it. Me'n Jim'n Wyatt, we'll all be moving on soon. Don't know where, but in any case, with your taste for living, and"—he grinned—"the kind of living you have a taste for, I don't figure Dodge City'll be a place where you'd want to sink your roots."

Hell no, thought Major Lowell, but he held his tongue.

"I dunno, Sheriff," said Lucia slowly. "I've got a perfect set-up."

"Hm?"

"Nellie's place. It would convert perfectly to a school."

Bat Masterson smiled broadly.

"Or maybe I'll just keep on running it the way it is."

The Major scowled heavily. "I don't think that'd be entirely proper, Lucia."

Lucia smiled sweetly. "I didn't notice that you worked hard to avoid it, Father dear."

The Major sighed. "If the only way you can use that expression, Lucia, is with sarcasm, however light—"

"What expression?"

"Father, as in 'Father dear'. . . ."

"Oh."

"Then I'd rather you not use it at all."

"All right. Major."

The Major nodded.

"And I certainly prefer Ben Lloyd to Brewster Lowell. What do your friends call you, Brew?"

The Major thought, despairingly, that it might

take some time, training this boisterous young filly.

"I do want to go to Denver with Paul, and to San Francisco to meet my brothers and sisters."

That was more like it, thought the Major. "Paul, errrr, what do you know about the railroad business?"

"Major—"

"Keep still, Lucia. I have to watch out for your future. Now, Paul, what kind of educational background—"

"Father! Don't interfere. I can take care—"

"Nonsense! This is business, Lucia, between us men. You just sit there and eat that—stinking cheese and mind your manners, young lady!"

The Major thought he'd fared rather well in that exchange.

But Lucia was thinking, Gol-lee. Here she'd crossed the entire country by herself, tracked down her mother, or the next best thing, and survived several attempts on her life. When were they going to realize that women could take care of themselves?

Authority sat well on her father's shoulders. Too damn well. He needed to be taken down a peg.

"Major? Errr, Father?"

She was sounding better, thought the Major.

"Yes, daughter?"

"Have you ever gone snipe-hunting?"

"Snipe-hunting? Wasn't that what those men were doing when they rescued you?"

Paul Brooker immediately feared for his own future. "Major Lowell—" he began.

Bat Masterson interrupted.

"Yes, they were Major, and it's a fine sport."

"Brooker?"

Brooker responded queasily.

"Don't know a thing about it, Major."

"I think you can call me Brewster, Paul—or Ben, as my daughter seems to prefer. I'd say we were friends now, at the very least, are we not?"

"Indeed," said Paul Brooker.

"So let's get on with this snipe-hunting," the Major said enthusiastically.

Lucia Bone, her blue eyes sparkling as she fought to suppress a grin, exchanged meaningful looks with Bat and Paul, and they all burst out laughing in unison.

The End

First in the Series

WOMEN WHO WON THE WEST

VOLUME 1

Tempest of Tombstone

by Lee Davis Willoughby

Sally Sewell was stranded in Tombstone, a wide-eyed slip of a girl, abandoned by a ragtag troupe of touring players. Rescued—and seduced—by the most powerful man in Tombstone, she learned to fight for her rights in this, the rowdiest, hell-roaringest of all frontier boomtowns. Sally became the most powerful woman in Tombstone, and the prize in the explosive struggle between Wyatt Earp and John Behan—the man some called the Devil incarnate— the struggle that tore the town apart and led to the bloody Battle of the OK Corral.

ON SALE NOW FROM DELL/BRYANS